Lady Elect 2:
Lady Arykah Reigns

Lady Elect 2:
Lady Arykah Reigns

Nikita Lynnette Nichols

www.urbanchristianonline.com

Urban Books, LLC
97 N18th Street
Wyandanch, NY 11798

Lady Elect 2: Lady Arykah Reigns

ISBN 13: 978-1-60162-688-2
ISBN 10: 1-60162-688-6

First Trade Paperback Printing January 2015
Printed in the United States of America

10 9 8 7 6 5 4 3 2 1

Distributed by Kensington Corp.
Submit Wholesale Orders to:
Kensington Publishing Corp.
C/O Penguin Group (USA) Inc.
Attention: Order Processing
405 Murray Hill Parkway
East Rutherford, NJ 07073-2316
Phone: 1-800-526-0275
Fax: 1-800-227-9604

Other titles by
Nikita Lynnette Nichols

None But The Righteous

A Man's Worth

Amaryllis

Crossroads

A Woman's Worth

Lady Elect

Damsels In Distress

Contact the author at:
kitawrites@comcast.net
Facebook: Nikita Lynnette Nichols
Twitter: @nikitalynnette

Dedication

I wish to dedicate this book to my very best friend, Jamia Ray-Franklin. You are, undoubtedly, the strongest chick on this earth. I thank God for your loyalty, your friendship, and your overall compassion. I love you, girl.

Prologue

The clock on the nightstand displayed 3:53 a.m. Arykah tossed and turned in her sleep.

Praise and worship was in full swing. Bishop Lance Howell sat in the pulpit. Mother Pansie Bowak sat on the second pew. She clapped her hands and swayed as the choir sang.

"Come on in where the table is spread and the feast of the Lord is going on ."

Arykah fidgeted. She turned to her right side, not knowing that she had thrown the covers from her body.

The sanctuary doors opened. Arykah appeared at the entrance. Myrtle and Monique stood on opposite sides of her. Darlita, Chelsea, and Gladys were behind her. Arykah took the first step, and all of the ladies followed her .

Arykah mumbled, then turned to her left side. She rested her head against her pillow.

Two policemen forced Clyde's hands behind his back and locked cuffs on his wrists.

"Clyde Trumbull, you're under arrest for the rape of Arykah Miles and second-degree murder in the death of her unborn child," an officer stated as he read Clyde his Miranda Rights. As they escorted Clyde up the basement stairs, they saw a huge collage of photographs, taken of Arykah, along the staircase wall .

Arykah turned onto her back. Tears ran from the sides of her closed eyelids, passed her temples, and into her hair. She continued to dream.

Dressed in a light blue terry cloth robe and curlers in her hair, Mother Gussie was visibly frightened. She stood in the middle of her living room and shook her head from side to side when questioned by the police .

Arykah twitched, then mumbled.

As Arykah and the ladies slowly made their way down the center aisle, the congregation lost interest in praise and worship. Everyone stopped singing and clapping. They focused on Arykah's battered face. Arykah heard many gasps.

"Is that Lady Arykah? Oh my God. What happened to her?"

Mother Pansie turned around and looked up the aisle to see what had captured the choir and musicians' attention. Her eyes filled with disbelief when she saw Arykah and her posse making their way in her direction. She turned back around and sat on the pew frozen. She stared straight-ahead.

When Arykah had arrived at her side, Mother Pansie looked up at her, and then looked away.

The entire church was quiet. Everyone watched.

"You tried to break me, didn't you?"

Mother Pansie didn't respond to Arykah. She sat stoic on the pew.

Arykah knelt down and placed her bruised face directly in Mother Pansie's view. "Look at me!" she yelled.

Again Arykah twitched and mumbled, "No, no." Sweat beads formed on her forehead. She pressed the rear of her head down into the pillow.

Mother Pansie flinched. She hastily grabbed her purse and Bible from the pew and stood. She maneuvered past Arykah and collided with Monique, Chelsea, Myrtle, Darlita, and Gladys as they blocked her exit. She brushed past the ladies and hurried down the center aisle but stopped in her tracks when she saw Detective

Cortney Rogers and two female officers walking up the aisle. Nervously, Mother Pansie turned around and saw Arykah and her gang closing in on her. She was trapped. She had been caught.

Detective Rogers grabbed Mother Pansie's arms and pulled them behind her. Her Bible and purse fell to the floor as she was placed in handcuffs.

The church was in total shock. Many congregants looked on as their beloved Mother Pansie was arrested. "What's going on? What's happening?"

Arykah approached Mother Pansie and stood toe-to-toe with her. "Did you really think that you could keep me away from this church?" She clenched her teeth and poked herself in the chest. "I am Lady Arykah Miles-Howell."

Mother Pansie held no expression on her face.

"You tried to destroy me, but it didn't work," Arykah continued. "You came after my marriage, but that plan failed too." As tears ran down her face, Arykah's words broke. "You stole my baby from my womb, but guess what, Pansie? God is still holding my hand. That weapon you formed didn't prosper. It will never prosper."

"Oh my God, not Mother Pansie," Arykah heard many folks say out loud.

Arykah laughed emotionally. "You know what I'm gonna do for you, Pansie? As the first lady of this church, I'm gonna ask the Lord to have mercy on your soul."

Detective Rogers escorted Mother Pansie out of the sanctuary. Lance came from the pulpit and stood in front of Arykah. "You did it, Cheeks. I'm so proud of you."

Arykah turned onto her left side again and exhaled. She slept peacefully for the remainder of the night.

One

She relented and gave in just to shut everyone up. Lance, Monique, Adonis, and even Mother Myrtle Cortland had worked Arykah's last nerve. Her supporters were overbearing, and Arykah was at her wit's end. If any of them mentioned calling a therapist one more time, Arykah was willing to slit both her wrists, and even theirs. She couldn't take their nagging a moment longer.

It'll be good for you if you speak with a therapist . . . You've suffered a traumatic experience . . . Arykah, keeping your feelings and emotions bottled up inside will only cause ulcers . . . You have to talk about the rape . . . It'll eat you up inside if you don't. You'll never get past it if you don't open up to someone. Blah blah blah.

Yes, Arykah had been raped. Yes, she had been beaten. Yes, she had a miscarriage. And, yes, she was traumatized. But Arykah wanted to heal in her own way and absorb the trauma on her own terms. Not talking about it and dismissing it from her mind was the best medicine. But each and every day since she was released from the hospital, it was, *"Did you make an appointment with a therapist yet?"* Why couldn't everybody just shut up and leave her alone?

So, there Arykah sat, wasting her precious time on a Saturday afternoon, in a building, in a corner office in downtown Chicago, with a view overlooking Lake Michigan. The tides were high in early May. Arykah watched the waves crash against the shoreline.

"A penny for your thoughts," Lance said. He sat in a chair next to Arykah and caressed her hand inside his own.

She glanced at him briefly before returning her gaze back to the water. "Hmm? Just wondering how many people have drowned in the lake."

Lance frowned, then he chuckled. "What?" He wondered what on earth would make Arykah respond that way.

She kept her focus where it was. "Isn't that why you and everyone else pressured me to come here? So that I could *drown* in my sorrows? Ironic, don't you think? You brought me to a therapist to drown, when really all you had to do, Lance, was push me in Lake Michigan. You know my fat behind can't swim."

Lance shook his head from side to side. He didn't understand. "No, Cheeks. I thought it would be good for you to talk about what happened. I can't get you to open up to me. You refuse to discuss it with Mother Myrtle or Monique. It's obvious the rape and miscarriage are eating you up inside."

Arykah snapped her head in Lance's direction. "What the heck you mean, 'It's obvious'? Because I cry from time to time? *That* makes me a nutcase?"

Aw, heck, here we go, Lance thought. He knew it would take some time for Arykah to bounce back to her old self, sassy talk and cuss words surfing on the tip of her tongue. When they married, Lance had vowed to love Arykah for better or for worse, until death parted them. And Lance had accepted the fact that Arykah's healing wouldn't be easy. It would be stressful, difficult, and trying. But with each passing day since Arykah was assaulted, Lance had to walk on eggshells.

Right then, all Arykah wanted to do was cuss out everybody who was either on her last nerve or the one before it. There was a time when Arykah was honestly trying to curb her vulgar vocabulary, but since the day she was attacked, she was starting not to care what she said or whom she said it to. If Lance said "Good morning" to Arykah, she wanted to respond, "What in the hell is so good about it?" For now, though, it was just a nod and a smile. But the clock was ticking before the sailor in her showed itself. God help her!

She had Lance so confused he didn't know if he was coming or going. One moment Arykah was behaving as if the rape never happened, and the next moment she would be crying and hiding from the world on the floor of her closet.

Though Arykah had fought Lance tooth and nail about speaking with a therapist, he knew he had to get her some help, even if it meant dragging her to the therapist office himself.

He chose his words carefully before he spoke to his wife. "Of course you're not a nutcase, Cheeks. I'm concerned about you. We all are. Mother Cortland, Monique, and Adonis are worried that you may not be dealing with this matter in a healthy way."

She raised her voice. *"In a healthy way ?* Really? Well, why don't you tell me, Lance, the healthiest way to handle *this matter."* Arykah made quotation marks with her fingers. "You think it's healthy for me to spill my guts to a total stranger about how my loving husband was not around when a man beat me, raped me, and ripped my baby from my womb?"

Lance's jaw became tight. Arykah said it. She finally said what Lance had felt. He knew Arykah had blamed him, but she hadn't actually said the words. Had Lance known, on that Monday morning, that Arykah was in danger, he never would've gone to church. In his mind, Lance was a husband first and pastor second. He should have been home to protect his wife. Had it been him, instead of Arykah, who answered the doorbell, she wouldn't have been raped and beaten. Arykah would still be carrying their child.

Arykah seemed fine after she was released from the hospital. She had told Lance that she didn't miss being pregnant because she hadn't even known she was with child. And against her doctor's orders to not indulge in any intimate relations for four weeks, Arykah tried to seduce Lance a week after the rape and miscarriage. Lance wanted to take Arykah but remained strong and reminded her of the doctor's orders. But everything had changed three nights ago, almost four weeks after the assault.

An hour after Arykah had retired for the evening, Lance walked into the master suite and saw that she had fallen asleep with the bedroom light on. He sat on the bed and kicked his slippers off, then reached for the lamp on the nightstand. As soon as the room darkened, Arykah gave off a bloodcurdling scream.

"No! Please, God, no!"

Lance was startled. He switched the light back on and jumped out of bed and looked at Arykah. She was trembling, and her head was shaking vigorously. When Lance moved toward her, Arykah squeezed her eyes shut and turned away from him.

"Please don't hurt me! No more. Please no more."

Her words stopped Lance in his tracks. His heart beat so fast he thought his chest would burst. "Baby, it's me. It's Lance."

Arykah clutched her pillow to her chest and sobbed loudly. Lance saw that she rocked back and forth in a fetal position. Slowly he moved toward her.

Arykah began flailing her hands and legs. "Don't touch me, don't touch me." Arykah looked toward the bedroom door. "Lance! Lance!" she called out.

Lance sat on the bed at her side and tried his best to console her. He placed his hand softly on her thigh. "Arykah, it's me. I'm right here."

Arykah fought off the man next to her. She swung at Lance, striking him repeatedly in his chest and neck area. "Get out!" she yelled. "Get out!"

Lance stood, but his feet were glued to the hardwood floor. He didn't know what to do.

"Move away from me. Get away!"

Arykah's screams sent him running from the bedroom to the kitchen. He yanked the telephone from the wall and dialed Monique. He was breathing heavy in her ear. "You better get here quick."

"What happened?" Monique asked in a panic.

Lance ran his hand over his bald head. "I don't know. She's screaming and yelling. She won't let me near her."

Monique was already jumping out of bed and running to her closet to change her clothes. "I'm on my way."

Lance didn't return to the master suite. He sat in the living room, waiting a half hour for Monique to arrive. He slept in one of the four guest rooms that night while Monique and Arykah stayed behind the closed door of the master suite.

"You think that I don't blame myself, for one second, that I wasn't home when you were attacked? It kills me that I couldn't protect you. I failed you, and I will never get past that."

There was a soft knock on the door before it opened slowly. An African American female entered the room. The first thing Arykah noticed was her cute short crop haircut and beautifully made-up face. Arykah had expected to see someone wearing a white lab coat, but the lady was dressed in a form-fitted dark blue jean button-down dress. She guessed the lady to be about a size fourteen. The last time Arykah wore a size fourteen was when she *was* fourteen. At thirty years old, Arykah fit comfortably in a size twenty-two. She was a big girl who took pride in her appearance. Arykah paid good money for her expensive clothes and shoes. She never allowed her size to interfere with looking her absolute best.

Arykah glanced at the lady's feet and saw a pair of black leather mules and frowned. *Why couldn't she have slipped into a pair of plain black stilettos to set that blue jean dress off?*

Arykah, a self-proclaimed shoe whore, thought that a lot could be said about a woman by the shoes she wore. The lady's crop haircut . . . *check* . Her face was made up nicely . . . *check* . The blue jean dress hugged her curves perfectly . . . *check* . The black leather mules . . . *epic failure*. Perhaps, when they were done, Arykah thought that she and the lady could switch seats. She needed a lesson and obviously some serious therapy on how to upgrade her shoe game.

"Mr. and Mrs. Howell?"

Lance stood from his chair and extended his hand. "Yes. I'm Lance." He shook the lady's hand and turned to face his wife. "This is Arykah."

The lady looked at Arykah who was still seated. "Hello, Arykah. I'm Doctor Santana Lovejoy." She sat down at her desk and noticed that Lance was still standing. "Lance, please sit."

Lance sat, and Doctor Lovejoy retrieved a notebook and ink pen from the center drawer of her desk. She looked up at both Arykah and Lance, then smiled.

Arykah was drawn to her hazel eyes against her dark mocha-colored skin. *Cute.* She could not really deny that Dr. Santana Lovejoy was strikingly beautiful. Arykah rated her a nine. She could've been a ten for sure had she worn the correct shoes.

Doctor Lovejoy had read Arykah's file before she and Lance had arrived. She looked at Arykah."How can I help you today?"

Arykah didn't want to be there. She concentrated on her hands and wondered when was the last time she had visited a nail shop. Since Lance thought the session was necessary, Arykah decided to let him and Doctor Lovejoy have at it. Arykah glanced at her cuticles. She was overdue for a fill-in. *I could be somewhere getting my nails done right now* .

Lance waited for Arykah to speak, but she didn't say a word. "Honey, you wanna start?"

When Arykah didn't respond Lance nudged her arm. While she kept her focus on her nails, Arykah nudged him back much harder.

Lance gave Doctor Lovejoy an embarrassed smile. He cleared his throat. *Maybe this wasn't a good idea after all*, he thought to himself.

"Why don't *you* start, Lance?" Doctor Lovejoy asked him.

That was the second time she had said his name. The way she said it caused Arykah to snap her head in Doctor Lovejoy's direction. *Lance? Lance? It's like that?* She said his name like they had been acquainted. Like they knew each other. Like they go way back. Like they may have been intimate before. Doctor Lovejoy sounded like that chick from *The Cosby Show* when she whined her boyfriend's name. "Oh, Laaannnce." Arykah cringed every time she watched those particular episodes.

"You two know each other?"

Both Doctor Lovejoy and Lance looked at Arykah curiously.

"You're on a first-name basis. I thought that maybe you were old friends."

"Actually, this is the first time that I'm meeting both of you," Doctor Lovejoy said. "I find that using last names in sessions doesn't break the ice with my patients. I prefer to be on a friendlier term."

Arykah couldn't say for sure that Doctor Lovejoy was flirting with Lance, but she decided to go ahead and participate so she could get the heck out of that office, and her man away from that woman. Arykah would really hate to have to flip the desk over on the broad in their first session.

"I was raped. I was beaten," Arykah started. "It caused me to miscarry. Now I'm crazy, and that's why we're here." Arykah looked at Lance. "Isn't that right, Babe? Go ahead and tell *Santana* all about your crazy wife."

By saying her first name and putting special emphasis on it told Doctor Lovejoy and Lance that Arykah didn't appreciate being there or the way Doctor Lovejoy had said Lance's name.

Doctor Lovejoy was taken aback by Arykah's straightforwardness. She was caught off guard and didn't know how to respond. She was confused. All she did was ask the couple how she could help them. "What just happened here?"

Lance pulled on his necktie to loosen the knot. All of a sudden the walls closed in on him. He felt claustrophobic. Lance knew Arykah was going to put on a show, and he had to be ready for when she popped off. Clearly, he'd made a mistake by convincing Arykah to speak with a therapist. She kept telling him that she wasn't ready, that she needed more time, that she would open up on her own. Lance wanted to leave the session and apologize to Doctor Lovejoy for wasting her time, but that would only cause him further embarrassment.

"I'll tell you what just happened here," Arykah offered.

Lance twitched in his seat and silently prayed. *Lord, please write on her tongue.* Sweat beads had formed on his brow.

"The truth is," Arykah started, "my husband is the head of our household. And because he's the head, I'm obligated to do things he asks of me, even when I don't want to. Like coming here today. I didn't want to. But Lance insisted. So, let's talk and get this session over and done with 'cause I gotta get to the nail shop." *And you need to get to DSW* .

"Okay," Doctor Lovejoy said as she wrote the words, *pissed off, mad, gonna be a handful,* on her notepad. She looked up at Arykah. "I hear you, Ary . . . um, Mrs. Howell." Doctor Lovejoy chose to call Arykah by her last name. Obviously calling Lance by his first name had set Arykah off. She was about to detonate.

"Who are you angry at?" Doctor Lovejoy asked her.

"She blames me," Lance said.

Arykah looked at Lance, then connected eyes with Doctor Lovejoy before staring out the window at the interesting waves again.

Doctor Lovejoy asked the same question in a different way. "Who pissed you off?"

Lance opened his mouth to speak but Doctor Lovejoy raised her palm to silence him.

"Mrs. Howell, are you angry at your husband? Are you angry at the man who attacked you? Are you angry at God?"

Arykah looked at Doctor Lovejoy. "All of the above." She glanced out of the window at those waves. "All of the above," she said in a very low voice almost speaking to herself. "All three of them pissed me off." Arykah's last words were just above a whisper, but Doctor Lovejoy and Lance had heard her clearly.

Doctor Lovejoy wrote more words in her note-pad. "Tell me why you're angry with God."

Tears dripped from Arykah's eyelids. She didn't look at Doctor Lovejoy. She kept her focus on the waves crashing against the shoreline. "Because God is omniscient. He knows everything. He saw it coming but didn't stop it." She began to rock back and forth in her chair. "God saw that man on my street. He saw him walk up my porch steps and watched him ring my doorbell." Arykah stopped rocking. She turned her head to her right and looked her husband in his eyes. "You and God allowed that man to rape me."

All of the blood in Lance's body turned cold. Chills ran down his back. From the moment Lance answered Arykah's call on that dreadful day, he had felt guilty that he wasn't home to protect his wife.

Lance saw his home number flashing on the caller ID on his cellular telephone. "You miss me already, don't you?" he joked upon answering the call.

She was crying. She was coughing and choking to get the words out. "He hurt me."

Lance frowned. "Cheeks?"

Arykah's sobbing became louder. "I was calling for you. Where were you?"

Still frowning, Lance didn't have a clue what she was saying to him. "What?"

Arykah screamed into the telephone. "He raped me!"

Lance jumped up from his desk at church. "What?" He was already running from his office. "Baby, I'm on my way. I'm on my way, Cheeks!" When Lance ran past the church secretary's desk, he yelled, "Sharonda, call the police and an ambulance to my house. Right now!"

Lance ran down the church steps, out the door, and got into his car at the speed of lightning. He had tears in his eyes. The thought of a man violating his wife infuriated him. "Baby, hold on. I'm coming home."

Waiting for her husband to get to her, Arykah lay on the living-room floor moaning and crying into the phone. "Lance? Lance?" Her words were just above a whisper.

"Cheeks!" Lance yelled into the telephone. She didn't answer him. Lance was worried that Arykah had lost consciousness. "Arykah! Arykah!"

Lance had blamed himself for not doing what he was called to do. Yes, he was the bishop of Freedom Temple Church of God in Christ, but he was also a husband. He didn't protect his wife. He felt less of a man. "Cheeks, if I could go back and change everything that happened, on that day, I would. You *know* I would."

Doctor Lovejoy's eyes grew wide. She wished Lance hadn't spoken those words. But he'd said them so fast, she didn't have time to stop him. She knew the session was over when Arykah jumped up from her chair and glared at Lance.

"You can't change it, Lance! You weren't there to protect me!" she screamed. "You weren't there! You weren't there!" Arykah moved past Lance, opened the door, and ran out of the office crying hysterically.

Lance leaned forward in his seat and placed his face in his hands. He exhaled loudly. "My God."

"Go after her," Doctor Lovejoy said.

Lance stood and exited the office. "I'm sorry," he said over his shoulder.

Arykah was already sitting in the passenger seat of their late-model Land Rover when Lance got to the parking garage. He opened the driver's door, got inside, and looked at her. "Cheeks, I'm so sorry."

Arykah stared straight-ahead at the wall in front of them. She didn't respond.

He reached out to touch her left arm when he saw that she was shaking. "Cheeks?"

Arykah snatched her arm away from his touch.

"I'm really sorry, Babe."

"Let's just go." She wiped tears from her eyes.

Lance started the engine and pulled out of the parking garage.

They had been riding in silence for ten minutes before he glanced over at Arykah. "I shouldn't have pushed. You weren't ready to talk about it, and I kept insisting. I just thought that if you got your emotions out, things would get back to normal faster."

Arykah was looking out of the passenger-side window. She didn't respond to him. As Lance drove, she watched people walk past all of the showcase windows on Michigan Avenue. Lance wanted to do something to cheer her up. He always kept a wild card in his back pocket for when Arykah was in a foul mood. "I feel like spoiling my wife today," he said. He glanced over at her with a smile. "How about we stop at Macy's? Let's see how long it'll take you to put a dent in their shoe department?"

When she didn't react, Lance frowned. That was the first time Arykah hadn't been fazed when he mentioned shoes. He knew then that something was really wrong. More wrong than he had thought.

"Are you hungry, Cheeks? We're not too far from the Cheesecake Factory."

Nothing from her.

Lance glanced at her again. "Don't they have the banana cheesecake you're always raving about? That's your favorite, right?" Lance chuckled when he recalled that Arykah always ate her desserts before her meals whenever they dined at restaurants.

Still no response. No facial changes, no body movements. Nothing.

The only thing Arykah loved more than shoe shopping was eating. Especially a sweet treat. Lance thought for sure that he'd get her hyped up for stilettos or something delicious to eat. When she didn't respond to either, he silently prayed, *Lord, please bring my wife back.*

"That's him!" Arykah hollered out. She pointed to a man walking along Michigan Avenue. "That's him, Lance! That's the guy who raped me!"

Lance slammed on the brakes and pulled over to the curb. He saw the man Arykah was pointing at. He wore a gray sweatshirt with stonewashed blue jeans. Lance understood why Arykah would think the man was the guy who attacked her. He was dark and bald just like Clyde Trumbull. "No. That's not him, Cheeks. We got the guy, remember? Clyde Trumbull. Mother Pansie's nephew."

"Oh," was all Arykah said. She settled back in the passenger seat.

Arykah wasn't present at church the Sunday morning when Detective Cortney Rogers arrested Mother Pansie for soliciting her nephew, Clyde Trumbull, to rape and beat Arykah at her home. After the fiasco at church, Lance came home and told Arykah what happened at Freedom Temple and that Clyde Trumbull had been arrested too.

Lance proceeded to drive down Michigan Avenue. "So, what do you wanna do tonight? How about we take in a movie?" He glanced at her. "You feel up to it?"

"That's him!" Arykah shrieked. She pointed to another bald, dark-skinned man. He wore a navy blue suit and carried a brown briefcase. "That's him, Lance! That's the guy!"

At that moment, Lance knew for sure that Arykah was in trouble. He had lost her. Her mind was gone. His voice quivered. "That's not him, Cheeks."

She pointed to a different dark, bald man wearing a beige button-down shirt with khaki pants. "That's him! That's him, Lance! That's him!"

Lance grabbed Arykah's left hand and squeezed it tight. Tears flowed from his eyelids. His vision became blurred as he drove his wife home. Between Doctor Lovejoy's office and their home, Arykah had accused a total of seven dark, bald men as being her attacker.

Two

The next morning, Arykah emerged from her closet dressed in a pale pink, floor-length sari wrap, Diane Von Fürstenberg dress. Made up of Viscose Georgette material, the dress was airy, and it blew gracefully behind her as she walked. She had fallen in love with the dress when she saw it in a bridal magazine. Her eyes were drawn to the gold silky soft bamboo pipe stitching along the neckline, wrists, and hem. "What do you think of this one, Bishop?" The gown was the second outfit Arykah had tried on and modeled for Lance. Being the first lady of a church, Arykah took pride in her dress code.

In his usual position for Arykah's Sunday-morning fashion show, Lance lay back on the bed with his hands suspended behind his head against the headboard. Arykah's teacup-size Yorkie, Diva Chanel, was lying on the bed next to him. "It's stunning, Cheeks." He called her by the nickname he'd given Arykah because her backside resembled two puffy cheeks. Lance thought about his words. "Correction, *you're* stunning in that dress."

Arykah opened the long flap of the dress to reveal 6¾-inch, peep-toe, satin, pale pink platform stilettos. "Boom! Pow! Bang!"

Lance laughed out loud. That was the Arykah that he loved. In the five months that they'd been married Lance had mastered a way to bring Arykah out of a funky mood. All he had to do was mention the word *stiletto* and her attitude would immediately change for the better.

Three months ago when Arykah and Lance had an argument, she had gone to bed angry. At four a.m., Lance had gotten up and walked around to Arykah's side of the bed. He bent over and whispered, "Stiletto."

Arykah rose up quickly with her eyes closed, said, "I'll take it in a size eight," then fell back into a deep sleep.

Lance fell to the floor laughing. When he told Arykah, the next morning, what she did in her sleep, she didn't believe him. Lance got his cellular phone and brought it to her. He had recorded the whole thing. When Arykah saw herself on video she had to laugh too. And she had completely forgotten what she was angry with Lance about.

"I have a beautiful wife," Lance said, after Arykah stripped and laid her dress on the bed. She stood before him naked.

Arykah smiled shyly and walked away because she saw something in Lance's eyes. She knew what was coming next. She grabbed her robe from her closet and put it on, then went into the bathroom and sat at her vanity. Diva Chanel jumped off the bed and followed her.

"We're in the clear now," Lance said from the bedroom.

Arykah squeezed her eyes shut. *He wants to have sex.* It wasn't that Arykah wasn't attracted to Lance. She loved her husband very much. In her mind, Lance trying to seduce her meant that he wanted to be in charge of her body just like Clyde Trumbull had been in charge when he forced himself on her. Arykah wanted to tell Lance that she'd be willing to make love to him if he didn't use his hands to touch her, but she knew he'd never go for that. Lance enjoyed grabbing her, squeezing her, caressing her, and fondling her. Arykah felt very different than she did weeks ago. Then she was willing. Her hormones had shifted.

Lance came into the bathroom and stood behind her. He put his hands softly on her shoulders. At his touch, Arykah jumped. She didn't want to be touched.

"Your doctor gave us the go-ahead, Cheeks." It had been five weeks since Arykah's rape and Lance craved her touch, her warmth, the feel of her body against his. When he tried to hug Arykah, she'd pull away from him. Whenever he tried to kiss her, she would turn her face away. They shared a California king-size bed, and Arykah made sure to leave enough space for four more people between herself and Lance.

"I miss our showers together in the morning," he said glancing at her reflection in her vanity mirror. "I miss my wife."

Arykah looked at Lance in the mirror. "I haven't gone anywhere. I'm right here."

Arykah may have been present in the flesh, but her mind and spirit could not be found. She had checked out. She completely dismissed what happened in the car on Michigan Avenue the day before. She refused to talk about it.

"Join me in the shower," Lance pleaded. Their love-making on Sunday mornings always started in the shower.

Arykah picked up a bottle of Neutrogena hand and feet moisturizer and poured a small amount in the palm of her hand. "I've already showered. Besides, if we get something started now we'll be late for church, Lance. I've been gone for five Sundays. It's my first day back at church, and I don't wanna be late." Arykah saw Diva Chanel sniffing around the bathroom. "And I still have to dress Diva Chanel."

Lance hung his head and turned away from Arykah. She watched as he started the water in the shower before stepping inside. She felt horrible that she denied her husband, but she couldn't get past the fact that Lance wasn't home when she was attacked. He should've been there. Lance could have prevented her from losing their baby. Everything was his fault. The rape. The beating. The miscarriage. It was all Lance's fault. And for some unexplained reason, she just didn't want to be touched.

After massaging the moisturizer into her hands and feet, Arykah exited the master bedroom. She ascended the spiral staircase and entered the first bedroom on the left, Diva Chanel's room. The Yorkie followed her master closely. Arykah sighed when she saw that the room was a mess.

"Diva Chanel," she started. "This room is terrible."

There were lots of toys next to the pink plush princess doggie bed. Stuffed teddy bears, small stuffed baby dolls, and small toy balls were scattered all around the room.

Arykah picked up the toys, teddy bears, and dolls and placed them inside a small pink netted basket. "How many times have I told you that you gotta keep your room decent and in order?"

Diva Chanel's tail wagged as she watched Arykah put away her toys. When the room looked tidy enough for her liking Arykah went to Diva Chanel's closet and opened the door. She stood before three racks filled with petite clothing for dogs.

"Okay, Miss Diva Chanel," Arykah said. "Today is your debut at church."

Monique and Adonis had bought Arykah the tea-cup-size Yorkie after she was attacked. They felt the dog would help distract Arykah's mind. She fell in love with the dog the first moment she saw her. Arykah and Diva Chanel had become joined at the hip.

"Mommy wants her little girl to be very pretty," Arykah said to Diva Chanel. She selected a small pink and yellow polka-dot dress with a small purse attached by Velcro. "This will be cute with the pink ribbons in your hair."

An hour later, the only thing Lance could do was shake his head from side to side when he saw Arykah and her mini-me dressed in matching pink and yellow outfits. "Oh my God. I have two of them."

Arykah kissed the tip of Diva Chanel's nose. "Isn't she cute, Lance?"

He exhaled. "Arykah, you're so extra."

"You're extra right, and I extra agree."

"I didn't think you were serious. You can't take Diva Chanel to church."

She looked at Lance in his eyes. "Of course I can."

"Dogs do not belong in church."

"Shhh," Arykah silenced Lance. "Do not call her that. She has feelings."

Lance frowned. "Call her what? A *dog*? That's what she is. She has four legs, a snout, she's hairy all over, and she has a tail. Diva Chanel is a dog, Arykah, and she's not going to church."

Arykah glared at Lance. "She *is* going to church."

Time was of the essence. Lance couldn't spare another minute arguing with her. "You're gonna leave her upstairs, in your office, right?"

"Lance, she fits right in my handbag. No one will even know she's there."

Lance exhaled. "So, what if someone else wants to bring their dog to church?"

"Everybody can't do what I do." Arykah walked past him. "Come on. I have a meeting at ten o'clock."

The five ladies, affectionately known as *"Team Arykah,"* sat in the first lady's office at Freedom Temple Church of God in Christ. Mother Myrtle Cortland, Chelsea Childs, Darlita Evans, Gladys Blackmon, and Arykah's best friend, Monique Cortland, occupied chairs around Lady Arykah's desk. It was after Arykah had purchased each of them a pair of Christian Louboutin stilettos and treated them to a spa day when the ladies had nicknamed themselves.

Arykah had summoned each of the ladies to her office before morning worship began.

"What do you think Lady Arykah wants to speak with us about?" Darlita asked the team.

Monique shrugged her shoulders. "Beats me. She wouldn't go into detail when she called this morning and asked that I meet her here."

"All I know is," Gladys started, "when Lady Arykah calls a meeting, something is up."

Myrtle nodded her head in agreement with Gladys. "She sounded mysterious when she called me this morning. Her only words were, 'Mother Cortland, I need you to meet me in my office at ten o'clock.'"

Chelsea chimed in. "Uh-huh. That's what Lady Arykah said to me too. I asked her what the meeting was about and she wouldn't tell me anything. She said she wanted to wait and share it with all of us together."

The door to Arykah's office opened, and she walked in carrying Diva Chanel in the palm of her hand. She saw her team sitting, dressed in their Sunday best, around her oak wood desk. Arykah didn't offer a greeting. She gave each of the ladies a somber look.

The ladies didn't know what to think or say. The first thing they noticed was Arykah's beautiful pink floor-length dress. Her wide-brim pink and yellow preacher's wife hat was pulled down on her face. Arykah wore the hat tipped to the right side so that it covered her right eye. In her hand she held a yellow Hermès Birkin bag that she paid a whopping $16,000 for. Arykah's pale pink, high-heeled, strappy stilettos represented pure elegance. She didn't disappoint. She never did. As always, Lady Elect was as sharp as a two-edged sword.

Gladys, Darlita, and Chelsea all cooed at Diva Chanel's pink outfit. Myrtle and Monique had already seen Diva Chanel's wardrobe. Her closet was almost as big as Arykah's.

The ladies, along with the entire Freedom Temple Church family, looked forward to seeing what their first lady would wear to church every Sunday. When she and Lance stood at the door to the sanctuary, right before morning worship began, the praise and worship leader would ask the congregation to stand and receive Bishop Howell and Lady Arykah.

Lance, in his tailor-made suits, and Arykah, dressed to the nines, strutted down the center aisle. Arykah always felt the heat from all the eyes that would scan her from head to toe. And even though the organ and drums made plenty of noise, Arykah could still hear, *"Wow , look at that dress . . . Oh my, those heels . . . She's beautiful."* Arykah felt like a young bride each Sunday as Lance escorted her to the front pew before taking his seat in the pulpit.

Darlita wanted to rise from her chair to hug and kiss Arykah. She hadn't seen her since the Sunday before she was attacked. But the mood that Arykah exuded kept the ladies in their seats with their mouths closed. No one wanted to be the first to mumble a word.

Only Monique and Myrtle had seen Arykah since she had been attacked. Monique was Arykah's best friend, and Myrtle was the mother she never had. Arykah couldn't keep them away. She had refused visits from Chelsea, Gladys, and Darlita. But each of them had given Lance their love to pass on to Lady Arykah.

Without uttering a word, Arykah took off her wide hat and hung it on the coat hanger just inside her office door. Her hair was pulled back into a tight princess bun. Not a single strand was out of place. She came and sat in the high-back leather chair behind her desk. Arykah put Diva Chanel down on the floor to allow her to sniff her surroundings.

First, Arykah looked at Monique, her friend since childhood. Arykah considered Monique to be her sister. They had been through thick and thin together. There wasn't anything that Monique didn't know about Arykah. Monique had always had Arykah's back. They had fought together. They had smoked dope together. And they had lied and cheated together. Arykah knew, without a shadow of a doubt, that if there was one person she could depend on, it was Monique. She was Arykah's ride-or-die chick.

Next, Arykah looked at Chelsea. She had grown on Arykah. Chelsea was originally a member of Mother Pansie's and Mother Gussie's team. Chelsea, along with most of the other women at Freedom Temple, was told that they had to hate Arykah. But one cold Sunday morning, Chelsea had complimented Arykah on her boots. When Arykah had given Chelsea a business card for a guy that made boots to fit thick calves, Chelsea had confessed to Arykah that she was the mothers' pawn. Chelsea apologized to Arykah and hugged her. Arykah accepted Chelsea's apology, and they had been close ever since.

After a moment, Arykah looked at Gladys. She'd never forget the day that Gladys had brought her fifteen-year-old pregnant daughter, Miranda, to her office. Miranda wanted to terminate her pregnancy against her mother's wishes. Arykah had counseled Miranda and convinced her that her baby was a miracle and all babies come from God no matter how they were conceived. Arykah had also saved Miranda the embarrassment of Mother Pansie's rule that all unwed mothers must stand before the church and confess their sins of fornication and ask the church for forgiveness. Gladys appreciated Arykah coming to her daughter's defense and vowed, from that day on, to support her pastor's wife.

Then Arykah looked at Darlita. Darlita was a mess when she had met Arykah. She was in a loveless marriage with a serial adulterer. Darlita's husband wasn't only unfaithful but also verbally abusive toward her. Arykah had to dig deep within herself to save Darlita. She shared with Darlita the abuse she had received from an ex-boyfriend.

Arykah had challenged Darlita to love herself and get out of that relationship. Darlita had taken Arykah's advice and moved in with her brother. She filed for divorce and is now living an abuse-free life. Darlita consistently thanked Arykah for saving her life.

Finally, Arykah looked at Myrtle. Arykah had known her for years. She had first met Myrtle when Monique was dating Myrtle's son, Boris. Myrtle, a no-nonsense woman, had captured Arykah's heart when she didn't defend her no-good son when he mistreated Monique. Arykah and Myrtle had joined forces and tried to get Monique to leave Boris and his ugly ways. But eventually fate stepped in, and Adonis had stolen Monique's heart right from under his own cousin's nose. And it was Myrtle who came to Arykah's rescue when she learned of all the dirty deeds the mothers at Freedom Temple were doing to Arykah.

The scene in Arykah's office was like mobsters sitting around the table waiting to be reprimanded by the boss. No one said a word. They waited for the mob boss to speak.

Arykah shrugged her shoulders and smiled. "I'm back."

Team Arykah relaxed and exhaled a sigh of relief.

Chelsea was pleased. "And not a moment too soon. You were truly missed."

"Had another Sunday gone by I was gonna put out an APB on you," Gladys chuckled.

"I wanna thank each of you for your prayers and the flowers and the cookies and the cakes and the pies," Arykah said patting her belly. "There's a saying that food is the way to a man's heart, but I gotta admit it's always been the way to my heart too."

"We know," Monique said. "How could we forget the story you told us about Bishop Lance cooking dinner for you on your first date."

"That man cooked a meal *and* baked a dessert. Shoot, I was hooked," Arykah said. "But when I saw him pour me a glass of grape Kool-Aid on ice . . . *Chile* . . . the bishop could've gotten it that night."

The women screamed out in laughter.

Myrtle chuckled. "Girl, you're a mess."

"I'm so glad you're back, Lady Arykah," Darlita offered. "It just hasn't been the same around here without you."

"It's good to be back, Darlita," Arykah stated truthfully. She was anxious to get her life back to normal. "But I wanted to meet with all of you before morning service just to say 'thanks.'" She looked at Chelsea, Gladys, and Darlita. "I am fully aware that you wanted to come by the house and visit, but I just wasn't up to it. Truth be told, my face was swollen, my mouth had stitches, and I didn't want anyone to see me that way."

"Lady Arykah, you don't have to apologize or explain anything to us. We understood."

Darlita and Gladys nodded their heads in agreement with what Chelsea had just said.

"And I'm aware of all the phone calls you made to me. I just didn't wanna talk because—"

"You're doing it again," Gladys said, cutting Arykah's words off. "There is no need to explain. We get it."

"Mother Cortland and Monique kept us in the loop," Darlita offered. "We were given a progress report almost daily."

"Very good," Arykah said. She exhaled and looked at all of them. "Now, what's the tea, ladies? Spill it. I wanna know everything that's been going on in my absence."

"Wellllll," Darlita sang, "there has been a lot of talk about how you had Mother Pansie falsely arrested."

Arykah's eyebrows rose. *"Falsely* arrested? Really?"

"Lady Arykah, there are women here who were raised in this church by Mother Pansie and Mother Gussie. The mothers ruled Freedom Temple for years before you got here. The majority of the congregation really thought that the mothers could do no wrong."

Arykah looked at Gladys. "But it's so sad that the congregation, especially the women, were mere puppets dangling from the mothers' strings."

"I know that to be true because I was one of them," Chelsea confessed.

"The bottom line is that you can expect to get the cold shoulder from folks, and then again, there are others here that sympathize with what the mothers did to you," Darlita said.

"And folks are asking questions," Chelsea added. "There has been some talk and rumors. No one really knows why, in detail, Mother Pansie was arrested at church."

Gladys chimed in. "And people are wondering why Mother Gussie hasn't returned to Freedom Temple. I hear that she hasn't taken any calls from anyone."

"What is her husband, Deacon Hughes, saying?" Arykah asked Gladys.

"He hasn't been to church since you were attacked."

"The bishop hasn't made a formal statement to the congregation," Monique stated. "When someone asks him where you are he simply states that you've taken some time off and that you'll be back soon."

That was news to Arykah. She had thought for sure that Lance had addressed the congregation. "I had no idea about any of this. I don't know why Lance didn't address the people."

"I think *you* should," Myrtle said to Arykah.

Arykah looked at her with a horrific expression. *"Me ?"*

"Well, someone should," Monique said. "If the bishop hasn't done it by now, then he probably won't do it at all. But the congregation should know what happened to you."

"I agree," Chelsea added. "And they should also know who was responsible. I think you should go downstairs and tell the entire church how cruel the mothers were to you and what part Mother Pansie played in your attack."

Myrtle shook her head from side to side. "Uh-uh. That's not the correct way."

All of the ladies looked at Myrtle with raised eyebrows.

"Look at me however y'all want. The church does not need to know details. I agree that Lady Arykah should address the church." Myrtle looked at Arykah. "But you shouldn't disclose private information. It's okay to tell the folks what happened to you and why you were away from church for five weeks but leave it at that. Ain't nobody stupid. They already know why Mother Pansie was arrested. The detective read her, her Miranda Rights as she was taking Mother Pansie out of the sanctuary. Folks also know why Mother Gussie ain't been back to Freedom Temple."

"I'll make a statement right after praise and worship before Lance takes his text."

"And just be classy about it," Myrtle advised Arykah. "No need to get ghetto and say, *'Mother Pansie had me raped and that's why her wrinkled, old butt is locked up.'* I can see you now waving your hands and rotating your neck. That's *so* ghetto."

The ladies laughed because they knew Myrtle was speaking the gospel truth about Arykah.

"But I *am* ghetto," Arykah admitted. "That's how I do it. I'm going downstairs and get it turned up."

"Not in the church," Myrtle said sternly. "You ain't turning nothin' anywhere. You're the bishop's wife. You're a first lady, Arykah, and you should conduct yourself accordingly."

Darlita, Gladys, and Chelsea liked the ghetto side of Lady Arykah and would have loved for her to put on a show, but they also knew that Myrtle was correct in the way Arykah should handle the congregation.

Arykah threw her hands in the air and surrendered. "All right," she said. She looked at Myrtle. "For you, *and only you*, I'll be delicate." She looked at Gladys. "Now, Gladys, I wanna know your plans for Miranda's baby shower."

Gladys exhaled. "Lady Arykah, I'm just gonna be real with you. You know I work two jobs just to make ends meet. As much as I would like to give Miranda a shower, I just can't afford the food and decorations. And besides, my two-bedroom apartment isn't in the best condition. I wouldn't wanna host a baby shower there anyhow."

"Well, the girl needs a shower, Gladys. You can't afford to buy a crib, high chair, diapers, swing, stroller, and everything yourself. So, guess what?"

Gladys and all of the other ladies looked at Arykah mysteriously. "What?" They all said in unison.

"Freedom Temple Church of God in Christ will host its first baby shower."

All five ladies gasped at the same time. They sucked all of the air out of Arykah's office.

"How are you gonna pull that off?" Gladys asked Arykah. "Miranda is an unwed mother. The church would never go for that."

Arykah veered at Gladys. Her neck danced as she spoke. "The church doesn't have to go for anything. *I'm* the first lady of this church, and if I wanna throw a baby shower in the fellowship hall, then that's what I'm gonna do. I'm not using any of the church's money, just the space."

"I love it," Monique hollered out.

Chelsea chuckled and shook her head from side to side. "If Mother Pansie and Mother Gussie were here, they would spit fire."

"Well, they ain't here," Myrtle said.

"Lady Elect Arykah Miles-Howell is here, honey," Darlita offered, snapping her fingers in the shape of the letter Z.

Monique smiled. "And she reigns."

Lance knocked on Arykah's office door before opening it and poking his head inside. He saw that she was in the presence of her supporters. "Praise the Lord, ladies."

"Praise the Lord, Bishop," everyone but Arykah responded.

Lance glanced at Arykah and smiled as he did every Sunday morning when he poked his head inside her door. "It's time to head down to the sanctuary."

"You go ahead without me."

Myrtle looked at Arykah curiously and cocked her head to the side. She knew that Arykah absolutely loved walking into the sanctuary with her strong and handsome arm candy by her side. She wondered why, on Arykah's first Sunday back at Freedom Temple, she was reluctant.

Lance frowned. He and Arykah had always entered the sanctuary together. He was looking forward to escorting his wife to the front pew on her first Sunday back in weeks. "Are you sure?" he asked her.

"Yes, I'm just gonna finish up some things with the ladies." Arykah forced a smile at Lance.

Myrtle saw right through Arykah's façade.

"Okay then," Lance said to Arykah. He looked at her one last time before shutting the door.

"Where were we?" Arykah asked the ladies.

Myrtle was not happy with the way Arykah had just dismissed her husband. She wanted to speak with her about it, but not in the presence of the team. She addressed Darlita, Gladys, Monique, and Chelsea. "Service is about to start. You all go ahead." She looked at Arykah in her eyes sternly. "I wanna speak with Lady Arykah."

Arykah could tell by the expression on Myrtle's face that she was in trouble. She didn't know why but knew that as soon as she and Myrtle were alone she would find out.

The ladies stood and gathered their things. On the way out of her office Chelsea, Darlita, Gladys, and Monique gave Arykah a welcome back hug.

Arykah saw Diva Chanel sniffing around a potted plant in the corner of her office. "Come on, Diva. It's time for church."

"Sit down." Myrtle's words were not a request but a demand. Lance had informed Myrtle the day before of Arykah's actions at her therapy session as well as in the car on the way home. Lance pleaded with her to do all she could to help Arykah.

Arykah looked at Myrtle's face and knew that she'd better take heed. She sat down in her chair.

"What's going on with you and the bishop?"

Arykah shrugged her shoulders. "What do you mean?"

"Every Sunday, you're so giddy for him to escort you down to the front pew. What's changed?"

"Nothing has changed. I just wanted to catch up with you and the girls."

Myrtle lowered her head a bit and glared at Arykah. "Don't lie to me, li'l girl. Something ain't right between the two of you."

Arykah looked away from Myrtle and focused on what Diva Chanel was doing.

Myrtle leaned back in her chair and crossed her ankles. "I got all day if you do."

Lance told Myrtle that Arykah blamed him for her attack confidence in. Myrtle wanted to tear into Arykah for doing so but needed Arykah to confess it first.

They heard Lance ask the congregation to stand for prayer.

Arykah would rather be anywhere else other than where she was at that moment. She didn't feel like being interrogated, especially by Myrtle Cortland. She had a way of pulling things out of Arykah that she didn't want to release. Myrtle was an intercessor; she knew how to reach Jesus on others' behalf. Arykah truly believed that Myrtle had missed her true calling. She belonged in a courtroom. She felt that Myrtle would have been a great prosecutor.

"Service has started, Mother Cortland. Shouldn't we head down to the sanctuary?"

Myrtle couldn't care less about what was happening down in the sanctuary. She was going to deal with Arykah right then. She ignored Arykah's question and asked one of her own. "Are you and the bishop fighting? I told you once before that you can't wear your emotions on your sleeve in this church. Women will use that to come between the two of you."

Arykah knew she wasn't going to get out of her office until she opened up to Myrtle. She shook her head from side to side. "No, it's nothing like that. Lance and I are not fighting."

"Well, what is it then? Why didn't you let your husband escort you down to the sanctuary like you normally do?" Myrtle patiently waited for Arykah's confession. *Go ahead and tell me that you blame him for what happened to you. Go ahead.*

Arykah really didn't want to talk about it, but she had no choice. "Lance wasn't there for me. Everything was his fault."

Myrtle needed clarity. "What was his fault?"

"The rape, Mother Cortland !" Arykah said irritably. "My miscarriage too. All of it was Lance's fault."

They could hear the congregation and choir singing. Myrtle didn't care. She was stunned at what Arykah had just said to her. "What do you mean? How is the bishop at fault?"

Arykah looked at Myrtle directly in her eyes. "He wasn't where he was supposed to be. Had Lance been home that morning, I wouldn't have been raped."

Myrtle looked at Arykah as if she had two heads. That was the most ridiculous thing she had ever heard. Myrtle knew that Arykah was delicate. Her response to Arykah had to be a soft one. "The bishop was here, at the church, when you were attacked. So, he *was* where he was supposed to be. You can't possibly be serious, Arykah. Are you *really* punishing him for not being at home that morning?"

Arykah looked at Myrtle. "You're taking his side." Myrtle had been married before. Arykah thought for sure that she would understand that it was a man's job to protect his household.

Myrtle shook her head from side to side. "No. There is no side to take. That Monday morning, Lance left you alone and went to work just as he does every morning. How can you fault him for not knowing that a lunatic was gonna ring your doorbell? You think he's a psychic, a fortune-teller, a wizard, or a genie? Lance isn't any of those, Arykah. He's a man. He has flesh and bones, just like you. He's only a pastor. Okay? Lance doesn't have superpowers that allows him to see into the future and stop disasters from happening."

Arykah exhaled. "You don't understand, Mother Cortland."

"See, *that's* where you're wrong. I *do* understand. *I* was raped before."

Arykah's eyes grew wide. She didn't know that. The two of them have had some deep conversations in the past, but that was a secret Myrtle had kept.

"And I did *exactly* what you did. I opened the door."

Tears appeared on top of Arykah's lower eyelids. "Oh my God," she cried out.

"My next-door neighbor saw my husband leave for work one morning, then came and knocked on my front door. I heard him calling my name, '*Myrtle, Myrtle, you gotta come! I need your help!'*"

Arykah was in disbelief. She covered her mouth but said, "No."

"I thought that maybe something was wrong with his wife. She and I were friends. Then again, I thought that maybe their house was on fire. I really didn't know what happened, but it was the urgency in his voice that made me open the door in a panic. Then he forced his way in and raped me."

"Oh my God," Arykah said again. That exact thing happened to her. "Why haven't you told me this before today?"

Myrtle shrugged her shoulders. "There wasn't a need to tell anyone until now. It wasn't my husband's fault that I was raped. And I want you to understand that it isn't the bishop's fault that *you* were raped and beaten. You can't put that type of guilt and burden on his shoulders, Arykah. It's not fair."

The tears dripped onto her cheeks. "But I gotta blame somebody, Mother Cortland. I wanna be mad. I wanna spit. I wanna cuss. I wanna throw things. I wanna . . ." Arykah was getting all worked up.

Myrtle reached across the desk and patted Arykah's hand to calm her. "Of course you can be mad, Sugarplum. No one would fault you if you spat, cussed, or threw something. You certainly have every right to do all of that, but when it comes to being mad, Arykah, be mad at the right person. *You* opened the front door without looking through the peephole. *You* did that. *You* opened the door."

Arykah pulled her hand from underneath Myrtle's and reached for a Kleenex tissue from a box that sat on top of her desk. She wiped the tears and blew her runny nose. "I don't understand why this happened to me."

Myrtle smiled slightly. "You're a pastor's wife. That's why it happened. You gotta have a testimony."

Arykah didn't understand. She looked at Myrtle. "Huh?"

"There are over 400 women on the roll at this church. What would you do if one of them came to you and said that she had been raped? How would you counsel her if she told you that she blamed her husband because he wasn't there to protect her? What would you do? What would you say to her?"

Arykah thought about the questions Myrtle had just asked her. "I would console her. I'd hug her and pray with her. I'd ask God to heal her heart. I would also recommend that she speak with someone, a professional."

"You mean like the way you allowed your husband to hug, console, and pray with *you*? Like the way he recommended you to speak with a therapist? The therapist you ran out on yesterday?"

Arykah's eyebrows rose. She didn't know that Myrtle knew about that.

"Oh, yeah, the bishop called me while you were taking a nap yesterday. He told me all about the way you ran out on your session. So, let me get this straight. You would advise a woman to do what you won't do? Is *that* what I'm hearing?"

Arykah sat in her chair boiling on the inside. How *dare* Lance tell Myrtle her business? "I can't believe he told you. That wasn't his place."

"It was *absolutely* his place. The man loves you. You blame him for your attack. You won't let him anywhere near you. You left your first therapy session abruptly. And you freak out at every dark, bald man that you see when you know your assailant has been arrested. Of course it was the bishop's place to call me. *Someone* has to get through to you."

Myrtle was the mother that Arykah never had. Having been passed around from foster home to foster home when she was a child, Arykah had basically raised herself. She was twenty-five years old when she met Myrtle. She served on the mother's board at their previous church, Morning Glory. Arykah and Myrtle were a lot alike in character. They were both short-tempered and quick to get someone told. The two of them had become like mother and daughter. Myrtle had been at Morning Glory for twenty years before she recently joined Freedom Temple to be at Arykah's side.

It was at Morning Glory that Arykah was chastised by Myrtle for dating three men at once. It was Myrtle who called Arykah out when she overheard Arykah using not-so-holy language. And it had always been Myrtle who Arykah had gone to when she needed counsel or advice.

"So, is this what this little meeting is all about? Gettin' through to me? You call yourself checkin' me?"

At Arykah's attitude a small sarcastic chuckle escaped Myrtle's lips. Back in her prime, Myrtle would have had both of her hands around Arykah's neck in a split second. Myrtle wanted to reach across the desk and squeeze the life out of her right then. "It would really be in your best interest, *li'l girl*, to realize who you're talking to." She leaned forward in her chair and raised her eyebrows. Myrtle gritted her teeth as she spoke to Arykah. "Don't let the gray hair fool you. The bishop may allow your lips to get loose with him, but I ain't the one to try, *and you know I ain't*." Myrtle's neck danced. "Trust me when I tell you this, Honey. You ain't the first pastor's wife that I done *checked* , okay? You're a rookie. I'm trying to teach your young, wet-behind-the-ears, inexperienced behind something about being a wife. Try closing your smart ass mouth and opening your ears up to learn a thing or two before you destroy your marriage.

"And if you believe, for one second, that Lance is gonna just let you do him any kind of way because you're throwing hissy fits and having baby tantrums, you got another thing coming. He ain't gotta settle for your crap. Not when he's got unlimited coochie standing in line just waiting for you to screw up."

Arykah realized that she wasn't the only one with a raw tongue. Myrtle shut her all the way down. *You gotta reach the people on their level, Arykah* , is what Myrtle had told her. *You can't be sugarcoatin' thangs in your counseling sessions. Just tell it like it is.* Arykah had learned from the best, and she herself was getting counseled by the master.

"What makes you think you're the only woman with a hole between your legs? Lance may be a pastor, but he's a man first. You know who Sally is, don't you?"

Arykah frowned and shook her head from side to side.

Myrtle sang, *"Rise , Sally, rise. Put your hands on your hips and let your backbone slip."* Myrtle glared at Arykah. "Sally will shake her tail to the east for your husband, then she'll shake it to the west for your husband . . . if *you* don't. There are Sallys down in the sanctuary just waiting."

Arykah sat in her chair stunned and speechless at the same time. Yes, indeed, she had just been checked. She looked at Myrtle but didn't utter a word.

Arykah's silence told Myrtle that her point had been made. She leaned back in her chair and crossed her ankles again. "Now, what happened to you wasn't Lance's fault. Sometimes, there are things in life that God allows us to go through so that we'll have a testimony to help someone else. What you experienced was horrific, but God will use your brokenness for His greatest and highest good. You have to snap out of this anger that you have toward your husband and do the work that God has called you to do. You married a minister, which means you involuntarily became a minister as well. You don't just get to play dress up. There's more to being a pastor's wife than wearing beautiful gowns, big hats, and high heels, Arykah. You can't just show up at church and sit on the front pew like a statue for folks to stare at and admire." Myrtle chuckled. "Is that what you thought being a pastor's wife was supposed to be like? You have a calling on your life, Sugarplum. And you have work to do. You are destined for greatness. Now get yourself together. I've seen victory too many times to let defeat have the last say-so.

"You and Bishop Lance, in ministry together, would be powerful. God had to break you to get you to where He's going to take you. This had to happen, and it's all for His glory. There are women downstairs that are hurting, broken, and miserable. Some are on the verge of suicide. How can you help and guide them if you don't know where they are or where they've been?"

Arykah pulled another Kleenex tissue from its box and wiped the new tears that had fallen on her face. She thought about her makeup and knew she must look like a hot mess. But for the first time in a long time, Arykah didn't care about her appearance. Myrtle was messing her up.

"You know Lance loves you, but God loves you so much more. To whom much is given, Arykah, much is required. You live in the biggest house that I've ever seen. Your wardrobe is ridiculous, and we won't even discuss your shoe collection. I know what's parked in your garage and taking up space in your driveway. You can drive a different car each day of the week if you wanted to. You may have spent money on those things, but do you really think that you don't have to pay for that stuff spiritually? Well, let me tell you something, Honey. You owe God for the lavish lifestyle you're living, and He's collecting His due." Myrtle glared at Arykah. "It's time to pay up."

Bishop Lance had already preached a short sermon and service was just about over when an usher escorted Arykah and Myrtle down the center aisle to the front pew. Arykah waited for the associate pastor and Bishop Lance's right-hand man, Minister Carlton Weeks, to bless the tithes and offerings. When the blessing was over Arykah went and stood at the podium directly in front of her with Diva Chanel cradled in her arm. She looked at all the people staring at her and suddenly became nervous. She turned and looked toward Lance who sat in the pulpit. He winked his eye at her. That expression of love was what Arykah needed to get through that moment.

"Good afternoon, Freedom Temple."

"Good afternoon, Lady Arykah," all the people responded.

"Um, I know there are questions about my absence over the past five weeks. Some of you know what happened to me, and some of you may not know." She looked at Myrtle who nodded her head toward Arykah. "A little over a month ago, on a Monday morning, I was attacked in my home. I . . . um . . . I answered the doorbell and was immediately hit in the face. I was dragged to my living room where I was raped and beaten very violently."

Many gasps for air could be heard throughout the sanctuary.

"So, for the past month, I've been at home recuperating and just dealing with this whole thing mentally." Arykah's voice started to quiver. She looked toward her team sitting on the front row. She pointed at them. "I wanna thank these ladies for holding me up in prayer and seeing about me and just making sure that I was okay." She turned to Lance. "And, Bishop, thank you for being the loving husband that I needed you to be. I thank you for your patience and for being by my side this whole time."

Lance gave Arykah an encouraging smile.

Arykah faced the congregation. She was very emotional. She struggled to get her words out. "And I'd like to thank the entire Freedom Temple family for your support. I'm happy to be back where I belong."

Gladys, Myrtle, Chelsea, Monique, and Darlita all gathered around Arykah and hugged her. A young woman left the fourth pew, walked up to Arykah, and stood before her. She removed a pearl necklace from her neck and placed it around Arykah's neck. She hugged Arykah and walked away. Two of the elderly deacons stood from their pews and approached Arykah. Each of them hugged her and both whispered encouraging words in her ear.

A man that Arykah didn't know walked up and extended his hand to her. "It's good to have you back, Lady Arykah." His skin was dark, and he was bald.

Arykah's eyes grew wide. Her whole body froze, and she held on to Diva Chanel for dear life. Lance saw her pause and rushed to her side. "Honey, this is Brother Henry McClendon. He drives some of the seniors to and from church every Sunday."

In that moment Arykah was able to shake her fear of him. She released a sigh of relief. "Oh." Arykah accepted Henry's hand into her own. "It's good to meet you, Brother Henry."

Lance stayed at her side. A lady came and placed a shawl around Arykah's shoulders, hugged her, and walked away. One by one, the congregation at Freedom Temple Church of God in Christ stood in line and gave Arykah jewelry, money, articles of their own clothing and many hugs. Finally, Arykah was accepted. She had earned the title as Lady Elect.

But it was Monique who noticed two women still seated on a pew at the rear of the sanctuary with their arms folded across their chests. They were whispering to each other and looking at Arykah. Monique moved closer to Darlita. "What's up with those women back there?"

Darlita looked at who Monique was referring to. "Oh, girl, don't worry about them. They are Mother Pansie and Mother Gussie's pawns. The one wearing the yellow blouse is Mother Gussie's granddaughter, Sharonda."

"That's Sharonda ?" Arykah had told Monique that a lady named Sharonda replaced Mother Gussie as Lance's secretary and Arykah also said that Lance informed her that Sharonda had been incarcerated. She's had a crush on Lance for years. "What do you know about her? I heard that she was trouble."

"I can tell you this," Darlita started. "Sharonda is crazy about the bishop and has been for as long as I've known her. She's a bit wacko. Lady Arykah has nothing to worry about, though. The bishop keeps Sharonda at arm's length."

"I see. Who's the lady she's whispering to?"

"That's Angela Moore, the bishop's ex-girlfriend."

Monique snapped her head in Darlita's direction. *"What?"*

"You didn't know?"

"Heck no. And I'm sure Arykah doesn't know that her husband's ex is a member here. She would've told me that."

"The bishop and Angela were off and on for years. They've both been members of Freedom Temple since they were kids. It wasn't until when the bishop was called into ministry that he and Angela parted ways for good."

"Really? How come? She didn't want to be the first lady of this church?"

"Lance wasn't ready to take a wife yet. She couldn't accept his vow of celibacy. *That's* what broke them up."

Monique looked toward the back of the church at Angela. That was the first time she'd seen Angela. But she and Arykah had only been at Freedom Temple for five months and with over one thousand members on the roll, and the women outnumbering the men, Monique understood why she hadn't seen Angela's face before. "Humph. Arykah should know that his ex-girlfriend is lurking around."

Darlita looked at Arykah still receiving hugs and well wishes from folks. "Well, *I* ain't gonna tell her."

"Lance should have done that already," Monique said sternly. She wondered why he hadn't told Arykah. She looked at the two women. One has dealt with Lance intimately, and the other *wants* to deal with him intimately. *I smell trouble*, Monique thought to herself. *A whole lot of trouble.*

After the benediction, Arykah and her team ascended the stairs to her office. Arykah unlocked the door and walked inside. The first thing she did was kick off her stilettos. "Lawd Jaysus, my feet are singin' a song." Arykah's feet hurt so badly, she had to stumble barefoot over to her chair behind her desk. She plopped down. "Oh, my feet. My feet, Jesus."

"Don't call on the Lord about your feet," Myrtle said as she sat down in a chair across from Arykah and removed her hat. "He didn't tell you to put those high heels on."

Arykah set Diva Chanel down on the floor and watched her trot to her training pad in the corner of Arykah's office. "Well, sometimes, it's an inconvenience to be cute, Mother Cortland. I know you wore many a heel in your day."

Gladys sat down next to Myrtle. "The heels they made back then can't even compare to the kind of heels *you* wear, Lady Arykah. I just don't see how you do it."

"Practice makes perfect, Gladys." Arykah noticed three of her team members missing. "Where are Darlita, Chelsea, and Monique?"

"Darlita had to leave right after service," Myrtle answered.

"That accounts for one team member," Arykah said.

"You know that Chelsea is on the finance committee," Gladys said. "She's counting the tithes and offerings."

Arykah looked at Gladys. "Well, where's Monique? She has all of my gifts the members just gave me."

Both Myrtle and Gladys shrugged their shoulders.

Across the hall in Lance's office, Monique stood on the opposite side of his desk with her arms folded across her chest. "Who's Angela Moore?"

Lance looked up at her. He paused before he spoke. "She's a member." He didn't lie.

Monique raised one eyebrow. "*And* an ex-girlfriend."

He exhaled. "Yes."

"Does Arykah know?"

"I haven't told her."

"She should know that your old flame worships here. Arykah should know who Angela Moore is. And why haven't I seen her before today?"

"I don't know," Lance answered. "Maybe she purposely stays out of the way. Angela is in church every Sunday. She and I haven't dated in years, way before I was even engaged to Gwen."

Monique knew that Lance was engaged to a lady name Gwen when she died in a car accident. "Look, Bishop, I don't think you're living foul. I know how much you adore Arykah, but you have to tell her that your ex-girlfriend is here."

"I promise you that Arykah has nothing to worry about. Angela means nothing to me."

"Then why not tell your wife?"

"I honestly don't think it's relevant."

"It's relevant," Monique insisted. "*Tell* her."

Lance knew that if he didn't tell Arykah about Angela, Monique would surely do it. He exhaled. "Okay, I will tell Arykah about Angela."

"Today," Monique said as she turned and exited his office with Arykah's purse and gifts.

Three

Sunday afternoon Lance and Arykah were seated at their dining-room table surrounded by a feast. Mustard and turnip greens, ham hocks, sweet potatoes, hot water corn bread, and baked macaroni and cheese filled each of their plates. For dessert Lance had made banana pudding. It was a meal that he had half prepared early that morning before they left for church.

As soon as Lance completed the blessing, Arykah added, "And, Lord, please let my stomach be bigger than my eyes."

She and Lance indulged.

"You and Mother Myrtle missed a good service this morning. Three people gave their lives to Christ."

Arykah should have been grateful for the new souls joining the family of God but she decided to discuss the issue of why she missed morning service. "Well, had you not shared my personal business with Mother Myrtle, I would have been in service. Since when do you and I go outside of our marriage to discuss our marriage?"

"We needed help, Arykah, and you know it." Lance inserted a forkful of sweet potatoes in his mouth.

Arykah looked across the table into Lance's eyes. *"We ?* Did you say 'we'? As I recall, there was only one half of *we* present in my office when Mother Myrtle tore me a new butthole."

Lance shook his head from side to side. "Arykah, your mouth."

She raised her eyebrows and glared at him. "What about my mouth?"

"It's ridiculous," Lance complained.

"Humph, you ain't got a problem with what I do with my mouth in the bedroom."

Lance lay his fork down on his plate. "Don't do this. I don't wanna argue with you. Not after morning service was so good."

Arykah shrugged her shoulders. "How do I know how good morning service was? I was being yelled at while the saints were rejoicing."

"What did Mother Myrtle say to you? Why are you so mad?"

Arykah didn't want to let Lance know that Myrtle did, in fact, put her in her place. "Let's just say that she gave me a 'welcome back to church' present. But it wasn't gift wrapped and it wasn't pretty."

"Did she help you? Do you still blame me for what happened?"

Arykah drank sweetened iced tea and swallowed before she spoke. "No. And I'm sorry for what I put you through, Bishop. You didn't deserve to be treated that way."

Lance was relieved. *Thank God.* "I've counseled many couples over the years. Do you know what breaks up marriages more than finances and adultery?"

Arykah nodded her head. "Unforgiveness."

"Tragedies too." Lance nodded and said, "When parents lose children it puts a deep hole in their relationships. We didn't have our baby to hold, Arykah, but we still suffered a great loss. I've witnessed husbands and wives seek consolation elsewhere other than each other."

Lance's words made Arykah recall what Myrtle had said to her earlier that day. *And if you believe, for one second, that Lance is gonna just let you do him any kind of way because you're throwing hissy fits and having*

*baby tantrums, you got another thing coming. He ain't
gotta settle for your crap. Not when he's got unlimited
coochie standing in line just waiting for you to screw up.*

Lance snapped Arykah out of her daydream. "Cheeks?"

She focused on his face. "Huh?"

He chuckled. "Am I talking to myself? Where were you
just now?"

"I heard what you said, and we're not gonna end up like
other couples."

"We're good?" he asked her.

Arykah smiled. "We're so good, Bishop."

Moments later, Arykah's belly was filled to the max,
but she had one forkful of potato salad that she wasn't
going to let be wasted. She needed something to go with
the last of her potato salad. She looked across the table at
Lance's plate. "You gon' eat cho' cone-bred?"

Her rendition of the famous line from the movie *Life*
caused Lance to spit his food across the table. He hollered
out and laughed so hard his throat hurt. Lanced loved
Arykah's craziness. She was sassy, fun, and care free. He
never knew what would come flying out of her mouth.
There were times when Lance would literally bite his
nails down until they bled, worrying about what Arykah
would say. Then there were times when Arykah was the
funniest comic.

He pushed his almost empty plate across the table.
"You can have my cone-bred."

Arykah scooped up the corn bread and potato salad
and savored them. "You've outdone yourself today, Chef."

"There's dessert in the fridge," Lance said. "Banana
pudding."

Arykah looked at Lance seductively. "Grab a spoon and
bring it to the bedroom."

Lance's eyes lit up. She hadn't looked at him that way
in weeks.

Arykah stood from the dining-room table and walked toward their bedroom. Lance didn't need to be told twice. He quickly sprinted into the kitchen to the utensil drawer for a spoon. He then opened the refrigerator and grabbed the bowl of banana pudding. Lance entered their master bedroom like a child entering the gates of Walt Disney World for the first time. He was overexcited. He saw Diva Chanel on the bed next to Arykah. He gave Arykah the spoon and bowl, then scooped Diva Chanel up. "It's mommy and daddy dessert time." He set her outside their bedroom door and closed it.

An hour later Arykah was fussing. "Look at this mess you made, Lance."

Banana cream, whipped cream, and small bits of banana chunks had stained the expensive bedsheets.

"The mess that *I* made? I brought a spoon. Who decided that we would eat the pudding off each other? That would be *you*."

Arykah stood from the bed and looked down at her pudding-covered naked body. She lifted her left breast and a piece of a vanilla wafer cookie fell to the floor.

Lance laughed. "I was wondering what happened to the cookies."

Arykah lifted the lower portion of her belly and another piece of cookie fell to the floor. "That's how I know that I'm fat as heck. I have cookies falling from between the rolls on my body."

"You're beautiful, Cheeks. Even with the cookies falling out, you're beautiful."

Arykah turned toward the master bath. "I gotta take a shower." She left a trail of cookies behind her.

Lance admired Arykah's nakedness as she walked away from him. He had nicknamed her perfectly. He jumped up from the bed. "I'm sticky too, Cheeks. I'll join you."

"Good," Arykah said. "I may need your help. I'm sure there are cookies in places that I can't reach." She started the water in the shower and began singing Tamar Braxton's song. "When my hair look a mess, yea, he gon' tell me that I'm beautiful."

It took twenty minutes and a half bottle of liquid soap for Lance to find and remove all the vanilla wafers from Arykah's body.

Later that Sunday evening Lance found Arykah and Diva Chanel snuggled on the sectional in the great room. He scooped up the teacup-sized puppy and sat next to Arykah. "What are you doing, Cheeks?"

Arykah was typing fast on the keys of her laptop that she had propped up on her thighs. "Just checking the latest listings on million-dollar properties."

"Are you back at work tomorrow?"

"Yep." Aside from missing five Sundays from church, Arykah, a real estate agent, had taken five weeks off from work as well.

"Are you sure you're ready?"

"Well, as much as I would just love to be a housewife." Arykah looked at Lance. "Not. You know I'm not the type to lie around the house all day, Bishop. There are houses to sell and there's money to be made and there are—"

"Stilettos to buy and handbags to buy and big hats to buy." Lance completed Arykah's sentence perfectly.

Arykah laughed at her husband. "Is that all you think I do? Buy clothes and shoes?"

"Well, let's see here." Lance looked up toward the vaulted ceiling as though he was deep in thought. "I paid cash for this house. I pay the homeowners insurance, every utility bill, every car note, plus insurance on the cars. I fill your gas tanks every week. And I buy all of the groceries. Now what do you do with *your* money?"

Arykah mimicked Lance and looked up toward the same vaulted ceiling. "Well, let's see here. I buy . . ." she paused. "I buy . . ." she paused again.

Lance helped her out. "You buy stilettos, handbags, and big hats."

She could do nothing but laugh. "That ain't all that I buy, Lance, and you know it."

"Oh, yeah, I forgot about the expensive wigs and weaves. You may as well tell the truth and stay in church."

"I help out around here."

Lance nodded his head in agreement. "Yeah, I'll give you that credit. You do help out. Purchasing your own expensive clothes and shoes is a great help to me. And an occasional burnt meal is always appreciated."

Arykah chuckled, remembering the last meal she made for Lance resulted in the fire department beating down their front door. She had wanted to surprise him with breakfast in bed. It was a disaster. Arykah hadn't been near the stove since.

"And you do tip our housekeeper, Graciela, very well when she comes twice a month, but she's on *my* payroll."

"I never said that I didn't have it good, Bishop. I know that I'm blessed." Truth be told, Arykah was more than blessed. Her cup ran over. She and Lance shared a joint savings account that they used to travel or purchase things together. Both of their signatures were required to make a withdrawal.

Lance's personal checking account was used to take care of his household and spoil his wife. Arykah's commission checks from selling million-dollar homes are deposited in her own personal checking account. It's the money she uses to buy the shoes, handbags, and whatever else she desires. Arykah also had a personal savings account. Twenty percent of her commission checks were deposited and tucked away for a rainy day.

Arykah has offered, on many occasions, to pay the utility bills, but Lance had argued that it wasn't her responsibility. Once, when Arykah arrived home, she retrieved the mail from the mailbox. In the stack of junk mail were the gas and water bills. Arykah wrote checks for both, placed a postage stamp on the envelopes, and put them in the mailbox. Two weeks later, when Lance realized that he hadn't seen the gas and water bills, he mentioned to Arykah that he would call the companies to find out why he wasn't billed for the month prior. When Arykah confessed that she had already paid those bills, Lance reminded her that she didn't need to spend her money. He was the sole provider for them both.

"I'm having the girls over this Friday for our Fat Girl party. It's my turn to host again."

Every fourth Friday of each month, Arykah, Monique, her cousin Amaryllis, and Amaryllis's roommate, Bridgette, took turns hosting a Fat Girl party. Collectively, the ladies tipped the scale at almost 1,100 pounds. The Fat Girl parties were times when the ladies let their hair down, ate what they wanted, danced, and caught up on the latest gossip. The four ladies had established a rule that no one who wasn't a plus-size woman could join their party. It was strictly for fat girls.

"Can I hire you to cater the event?"

"*This* Friday evening?"

"That's right. Are you available?"

Lance, a gifted chef, often catered parties and events. "I am, but you're not."

Arykah looked at Lance curiously. "What do you mean?"

"This Friday night at the church is your first monthly *'Ask Arykah Anything'* night."

Arykah smacked her forehead. "Oh no. The triple 'A' session. I had forgotten about that. I set that up before my attack."

"Yep, you did, and it's still on the church's calendar. The women are looking forward to it."

"This will give the ladies of Freedom Temple a chance to get to know the real me."

"I think it's great that you're doing this, Cheeks."

"Me too. I'm hoping the triple 'A' sessions will break the ice between me and some of the women that still haven't accepted me as their pastor's wife."

"I'm optimistic. After the hugs and gifts you received today from the members, I'm sure your session will be a success."

Arykah kissed Lance on the lips. "You're such a loving and supportive husband." She went back to looking at listings on her computer.

Lance exhaled. He needed to tell Arykah about Angela Moore but didn't quite know how to do it. They had just made love for the first time in weeks. He and Arykah were in a good place. He dreaded that the subject of his ex-girlfriend at Freedom Temple would ruin it.

"Cheeks, do you know who Angela Moore is?"

She shook her head from side to side. "No. Should I?"

According to Monique, you should. "She's a member of the church. I know that you've only been at Freedom Temple for five months, and you haven't yet met all of the members."

Arykah tried to jog her memory. "I don't remember anyone introducing themselves as Angela Moore. Before today, only a handful of women have welcomed me. I would've remembered her if she had. What about her?"

Lance didn't answer.

Arykah looked at him. "What about her?" she asked him again.

"Angela and I dated."

Arykah's eyebrows lifted. "And you're telling me this because . . ."

"Well, I think you should know. That's all."

"But why now? I've been there five months, Lance."

"I'll be honest," he said.

Arykah's eyebrows lifted higher. "You better be."

"I wasn't gonna tell you about Angela until Monique approached me today."

"Monique?"

"Somehow Monique found out that I used to date Angela, and she asked me if I had told you."

"Well, I'm curious about why you *didn't* tell me."

Lance shrugged his shoulders. "Well, because it doesn't matter, Cheeks. Angela and I were over years ago. Even before I met Gwen."

"Did you screw her?"

Of course Arykah could have asked the question in a more delicate way like . . . *"Were the two of you intimate?"* or *"Was the relationship a sexual one?"* But Myrtle's words to Arykah to never sugarcoat were impacted in her brain.

Lance was very uncomfortable but knew that he had to be honest with his wife. "Yes."

"Were you in love with Angela?"

"We were together for three years, Arykah. I mean, I cared very deeply for her."

"Were . . . you . . . in . . . love . . . with . . . her?" Arykah overemphasized her words and spaced them apart.

"Yes."

"So, there was a soul tie. And you didn't feel the need to tell me? You don't think I have the right to know who's smiling in my face, Lance? Is she prettier than me?"

"Cheeks, ain't *nobody* prettier than you."

She looked at him. "You better had said that."

"It's the truth," Lance confirmed.

Arykah thought that if she used reverse psychology on Lance, he'd get where she and Monique was coming from.

"Suppose there was a guy at the realtor's office that I had knocked boots with and didn't tell you. How would you feel to know that I'm still working with him?"

Lance shrugged his shoulders again. "It wouldn't bother me. Your past, Cheeks, is your past."

Arykah turned her attention to her computer. "Well, good. I'm glad you feel that way."

Lance sat in silence looking at Arykah.

She felt his stare burning through her.

"So, you got an ex-boyfriend working with you?"

Arykah closed her laptop and stood from the sofa. "Come on, Diva Chanel," she said over her shoulder. She left Lance sitting by himself. *Two can play that game.*

At ten the next morning Arykah was greeted by her fellow real estate agents as soon as she entered the front door at Bowen Realty.

"Welcome back."

She displayed the widest grin. "Thanks, everybody."

Three female agents approached Arykah and hugged her.

"How are you?" Jacob, a male agent, asked Arykah.

"I'm good, Jacob. Thank you."

Arykah walked to her desk and was surprised to see a large bouquet of red roses. She smiled and removed the small card from the envelope.

Hope your first day back is a marvelous one. Have a superb day, Cheeks. Love, Lance.

Her smile got wider. "Aw, he's so sweet." Arykah withdrew a single rose from the bouquet, brought it to her nose, and inhaled the beautiful scent.

"You like the roses?"

Arykah looked up and saw Lance standing ten feet from her. She smiled at the thought that he would see to it that she made it to work safely. Once it hit her that there was another reason why he might have shown up unannounced, she frowned.

"What are you doing here?"

Lance looked over his shoulder and scanned the office almost like he was looking for a specific person. "I missed you so much that I wanted to see you one more time before I headed to the construction company."

Arykah looked at him shamefully. Lance was the chief operating officer of Howell Construction on the far north side of Chicago. He split his time between there and Freedom Temple.

"Really, Lance. You can't do any better than that?"

A handsome African American male agent approached Arykah. "Hey, Beautiful. I heard you were back." He hugged her and admired Arykah's wide-legged teal-green jumpsuit and cream-colored Granny Smith snakeskin peep-toe ankle boots. "You look good as always."

Lance looked from the guy to Arykah, then from Arykah to the guy.

For Lance's benefit, Arykah gave off a laugh like Betty Rubble from the Flintstones cartoon. She knew he was there to spy, and she wanted to give him something to see. She looked down at her outfit. "This old thing?"

Lance didn't know how long the jumpsuit had hung in Arykah's closet, but he definitely witnessed her remove the price tag from it that morning. He decided to make his presence known. "Ahem."

Arykah saw a stern expression on Lance's face. She loved it. "Um, Demetrius, please meet my husband, Lance."

Demetrius stepped to Lance and extended his right hand. "Oh, *you're* Lance. It's nice to meet you, man. I've heard a lot of things about you."

Lance accepted Demetruis' hand into his own. "It's good to meet you, Demetruis. How long have you known Arykah?"

"I was hired three months before Arykah took her leave of absence. She's really great."

"Yeah, she is," Lance confirmed. He concluded that Demetruis wasn't an ex-boyfriend.

"It's good having you back, Arykah," Demetruis said and walked away.

"You should be ashamed of yourself," Lance said to Arykah. "Trying to make me jealous."

Arykah laughed out loud. "Did I follow you to your office, or did you follow me to mine?"

"You don't believe that I missed you and wanted to see you?"

"Not even a little bit. Our home is southwest of Chicago, Lance. My office is *waaaaay* south of the city. Howell Construction is north. No. I don't believe you followed me here because you missed me."

It was true. Lance had driven an hour out of his way, but he wasn't leaving Arykah's office without the information he came there for. "Do you have an ex working here or not?"

Arykah sat at her desk and logged on to her desktop. "Thank you for the roses, Honey. You may go now."

He glared at her. "Arykah."

She looked up at him. "When I meet your ex, then you can meet my ex. Okay?" Arykah smiled and blew Lance a kiss. "Have a great day."

Five minutes after Lance left Arykah's office, her extension rang.

"Bowen Realty. Arykah Miles speaking."

"So you really did it, huh? You really left that California king-size bed and went to work?"

Arykah smiled at Monique's voice. "Girl, yes. I was bored at home."

"That's why Adonis and I bought you Diva Chanel. She was supposed to keep you company while you recuperate."

"That dog eats, sleeps, and poops more than I do. Okay? That's all Diva Chanel and I did. For the past five weeks, we ate a lot, slept all day, and pooped all night."

Monique laughed. "How does it feel to be back at the office?"

"It feels great. I'm ready to get back in the swing of things. Lance sent me a beautiful bouquet of roses."

Arykah was in a good mood, and Monique wondered if Lance had told her about Angela Moore.

"Speaking of Lance," Arykah started. "He told me about his ex-girlfriend."

Monique was relieved that Lance did the right thing because she didn't want to be the one to tell Arykah, but Monique was more than willing if Lance hadn't.

"I'm glad he did."

"How did you find out that Angela was a member at Freedom Temple?"

"Yesterday when you were receiving your gifts and hugs from everyone, I saw two women at the back of the church whispering to each other and pointing at you. So I asked Darlita who they were. She told me that Sharonda was one and said that the other was the bishop's ex-girlfriend, Angela Moore."

"Well, I thank you for having my back, Sis. If you hadn't threatened Lance, he probably never would've told me."

"He told you that I threatened him?"

Arykah chuckled. "No. But I know you. Of course, you threatened him."

Monique laughed. "Well, maybe I kinda sorta did. Hey, are we on for Friday night at your place?"

"Girl, I'm gonna have to host the Fat Girl party next Friday. I had forgotten that I had scheduled my triple 'A' session at the church this Friday night."

"Oh, that's right," Monique said. "I read it in the church bulletin yesterday and didn't put two and two together.

Are you sure you're up to being asked so many questions? You wanna expose yourself like that?"

"I don't have anything to hide, Monique. My life is an open book."

"Yeah, well, the problem with being an open book is that you allow everybody to read you any way they want to. You know how most of the women at Freedom Temple feel about you. What if someone asks you if you're a gold digger?"

"Then I'll open my checkbook and show them my eight-figure bank balance. That would clear that rumor up real quick."

"Well, alrighty then, Miss Thang. Do you need help with anything?"

"I'm glad you asked. I wanna give everybody a gift bag filled with candy and maybe a candle or something else that's small and cute."

"Sure, I can take care of that for you. You think fifty gift bags would be enough?"

"Mmm. Well, based on how many women welcomed me yesterday, I think we should prepare about one hundred fifty gift bags."

"You really think that many folks will show up?"

"Yeah, I really do. Plus, I'd rather have more than enough than not enough."

"Okay," Monique said. "What about food?"

"Lance has agreed to cater the event."

"Great. Anything else?"

"Yes. I need you to reach out to the team and ask them to meet me at the church, in my office, at six p.m. on Friday, and tell them to wear pink."

"Mother Myrtle too?"

"Definitely."

When Arykah disconnected the call from Monique she heard three knocks on her opened door. She looked and saw Sarah Zembowski, a Caucasian female coworker of hers. Like Arykah, Sarah was a top-selling real estate agent at Bowen Realty. Arykah and Sarah were fierce competitors but friendly with each other.

"Welcome back, Arykah."

"Thanks, Sarah. It's good to be back."

"How are you feeling?"

"Great. Ready to kick your butt in sells."

"As if you could."

"Oh, you *know* I can."

Sarah chuckled. "You have anything lined up this morning?"

"Not yet."

"I just received a call from my daughter's principal."

Arykah knew that Sarah's thirteen-year-old daughter, Jessica, was the apple of her mother's eye. Sarah had been a single mother for the past ten years. Her husband, a Chicago firefighter, was visiting his parents in New York City on September 11th when tragedy struck the city. That dreadful morning after the first airplane hit the first tower, Sarah's husband called her and said that he felt obligated to go and offer his services to the New York City fire department. That was the last time Sarah had heard her husband's voice. Along with the entire country, Sarah watched the towers fall. Her husband, among hundreds of other people, was trapped in the stairwell of the second tower. He was killed.

"Is Jessica okay?" Arykah asked.

"Her principal said that she was vomiting and has a fever. I'm going to pick her up and take her to the emergency room."

"Aw, that's too bad. I hope she'll be okay."

"I'm sure she will. It's probably just a bug."

"Well, I'll be praying for Jessica."

"Thanks. Before Jessica's principal called I was on my way to show a listing in North Barrington. I don't wanna cancel on the client because I had to reschedule with him once already. I wanted to give you first dibs on it before I offered the appointment to someone else. Are you interested?"

Kaching, kaching. Arykah heard the cash register ringing. North Barrington was considered one of the richest cities in Illinois. The top two sells of Arykah's career were in North Barrington. It was a shame that Sarah had to pass it along to another agent, but Arykah was grateful that it fell into her lap.

"Heck yeah, I'm interested. Tell me about the property."

"It's a seven-bedroom, six-bath, new construction on Forest Glen Parkway. It has a first-floor master, an in-law suite, a guest house, a full finished walkout basement, and an inground pool. It's listed for six-nine-nine."

The commission from a six million, 799 thousand-dollar sell would put Arykah over the top.

"The client is Randy Brown."

Arykah's heart skipped two beats. "The Chicago Bulls Randy Brown?"

"Yes, he earned three championship rings with the Bulls. Randy is now the assistant general manager of the team."

"He's married, isn't he?"

"Yes, his wife's name is Tamara. She will not be at the appointment. Mr. Brown is purchasing a home as a surprise for her birthday."

Arykah lowered her head and glared at Sarah. "Shut the front door. Girl, *what* ?"

Sarah laughed at the expression on Arykah's face. "Yeah, that's pretty much how I felt when he told me that." Sarah glanced at her wristwatch. "The appointment is in an hour. You better get going."

***

Arykah was standing at the head of the driveway next to the four-car garage when a charcoal-gray, late-model, Range Rover drove up and parked at the end of the driveway on the street. Randy Brown exited the SUV, and Arykah's body froze. He was dark skinned with a clean-shaven bald head.

She panicked. Her heart started to race. She panted for air. *Oh my God. It's him.*

"Mrs. Howell?" Randy Brown called from the end of the driveway.

Arykah heard him call her name, but she couldn't answer. Her entire being had shut down. Chills shook her body. She looked up and down the street for Lance but didn't see him. Silently, she encouraged herself. *Shake it off, Arykah, shake it off. You can do this. He's not the man that attacked you. Shake it off.*

Halfway up the driveway, Randy Brown called her name again. "Mrs. Howell?"

Arykah squeezed her eyes shut. He was getting close to her. She wanted to scream. *In the name of Jesus. Jesus, Jesus.* Arykah heard the voice of her Heavenly Father. "Fret not, my daughter, for I am with you."

Immediately Arykah's body loosened. When she opened her eyes, Randy Brown stood before her. She extended her right hand to him and smiled broadly. "Mr. Brown, it's such a pleasure to meet you. I must admit that I am a huge fan."

He returned her smile and shook her hand. "Thank you."

"Welcome to North Barrington," Arykah said.

Randy Brown looked around at the mansions next door and across the street. "It's really nice here."

"Sarah wanted me to apologize again that she couldn't meet with you."

"Yes, she had an emergency with her daughter, right?"

God, he smells good. "That's right. She didn't want to disappoint you a second time, so I offered to step in and show you this beautiful home. Is it true what Sarah told me? Are you shopping for a home as a birthday gift for your wife?"

"As a matter of fact, I am."

"Wow. She's a very blessed woman."

"Not as blessed as I am to have her. Tamara is my everything."

"Well then," Arykah said, "shall we take a look inside?"

Randy extended his right hand toward the front door. "After you."

Forty-five minutes later, Arykah was screaming in Lance's ear.

He sat at his desk at Howell Construction with his desk telephone pressed against his left ear. "Cheeks, I can't understand you."

"Babe. Oh my God, Lance," she cried out. She sat in her car with the air conditioner on full blast as she watched Randy Brown's Range Rover drive away and turn left at the corner.

The last time Arykah had called Lance screaming and crying was the day she was raped. Lance's car keys lay on his desk. He gripped them and stood. He was ready to run out of the office. "Arykah, are you all right? What happened?"

"He bought the house, Babe!" she yelled in Lance's ear. *"He bought the house!"*

Lance frowned and yelled back. *"Who bought what house? Where are you?"*

Arykah took two deep breaths. "I'm in North Barrington. Sarah couldn't show an estate because she had to take her daughter to the hospital. She didn't want to cancel a showing that she had scheduled this morning." Arykah was breathing heavy. "She offered the listing to me, and, of course, I had to take it. I mean, heck, it's North Barrington—why *wouldn't* I take it? But, Babe, the client was Randy Brown."

Lance's eyes grew wide, and he gripped his keys tighter. *"The Chicago Bulls Randy Brown?* No way."

"Yes, it's true. And he bought the house. Bishop, your wife sold a house for seven million. Randy Brown bought it for the full asking price." Arykah laughed. *"Bam!* Whatcha gotta say about *that* , Husband?"

"Did you get his autograph for me?"

Arykah sighed. Lance blew her high. That wasn't the response she was hoping for. "Really, Lance? I tell you that I just sold a seven million-dollar estate, and that's the best you can do? Are you serious?"

"My bad, Cheeks," Lance said. "Congratulations. Did you get Randy's autograph?" Lance was happy that Arykah was happy, but she sold million-dollar homes all the time.

She shook her head from side to side. "As a matter of fact, I did. And I also scored two tickets for when the Bulls host the Miami Heat at the United Center in November."

"Yeeeessssssss," Lance yelled out. "That's my baby."

"I can't wait to tell Monique that she gets to sit courtside, with me and stare at LeBron's triceps. She and I will have a good time at the game."

The next thing Arykah heard coming through the telephone was, *"What?* Come on, Cheeks. Are you really gonna do me like that?"

Arykah had to laugh at Lance's disappointment. She could only imagine the sad expression on his face. She had every intention to give him the tickets, but she wanted to make him sweat for them. "Relax, Bishop. You and Adonis can have the tickets, but when I tell you that I sell a seven million-dollar estate you better jump for joy."

"Woo-hoo!" Lance cheered. *"Way to go, Cheeks! Bravo! That's what I'm talkin' 'bout. You go, girl. I knew you could do it. I'm rolling out the red carpet for you, Baby, Baaabaaayyy,"* he sang. Lance ran with it and shouted, *"Hallelujah!"*

"Okay, stop it," Arykah said when Lance started speaking in an unknown tongue.

Four

On Friday evening, Arykah's team, all dressed in pink, assembled in her office. She wondered why Darlita, Gladys, or Chelsea hadn't told her that Lance's ex-girl-friend was taking up space on the pews.

They had been to her home, ate at her dining-room table, received expensive stilettos, and enjoyed a spa day at Arykah's expense. If Arykah was honest with herself, she'd admit that she felt betrayed. On the other hand, Darlita, Gladys, and Chelsea were lifelong members of Freedom Temple just as Lance was. They had grown up with him. Now he was their pastor. They had a personal relationship with Lance and were friends with him. Arykah understood that the ladies may have kept quiet out of loyalty to Lance, and she couldn't be angry at that. She expected and did have that same type of loyalty from Myrtle and Monique.

"I had a conversation with the bishop last Sunday night. He told me all about Angela Moore."

The ladies', with the exception of Myrtle, eyes bulged. Chelsea, Darlita, and Gladys looked at Arykah, then at each other, then back at Arykah again.

Arykah nodded her head. "Yep, he told me."

Gladys waved her hand to dismiss the very subject of Angela Moore. "Well, you ain't got nothin' to worry about. The bishop makes it perfectly clear to her that he's not interested."

Arykah cocked her head to the side. *Interested in what?*

Gladys was speaking in the present tense. *"Makes* it clear" not *"Made* it clear," like maybe months ago before Lance and Arykah were married. Arykah heard it clear as day. Gladys said, *"Makes it clear."*

"Angela's well is dry. She's thirsty. She's missing her water," Chelsea said. "She's desperate for his attention. You'd think that when the bishop announced you as his wife, she'd stop."

Arykah cocked her head to the other side. *Stop what?*

"Angela wants what she can't have," Darlita added. "She let a good man get away. Now that he's married, she can't take 'no' for an answer."

"Wait a minute," Arykah started. "She's chasing Lance?"

Darlita, Chelsea, and Gladys looked confused, and so did Myrtle. She didn't know who Angela Moore was.

No one answered Arykah so she rephrased her question. "Is Angela Moore pushing up on my man?"

"Yeah," Chelsea answered. "You just said that the bishop told you about her."

"He told me who Angela Moore was. But he didn't tell me that she was trying to get back in his drawers."

Oh, Lord, here we go, Myrtle thought. She knew Arykah was getting ready to do bodily harm to whoever Angela Moore was. When it came to her husband, Myrtle knew that Arykah didn't play. She'd made it very clear. *"Don't f*!k with my husband,"* Myrtle heard Arykah say awhile back when she was venting about the dry cleaners and Lance's suit jacket scheme that Mother Gussie tried to pull.

Gladys gasped. "Oh my God. We thought you meant that he told you that Angela was pursuing him."

"Nope, y'all just did."

Darlita became nervous. "What did we just do?"

"You inadvertently told the truth. *That's* what you did," Arykah said. "But that information should have come from Lance."

"Lady Arykah, we are so sorry."

"You ain't gotta be sorry, Gladys. Don't you think that I should know that a dirty broad is grinnin' in my man's face?"

"Of course, I do, but . . ." Gladys paused.

"But he's your pastor," Arykah said. "Hey, I understand why y'all didn't say anything, and I respect it."

"Please know that the bishop ain't thinking about that tramp. You got that man's nose so wide open, all he sees is you."

"Chelsea, trust and believe that I am not insecure in my marriage. I'm not the jealous type. I know exactly who I am. Ain't no woman finer than Arykah. Ain't no woman *better* than Arykah. When it comes to my husband, I know what to do to keep him faithful. I don't worry if he's coming home at night. I know Lance loves me, *but . . .*" Arykah paused, "he ain't perfect. No man is. I don't want *any* woman tempting him to betray me. And if Angela Moore doesn't understand what the word 'no' means, then perhaps she needs to hear *my* definition of it. So when we get downstairs I want y'all to point the ho out."

Darlita, Chelsea, and Gladys gasped.

"Arykah!" Myrtle shouted out.

Arykah was on level ten. "Mother Myrtle, don't act like you don't know me. You *know* I don't tolerate no crap when it comes to my husband. Just ask Mother Gussie Hughes. She learned that the hard way. Lance is *my* man. Okay? He belongs to *me*. In hell will I lift up my eyes before I allow a tramp like Angela Moore to come between me and what's mine."

"I understand that," Myrtle said, "but you need to calm down."

"This *is* calm," Arykah said with her eyes blazing. "It's my job and my duty, as Lance's wife, to make sure that our covenant remains pure. Ain't no chick gotta like me, but I'll be *damned in hell* if I'm not gonna be respected. Now this conversation is over. I'm not gonna discuss it anymore."

If a pin had dropped on the carpet in Arykah's office, it certainly would have been heard loud and clear. No one said a word. Chelsea, Darlita and Gladys finally got their chance to see Arykah pop off and they actually feared what she would do to Angela Moore.

Whoever Angela Moore was, Myrtle silently prayed that she wouldn't show up at the church that evening.

Arykah broke the silence. "I guess I need to get ready."

"I can't believe you're doing this, Lady Arykah," Gladys said. "This Ask Arykah Anything could go way wrong."

Arykah looked at Gladys, Myrtle, Chelsea, and Darlita as they sat around her desk. Each of them had called her during the week and pleaded with her to cancel the evening. "All of you worry too much. What could go wrong? I'm offering the members, *my members*, especially the women of this church, an opportunity to get to know their pastor's wife on a personal level."

"How personal are you willing to get?" asked Myrtle. "What if someone asks you how much you weigh?"

Arykah looked into Chelsea's eyes. "Why would someone ask me what my scale says?" Arykah shrugged her shoulders. "Who does that?"

"Broads that ain't got an ounce of respect for no one," Darlita answered. "You gotta remember, Lady Arykah, you've only been here at Freedom Temple a short while. And I know that you were given a warm welcome down in the sanctuary last Sunday; however, Mother Pansie and Mother Gussie still have supporters here." Darlita thought back to when Monique pointed out Angela Moore and Mother Gussie's granddaughter, Sharonda, huddled up in the rear of the sanctuary. They were whispering and pointing at Arykah.

Chelsea had a thought. "Hey, I know what we can do. I'll give everyone a pencil and a sheet of paper and tell them to write their questions down. Then the team can screen the questions and throw out any that may be inappropriate."

Myrtle nodded her head. "I like that, Chelsea. That's a great idea."

"No," Arykah said sternly. "I don't want to give anyone the impression that they can't approach me. I need to establish a relationship and trust with these folks."

"And that's all fine and dandy, Sugarplum, but let's get real. You are not well liked here."

"And I'm trying to change that, Mother Myrtle. I want people to feel that they can confide in me and know that I'm their covering. I honestly don't believe that anyone will get out of pocket."

"But what if someone does?" Chelsea asked.

Arykah looked at her. "Then I'll handle it."

Myrtle was worried. "*How* will you handle it?"

Last Sunday morning before Arykah addressed the church about her five-week absence, Myrtle made her promise to conduct herself accordingly in the sanctuary.

Arykah looked at Myrtle and sneered. "This ain't Sunday morning, and we won't be in the sanctuary. If someone gets out of pocket . . . then I will too."

In the fellowship hall fifteen round tables were covered with pink tablecloths. Lance, with the help of a few men, had assembled ten chairs for each table.

"Somebody having a party, Bishop?" Twenty-year-old Tyler Armstrong asked Lance.

"Lady Arykah is throwing a small reception for the members."

"Really? There will be girls in here?" Tyler asked mischievously. "I certainly don't mind spending a Friday night in a room full of females."

Tyler was a thorn in Lance's side. He was girl crazy, and Lance was constantly pulling his coattail. There wasn't a female at the church between the ages of eighteen and twenty-five that Tyler hadn't chased.

"Well, it's too bad you'll be upstairs in the young adult choir rehearsal."

"Aw, come on, Bishop. I could get a whole bunch of telephone numbers tonight."

Lance exhaled. "Tyler, this room is off-limits to you tonight. Understand? Go to rehearsal and give the ladies a break."

Monique and Adonis came into the fellowship hall carrying large black plastic bags. They approached Lance. "Hey, Bishop," Monique greeted, "is there a table that I can use?"

Tyler's eyes lit up. "Hey, Sister Monique. You look pretty tonight."

She chuckled. Tyler always flirted with her. "Thank you, Tyler."

He admired Monique's pink chiffon blouse and pink jeans. "You look *real* pretty."

Adonis often had to shoo Tyler away from his wife. "Man, don't you see me standing here?"

"I'm just admiring a beautiful woman."

"Well, this one is taken," Adonis confirmed.

Monique chuckled. "Calm down, gentlemen. There's enough of me to go around."

"No, it ain't," Adonis said. He eyed Tyler. "You have someplace else to be."

"Like where," Tyler asked.

"Like the choir stand. Let's go." Adonis kissed Monique's cheek and escorted Tyler from the fellowship hall.

"That boy is a trip," Monique said to Lance.

"One day he's gonna roll up on the wrong woman. Every husband won't be as tolerant as Adonis."

Lance led Monique to a long rectangular table in the corner of the fellowship hall.

"Will this table do?"

"This is perfect," she said.

Lance left her alone and walked across the room to check on the buffet table. Arykah had requested a mash potato bar with all of the trimmings. At the beginning of the table sat stacks of martini glasses. Also on the table was an extremely large and very deep aluminum pan filled with hot buttery mashed potatoes.

When a guest filled the martini glass with a scoop of mashed potatoes, they would move farther down the table where the choice of toppings in large plastic bowls were plentiful. Sour cream, chives, bacon bits, shredded cheese, and more butter were placed decoratively on the table. A loaded baked potato, minus the skin, in a martini glass created the perfect mashtini.

On an adjacent table was a chocolate fountain that Lance had rented. It was surrounded by trays of pineapple chunks, sliced bananas, and whole strawberries.

Monique decided to do without the gift bags and surprise Arykah with a pink sweet table instead. Pink M&Ms, pink and white peppermints, pink gummy bears, pink Jolly Rancher candy, chocolate Hershey Kisses wrapped in pink foil, pink Starbursts, and pink licorice sticks were displayed in clear plastic bowls. Each bowl had its own pink scoop. Guests would be allowed to fill small clear cellophane bags with the candy as a parting gift. Monique was so busy decorating the sweet table she didn't notice what was happening across the room.

Lance dipped his finger in the melting chocolate and savored the taste.

"I see you still have that sweet tooth."

Lance turned around and saw Angela Moore. His eyes bucked out of his head.

"Do you remember what we used to do with melted chocolate?"

Lance looked across the room and saw Monique fussing with the sweet table. Thank God her back was turned. "Angela," he spoke.

Her jet-black hair was parted down the middle, and it flowed past her shoulders. She was sexy. Angela had always been sexy. Lance glanced down at her figure. *Oh my Gawwwd.* Jessica Rabbit came to mind. Angela had a body out of the world, and it used to drive Lance crazy back in the day. If she turned sideways, the top portion of her body was shaped like the lower case letter "q." The bottom portion of her body was shaped like a capitol letter "P." Back when they were hot and heavy, Lance would sing, *"Thirty -six, twenty-four, thirty-six. She's a brick house."* Surely The Commodores were referring to Angela when they sang that song.

She always knew how to accentuate her curves, and the crimson red dress Angela wore that evening may as well have been painted on. Lance was tempted to touch the dress to see if the color red would rub off on his fingers. "Can you breathe in that thing? Aren't you uncomfortable?" He looked at Monique again. She was still occupied.

Angela chuckled seductively. She looked across the room at whom Lance was watching so closely. "Apparently *you're* uncomfortable."

"That dress looks like it's taking your blood pressure."

Angela turned her arm outward and extended her wrist toward Lance. "You wanna feel my pulse?"

Men and women had started to mingle in the fellowship hall. Lance was happy that someone had approached Monique and engaged her in a conversation.

"What are you doing here, Angela?" Though the two of them haven't been a couple in years, Angela still flirted with Lance every chance she had. There were times when she'd hug him longer and tighter than the other female members would. Often her hugs came with a whisper, *"I don't have any panties on."*

It had gotten to the point that Lance would try his best to avoid any type of contact with Angela. If he saw her coming his way, he'd strike up a conversation with whoever was near him.

"I came to ask your wife some questions."

"Listen to me, Angela. Whatever you got planned for this evening, don't do it. You don't wanna fool with my wife."

"No, I don't. I wanna fool around with *you* ."

Lance gave off a sarcastic chuckle, shook his head, and walked away.

Upstairs in Arykah's office, Chelsea, Darlita, Gladys, and Myrtle, were making a fuss over Diva Chanel's pink sundress, pink hair bows, and pink diamond-studded neck collar.

Darlita held Diva Chanel and cooed at her wet nose. "Lady A, you dress her so pretty."

"That dog is spoiled," said Myrtle.

"I can't deny that, Mother Myrtle. She's my mini-me."

Arykah answered a knock on her door. "It's open."

Natasha and Miranda entered and Arykah smiled. "There are my girls." She stood from her desk, walked over to them, and hugged them both. "This is a surprise."

"Hey, Lady A," Miranda greeted.

Arykah looked down at Miranda's bulging belly. At eight months pregnant, the maternity blouse she wore stretched at the seams. "I see that baby is stretching on out there."

Miranda was once unsure about keeping her baby until her mother, Gladys, brought her to Arykah's office. Arykah had a heart-to-heart with the girl.

"Did your mom tell you that I'm throwing you a baby shower here at the church?"

Miranda smiled. "Yes. I'm so happy. Thanks so much, Lady Arykah."

"You're welcome, Sweetie Pie. How are you feeling? You been going to all of your doctors' appointments and eating healthy?"

"Yes, ma'am."

"I want you to think about a theme for your shower. We gotta select a date and get the ball rolling. We need to get you registered somewhere. Did you find out the sex of the baby?"

Miranda glanced at her mother and smiled. "Can I tell it?"

Gladys shrugged her shoulders. "It's up to you."

Arykah looked from Gladys to Miranda. "Well, don't keep me in suspense. What are we having?"

"A boy," Miranda announced happily.

Everyone in the office clapped and cheered.

Arykah clapped her hands together and squealed. "It's a boy!" She grabbed Miranda and hugged her tightly. She rocked Miranda back and forth and sang the words, "We're having a little snot-nosed, nappy-headed boy."

Arykah asked, "What are *we* having?" then said, "*We're* having a little snot-nosed, nappy-headed boy." She included herself as part of Miranda's family and made it easy for Miranda to do what she came to Arykah's office to do.

"Um, Lady Arykah, since this is Ask Arykah Anything night, and I can't attend because I have choir rehearsal, I want to ask you something now."

The look on Miranda's face was serious; therefore, Arykah became serious. "Okay. Is it personal? Do you want me to ask everyone to leave?"

"No, we're all staying for this," Gladys said. She knew what Miranda wanted to ask Arykah and wanted the team to be present for it.

"Okay, then," Arykah said to Gladys, then looked at Miranda. "What's your question?"

Miranda inhaled and exhaled. She inhaled again, then exhaled once more. She looked at her mother.

Gladys smiled and nodded her head.

"Will you be my son's godmother?"

Arykah's heart fell to the pit of her stomach. That was the absolute last question she had expected Miranda to ask her.

"That's so sweet," Darlita said.

Tears welled up in Arykah's eyes. Just five weeks ago she was pregnant with her own baby. But now, her womb was empty and Arykah thought Miranda's proposal to take on the responsibility to care for her son, if Miranda should ever be unable to provide for him, made Arykah feel good. She wiped the tears that had begun to fall onto her face. "Of course, I will. I'm so happy and honored that you asked me."

"I knew that day I left your office that I wanted you to be my baby's godmother. You saved us both."

"Well," Arykah said, "this certainly changes things."

"How do you mean?" Gladys asked her.

"I gotta start saving my pennies. I have a godson on the way." She looked at Miranda. "When are you due?"

Miranda rubbed her swollen belly and exhaled loudly. "I wish I could deliver today, but I have almost four more weeks to go."

Arykah did some calculations in her head. "Okay, that's good. He'll be a good ten months when I take him to New York for fashion week next April."

Everyone laughed.

"Oh, Lord, help the poor child," Chelsea said. "He ain't even been born yet and she's already putting him in Burberry."

Arykah looked at Chelsea, nodded her head, and winked. "And you know it."

Arykah noticed Natasha standing next to the door. "Hey, Miss Missy. What's up with you?"

"I'm graduating in two weeks," she said proudly.

Arykah raised both hands in the air and rejoiced. "Halleluuuuuuuujah," she sang. "Yay for Natasha. I'm proud of you."

"We all are," Gladys said. She and Natasha's parents were acquaintances.

When Arykah met Natasha she had overheard her speaking with another young female about having sex with a married man. Arykah interrupted the conversation and marched Natasha up to her office. She sat her down, ate a bag of Doritos doused with Louisiana Hot Sauce, drank half of a twelve-ounce bottle of Pepsi, then belched in Natasha's face.

"You do know that sleeping with a married man is a stupid thing to do, don't you?"

Natasha looked toward the floor.

"I told you to look at me. Why do you focus on the floor? We're having a conversation. If you're woman

enough to screw another woman's husband, then be woman enough to face the consequences for doing so. I heard you tell your friend that you had no problem sitting next to the man's wife and still screw him. That's what tricks do. See, tricks don't have any self-respect. They're easily persuaded to cheapen themselves while thinking they're on top of the world. Tricks hide. They sneak around. They settle for sex in the backseats of cars. A trick can never be number one; she'll always be the secret that no one can know about.

"A trick can't be seen on the arm of her man because she's not worthy. She's not even second best. She's told when to speak, when to sit, and when to breathe." Arykah swallowed more Pepsi, then asked, "How long have you been trickin'?"

Natasha wanted to crawl beneath a rock. Arykah had basically told her that she had no worth. She was wasting her life. She was nothing. She was useless. She was a cheap whore.

Arykah saw tears spilling from Natasha's eyes. "What do your tears mean?"

Natasha looked at Arykah as though she didn't understand.

Arykah rephrased the question. "Why are you crying?"

Natasha wiped her face with the back of her hand. "'Cause . . . I . . . I'm just . . . I don't know."

"You don't know what—that you're a trick? Because that's exactly what you are. You're a pretty girl, Natasha. You're on the honor roll and you're graduating in a few months. You have too much going for you to be treated as though you're nothing."

"My prom is next Saturday night," Natasha said.

"Oh, wow," Arykah said. "I know you must be so excited. You have your dress and everything?"

"Yep."

Arykah called for Natasha to come closer to her. She looked into Natasha's eyes sternly. "You ain't still messing with whom we talked about, are you?"

Natasha quickly shook her head from side to side. "Nah, Lady Arykah. I've been done with that situation."

She looked at her sideways. "He ain't your prom date?"

Natasha's eyes grew wide. "Nooooo."

"You been keeping yourself?"

Natasha nodded her head.

Arykah looked at Miranda. "You better have been keeping yourself. I can only afford one godbaby."

"Don't worry," Miranda said to Arykah. "I've learned my lesson."

"Okay, I'm just checking. I gotta stay on top of you young gals. Some of y'all can be as slick as hen piss."

The ladies screamed out in laughter. Myrtle shook her head from side to side. Arykah had no filter.

Natasha reached inside her purse, pulled out a small white envelope, and gave it to Arykah. "I wanted to give you this."

Arykah took the envelope and looked at Natasha. "This ain't no wedding invitation, is it?"

Natasha chuckled. "No."

Arykah flipped the envelope over and glanced at the back flap. "What's in this envelope, Natasha?"

"It's my Ask Arykah Anything question."

Arykah tore the envelope open and pulled out what looked like a movie theater ticket. She saw that it was an invitation to Natasha's high school graduation. She read it silently and placed her hand over her gaping mouth. She looked up at Natasha. "Is this mine?"

Natasha nodded. "I'm sorry that I only had four tickets. The other three are for my parents and my younger brother. My mom said that I could invite the bishop, but I chose to invite you instead. You think he'll be angry with me?" Lance had always favored Natasha and often referred to her as his favorite choir member. Natasha had made the decision to give the extra ticket to Arykah because she felt that Arykah had detoured her from going down a dark path.

"I'm sure he'll understand."

"Can you make it?" Natasha asked Arykah.

"Are you kidding me? Of course, I can make it. I'll be there with bells on."

"Natasha, we gotta go," Miranda said. "Choir rehearsal is about to start. And you know how Brother Adonis hates when someone is late coming into the choir stand."

Arykah looked at her wristwatch. "Oh, wow, it's already seven. I gotta change and get downstairs."

The fellowship hall was filled to capacity when Arykah entered the room. All fifteen tables with ten chairs each were spoken for. It was standing room only. Knowing that members of the church had come out on a Friday night to get to know their new first lady made Arykah feel good.

"Hi, Lady Arykah," a woman greeted when Arykah got near her.

Arykah looked at her. She didn't have a familiar face. "Hi. What's your name?"

"Evelyn Marshall." She pointed to the man standing next to her. "This is my husband, Nathaniel."

Arykah shook both their hands. "It's a pleasure to meet you both and thanks for coming out tonight."

"Lady Arykah?"

Arykah turned around to see a woman that she did recognize. It was the woman who read the church announcements every Sunday. "Hello. Stephanie, right?"

Stephanie smiled. "Yes. Stephanie Nichols."

"I appreciate you coming tonight."

Arykah worked her way through the fellowship hall and greeted as many people as she could. Some she recognized, and some she didn't. But Arykah was thankful and grateful that everyone greeted her with respect and a smile.

When Arykah had reached the sweet table she was happy to see that Monique had chosen to not prepare gift bags. She looked at all of the pink candy displayed beautifully. Monique had decorated the table with pink glitter. "Monique, girl, *you* did that?"

"I knew you'd like it."

"I love it. Everything is pink." Arykah looked at all the candy. "Where did you find pink Jolly Ranchers?"

"I had those flown in from Vegas," Monique said.

"From Vegas?" Arykah knew the shipment couldn't have been cheap. "Monique, how much did all of this cost you? You shouldn't have spent a lot of money."

"Don't worry about it. I wanted to do this for you. It's *your* night."

Arykah gave Monique the biggest hug. *Note to self . . . reimburse Monique for all the trouble she went through.* "Thanks, Sis."

Lance approached them. "Hey, Cheeks. You look beautiful, Babe."

Arykah was dressed in a white silk tank top with Lady Arykah spelled out across her chest in Swarovski crystals. She wore an ankle-length hot-pink silk skirt that featured a single line of white silk ruffles down the middle rear from her waist to her ankle. On Arykah's feet were six-inch white snakeskin granny boots that laced up the front. They were peep toe and stopped just above the ankle. Arykah's blond hair was pulled into a side bun. She wore a diamond chain headpiece that Indian women were married in. The chain held a pink teardrop diamond that dangled in the middle of Arykah's forehead. Her makeup was perfect. Arykah was stunning.

"Hey, Babe," Arykah said. She gave Lance a soft peck on the lips. She was careful not to ruin her Lips By Carla lip gloss.

"Where's Diva Chanel?" Lance asked her.

"I decided to leave her upstairs since there's food here."

Lance took her by the hand. "Come. I want to introduce you to some people." He brought Arykah to a couple. "Babe, this is Quincy and DaShawn. They're newly engaged."

Arykah smiled. "It's nice to meet both of you and congratulations."

DaShawn shoved her left hand in Arykah's face. "He proposed this morning."

Arykah looked at the ring. It was a single diamond surrounded by an eighteen carat gold band. Arykah squinted. She thought the diamond to be a fourth of a carat at best. It wasn't her taste, but seeing how DaShawn was so excited to show the ring off, Arykah obliged her. "Oh my, that's a beautiful ring." Arykah wished she had her reading glasses on. Maybe with them on she could actually see the little pebble.

"DaShawn and I would like to schedule marital counseling with you," Quincy said to Arykah and Lance.

"Absolutely," Lance said.

"I have some questions for you tonight, Lady Arykah."

Arykah smiled at DaShawn. "I can't wait to hear them."

"Please excuse us," Lance said as he took Arykah to the mashed potato bar.

"OMG, Honey, this is amazing," Arykah squealed. "It's *exactly* what I wanted."

Lance was proud that he was able to make Arykah's wish come true on her special night. "I thought about putting food coloring in the mashed potatoes and making them pink to go along with your theme. Then I thought that maybe it would have been too much."

"Yeah, a little bit," Arykah said. She looked around the room and saw everyone eating from martini glasses. "I love this."

"Lady Arykah, give me those shoes," Sharonda walked up and said.

You can't afford them. "Hey, Sharonda. How are you?" Arykah asked the question to be kind. She really didn't care for Sharonda and told Lance that he needed to hire a new secretary. Arykah wasn't satisfied with Mother Gussie's granddaughter handling her husband's affairs.

"I'm good," Sharonda answered. "And I think this is wonderful what you're doing tonight. Look at all of these people here just for you."

Arykah didn't respond to Sharonda. She didn't care to be in her presence, and Lance picked up on Arykah's silence.

"I think we should get started, Cheeks. You ready?"

Arykah inhaled and exhaled. "As ready as I'll ever be."

Lance took Arykah to the front of the room. He stood behind a podium and spoke into the microphone that was mounted on top. "Good evening. I'm gonna ask that everyone settle down." He waited for the commotion in the fellowship hall to calm. "Is everyone enjoying the mashtinis?"

"Amen, Bishop," some folks answered.

"They're very good, Bishop."

"Make sure you drink up—I mean eat them all up," Lance joked.

The folks laughed.

"I appreciate you all for coming out to Lady Arykah's 'Ask Arykah Anything' session. I think this is a great idea she had to meet and greet the members of Freedom Temple." Lance glanced at his wife standing off to the right side of him. "Arykah has a good heart."

"Amen," Chelsea, Darlita, Monique, Myrtle, and Gladys shouted out. They were all seated at a table at the front of the room. They wanted to be close to Arykah in case she needed their assistance.

"All of you know that when we lost Gwen, I had given up on love. I had decided that I would live out the rest of my days as a single man. But God didn't see fit to let that be." Lance looked at Arykah again. "When I had least expected it, God blessed me with a fine woman. Ain't she fine, y'all?"

The people laughed, and Arykah blushed.

"Ladies and gentlemen . . . Lady Arykah."

The fellowship hall was filled with a hearty applause. Team Arykah stood and cheered her on with encouragement. Lance stepped from behind the podium, kissed Arykah's cheek, and guided her to take his place behind the podium.

Arykah looked out at all of the people and became nervous. Suddenly she thought about what Chelsea had said earlier in her office.

This Ask Arykah Anything could go way wrong.

Backing out wasn't an option at this point. Arykah shook off the fear and spoke to her members. "Good evening, Freedom Temple."

"Evening, Lady Arykah," the people responded.

"You're beautiful," Arykah heard someone shout out. She looked to the middle of the room and saw that the words had come from a lady. She was seated at a table with nine other people that Arykah hadn't recognized. But Arykah did recognize the face of the lady that had shouted out to her. Last Sunday after Arykah had given her speech on what happened to her, the lady approached Arykah and wrapped her shawl around her shoulders.

Arykah looked at her and smiled. "Thank you. What's your name?"

"ParaLee Weatherall," the woman answered.

"I'm glad you're here, ParaLee. I appreciate you and the shawl. It was a kind gesture. Thanks so much."

The members seemed to be warm and engaging. Arykah thought that she could loosen up and ignore her nervousness.

"The purpose of this evening is to allow all of you to get to know me and for me to get to know all of you. Some of you I have already met, yet, I see faces that I don't recognize. This small, informal reception was planned so that I can answer any question that any of you may have for me. So, feel free to stand, introduce yourselves, and ask away."

Immediately, almost every hand in the fellowship hall went into the air.

Arykah pointed to a female to her left. "Yes. What's your question?"

The young woman stood. "Hi, Lady Arykah. My name is Karen Dobson. And I just have to say that I looooove the way you dress. The outfit you're wearing now is gorgeous. Where do you shop?"

That was a question that Arykah had been expecting. She knew that her wardrobe was the topic of many conversations. "Thanks for the compliment, Karen. Because I am a curvy woman, the majority of my dresses, blouses, and pants are tailor-made to fit my body. Even my winter boots have to be tailor-made to fit my thick calves. Believe it or not, the tank I'm wearing tonight is basic. I found it at Walmart. I took it to a place that bedazzles and blings out shirts. The tank is cheap, but the crystals are not. My skirt was custom-made for me. However, I do often run across websites that feature clothes for plus-size women. If I see something that I like in my size, I buy it."

Karen had a second question. "Is it true that your closet is the size of a two-bedroom apartment?"

Arykah blushed. She was embarrassed by Karen's second question. Arykah knew that it must've been Gladys who boasted how large her closet was. The night Arykah hosted a stiletto party at her home, Darlita, Chelsea, and Gladys asked for a tour. When Gladys walked into Arykah's closet, she said that it was bigger than her two-bedroom apartment.

Yes, Arykah was blessed, and Lance had often encouraged her to be honest when folks asked about her lavish living. Arykah feared that she would be frowned on or avoided by people who were less fortunate than she was. She never wanted to brag. She should've made the ladies sign confidentiality agreements before they stepped foot in her home.

"Well, Karen, a two-bedroom apartment is fairly large. I certainly wouldn't say that my closet is *that* huge but . . ."

"*I would!*" Gladys shouted out.

The people chuckled.

Arykah glared at Gladys and slightly balled her lips. *Would you shut your mouth?*

She brought her attention back to Karen. "Comparing my closet to a two-bedroom apartment is an exaggeration. It's not that big." Arykah looked out at the people. "Who's next?" She wanted to end that topic quickly.

Arykah pointed to a lady that was standing against the wall on the right side of the room. "Yes. What's your question?"

"Hi, Lady Arykah. You're gorgeous tonight."

Arykah smiled at her. "Thank you."

"My husband and I both agree that we need a housekeeper. The problem is that he wants to hire a young chick, and, of course, I know better than that. What should I do?"

"You already know what to do. Hire the oldest, wrinklest, non-English-speaking woman you can find."

The fellowship hall roared.

"What's your name, Honey?"

"Donna Avers."

"Listen to me, Donna," Arykah started. "Don't bring a young chick in your house. Temptation is too great so don't entertain it. *I* wouldn't. See, my husband likes to sit at the kitchen table and read his newspaper with a hot cup of coffee. A young chick will have just one time to conveniently drop the dish towel on the floor, then bend over and reach for it, but stop short with her butt in the air. *'Oh, I didn't mean to drop this towel. Tee hee hee.'*"

The people laughed.

"See, then y'all will read about me in the *Sun-Times* 'cause I done caught a case. And I ain't trying to bring shame on the church, okay?" Arykah shook her head from side to side. "Don't do it, Donna. Don't do it." She looked around the room. "Who's next?"

A man stood. "Lady Arykah, my name is Darryl Glenn." He pointed to the lady seated next to him. "This is my wife, Carol. My question is for the bishop, if I may."

"Absolutely," Arykah said. She invited Lance to come and stand next to her.

"Bishop," Darryl started, "I need your advice. Carol often asks for my opinion on different matters. And when I give it to her she tells me that I'm being unreasonable. So, tell me, do you experience that in your marriage? If so, how do you handle it?"

The room went silent. There was no walking, no eating, and no drinking. No movement whatsoever. Everyone wanted to hear how Lance would answer Darryl's question.

"You know, Darryl, that's a good question. Yes, I have experienced that. But I figured out a way to keep peace in my home. I just wait for Lady Arykah to *give* me my opinion, and I agree with her. Happy wife, happy life."

The people laughed until they were in tears. Lance stepped off the podium and gave Arykah the floor.

She was still chuckling at Lance's answer when she took another question. She pointed to a man across the room. "Yes, what's your question?"

"My name is Quincy Hudson. Do you feel that tattoos are an abomination against the Lord?"

Arykah thought about his question. "Well, Quincy, I can't say that I do. I don't have any tattoos because I don't find them attractive. Both of my ears are pierced though. I was brought up in a Baptist church where tattoos and body piercing was frowned upon. But, no, I don't believe tattooing and piercing offends the Lord. But I will say this; I don't agree with folks getting girlfriends' and boyfriends' names etched on their bodies. Relationships don't always last. While some folks may find it a loving gesture or a dedication to their significant other, things do happen. Then you're left with a person's name, a person that you may have grown to dislike, on you forever. So, Quincy, make sure you think before you ink."

Arykah pointed to a woman directly in front of her. "Yes. What's your question?"

The woman stood. "I'm Tyfani Whitaker. My cousin is trying to set me up on a blind date. I'm hesitant. Do you think I should go?"

"Chile, let me tell you," Arykah said.

The people chuckled. They knew she was gonna say something hilarious.

"I went on a blind date once, and it was the worst date I ever had. A coworker set me up with her boyfriend's brother. I actually liked my coworker's boyfriend because he treated her like a queen. I figured that his brother had been cut from the same cloth. So, I agreed to go to the movies with him. I didn't want the guy to know where I lived so I met him at my coworker's house. When I got in his car he asked if I was gonna want some popcorn or candy or something to drink when we got to the movies. I told him that I wouldn't. Well, when we sat in our seats, inside the theater, I saw that the couple next to us was sharing a huge bucket of popcorn and it smelled heavenly. So I said to my date, 'I changed my mind. I *would* like some popcorn and something to drink.' The fool got so irate and yelled, *'Didn't I ask you before we got here if you were gonna want some popcorn? I would've stopped by the dollar store and bought you popcorn and something to drink. The popcorn and drinks here at the movies cost too much!'*"

All the people yelled out in laughter.

"So, ten minutes into the movie, I excused myself and said I was going to the ladies' room. I left his cheap behind right there at the movies and took the bus home. I vowed to never go on a blind date again." Arykah looked at Tyfani. "But, Tyfani, I won't tell you not to go on a blind date. Your experience may be better than mine."

Arykah pointed to a man who stood across the room on her left side. She recognized him as a member of the church, and he also worked for Lance as a construction worker at Howell Construction. "Yes, Isaac. What's your question?"

"You're stunning tonight, Lady Arykah."

She smiled. "Thank you."

"I'm a single guy," Isaac said. "I make a decent living and have a few bucks in my bank account. A lot of people depend on me to help them make ends meet. But it seems like the more I give, the more people want. How do I cut moochers off without offending them?"

"Isaac, the best thing you can do for poor people is to not become one of them."

A bunch of "Amens" ricocheted throughout the fellowship hall.

"Now you're preachin'."

"Say that again, Lady Arykah."

Arykah looked at Isaac. "When you give and give and give, you become an enabler. As long as you don't mind giving away money, folks ain't gonna mind asking you for it. You're the one going out every day slinging heavy concrete. Tell me something, Isaac. The people that you're supporting, are they able to work?"

Isaac nodded his head. "Yes."

"Well, what would happen if you run into a snag and need a dime or two? Can you depend on them to carry you?"

He shook his head. "Probably not."

"It's time to shut the ATM down, Isaac. Hang an Out Of Order sign on it. And thanks to caller ID, you ain't gotta answer your phone."

A few folks applauded Arykah's advice.

Arykah pointed to another man seated at a table near the rear of the fellowship hall. "Yes. What's your question?"

"Lady Arykah, my name is Donald Bettis. I'm a twenty-three-year-old ex-con. I served six years in the penitentiary for selling dope. I'm rehabilitated, but I can't seem to catch a break with folks that want to remind me of what I used to do. I have a great job; I have a girlfriend that I love, and I love being a member of Freedom Temple. But it's mainly church folks that frown at me like I'm beneath them. How do I handle that?"

"Well, the first thing you gotta do, Donald, is get delivered from people."

"Come on now," Arykah heard a man say.

"Say that, Lady Arykah."

She felt her help coming on. Arykah walked to Donald and stood in his face. "The church is full of dream killers and destiny preventers. But you can't let what folks think of you keep you from receiving all that God has promised you. You see, Donald, justice is when you get what you deserve. Grace is when you *don't* get what you deserve. And mercy is when you *get* what you *don't* deserve."

More people applauded Arykah. Lance was impressed by his wife's wisdom. He could probably put Arykah in the pulpit—But he quickly dismissed that thought. *Arykah in the pulpit? Absolutely not.* Her sermon would be full of curse words.

"Do you understand what I just said, Donald?"

"Perfectly," he said.

"Don't carry around folk's negative thoughts of you. Ain't nobody got a heaven or hell to put you in. Understand?"

Donald nodded his head. "Yes, ma'am."

Arykah turned and walked back to the front of the room. She looked at her wristwatch and saw that it was getting late. "I think I have time for a couple more questions."

Arykah pointed to a woman seated at the table with her team. "Yes, what's your question?"

The woman stood. "Lady Arykah, my name is Josephine. I'm a housewife raising two kids. My husband, who isn't a member of Freedom Temple, supports our household on his salary just fine. But there are times when I'd like to buy a new hat or even treat myself to a spa. My husband feels that I don't deserve a spa because, in his mind, all I do is sit around the house all day."

Arykah immediately addressed all the women. "Ladies, don't let what a man brings to the table be all that you have to eat." She connected eyes with Josephine. "Who pays the bills?"

"My husband does."

"I mean who writes the checks and balances the bank book?"

"I do," Josephine said.

"When you pay the light, gas, cable, telephone, and mortgage, make sure you pay yourself too. A woman should always have her own money."

Lance's eyebrows rose. He didn't agree with what Arykah had just done. She told Josephine to go behind her husband's back and hide money. Lance stepped to Arykah and said, "Honey, if I may?"

Arykah allowed Lance to address Josephine.

"Sister Josephine," Lance started, "if your husband is willing, Lady Arykah and I would like very much to sit with the two of you and discuss any financial disagreements you may have."

"Okay. Thanks, Bishop." Josephine took her seat.

Arykah took another question from a man seated at a table near the rear of the fellowship hall.

"Lady Arykah, do you believe it's a sin to partake in swine?"

Arykah cocked her head to the side. "Is that a trick question? Do I look like I don't eat swine?"

The people laughed.

"I eat every part of the pig from the roota to the toota. And if it is a sin, then God must be *real* mad at me."

Everyone chuckled.

At the lateness of the hour, Arykah went back to the podium and spoke to everyone. "This was truly wonderful, and I'm happy that you all took the time to come out—"

"I have a question."

Arykah saw a woman in a skintight red dress come from the back of the room and stand directly in front of her.

"Oh my God," Lance mumbled.

Monique stood and so did Darlita, Chelsea, and Gladys.

Arykah heard the people talking and whispering amongst themselves, but she couldn't make out what anyone was saying. Arykah was focused on the drop-dead killer body that was in front of her. The red dress was gorgeous, and so was the woman's face. Arykah had to admit that God curved the woman in all the right places. Arykah couldn't hate. She was drawn to the woman's feet. Arykah's eyes bucked. She was wearing red Jimmy Choo high-heel sandals. The specific stiletto was called the "Freya." They cost $2,895 a pair, and Arykah had preordered them three months ago. The Freya design wasn't due to release until early August. How on earth could the woman have them on her feet in late May?

"I have a question for you, Lady Arykah," she said again.

Arykah brought her attention from the woman's feet up to her eyes. *I got a question for you too. How did you get those Jimmy Choos so early?* "Yes. What's your question?"

Lance held his breath and watched. Team Arykah was on standby.

"I was once in love with a man that I let get away from me. He's moved on now, but I really wanna get him back. Do you have any advice on how I should go about it?"

More mumbling came from the people. Arykah figured they were thinking out loud exactly what she was thinking. Why would a woman that gorgeous need to chase a man? Surely with her good looks, body to die for, and obviously great taste in clothes and shoes, she could have any man she wanted.

"Well, first of all, you're much too pretty to be chasing a man that has moved on. You can't hunt a hunter." Arykah realized that she didn't know the woman's name. "What is your name?"

"Angela Moore."

As soon as Angela announced who she was, Monique moved toward Arykah. She only hoped that she could get to Arykah before she put her hands around Angela's throat.

Arykah frowned. *Angela Moore?* It angered Arykah that Angela had the gall to approach her and ask how she should go about getting Lance back. Arykah became angry with herself because she admired Angela's appearance before she realized who she was. She stepped to Angela. "You're the one who's chasing after my husband?"

Angela stepped to Arykah. "I had him first."

Arykah stepped closer pressing her nose to Angela's nose. "That's right. You *had* him. Okay? He's *married* now."

"That can be changed."

The people gasped.

Arykah pushed Angela backward. She lost her balance and fell. Immediately, Arykah went toward Angela but was shoved out of the way. Arykah stumbled to the side, but saw that it was Monique who had shoved her and dived on top of Angela. People near the women scrambled to move out of the way. Lance ran to Monique and tried to pull her up off of Angela. Arykah joined in and began hitting Angela in her face and head. A few men in the fellowship hall came to assist Lance in breaking up the fight. Lance let go of Monique and locked his arms around Arykah's upper torso, then pulled her off of Angela. Three other men separated Monique and Angela. It was total chaos in the fellowship hall.

Arykah tried, with all of her might, to get free of Lance's bear hug. *"Turn me loose , Lance. Let me go,"* she yelled out.

Arykah outweighed Lance by ninety pounds, but he managed to keep his bear hug intact and get her upstairs to her office.

"What is the matter with you?" he yelled when they were behind closed doors.

Arykah's eyes were blazing. *"I'm gonna kill that ho!"*

The door to Arykah's office busted open and two men forced Monique inside. She was out of breath from fighting the men to release her.

"Sit down, both of you!" Lance ordered.

Lance sat behind Arykah's desk, and she and Monique sat in chairs on the opposite side of the desk. All three of them were breathing heavy. He looked at them both. "I can't believe what just happened."

"She had it coming," Monique said.

"Exactly," Arykah agreed. "I think that broad tattooed them eyebrows one too many times, and the ink soaked through her skull. She's brain dead. And what she did just now was buy herself a one-way ticket on the train of whoop-ass."

Myrtle walked into Arykah's office with fire in her eyes. She was huffing and puffing. She slammed the door shut and marched right over to Arykah and Monique. "I'm finta beat both y'alls tails."

Lance hung his head and shook it from side to side.

Before bed, Arykah was in her dressing room on her knees. "Father, I'm so sorry. Please forgive me. I brought shame on my husband and the church." Arykah's eyes welled up. She realized that she had embarrassed her husband. On the drive home, Lance hadn't uttered a word to her.

But before they left the church Myrtle gave her and Monique a tongue-lashing. Her words were so severe that Arykah wished that Myrtle had just put them over her knee and did what she said she was going to do to them. Beating her and Monique would have been less painful than what they had to sit through.

"Father, please don't let the church punish Lance because of my actions. Jesus, I promise that I'll do better with my temper and my language."

After prayer, Arykah found Lance lying on the bed staring up at the ceiling with his hands extended behind his head. Diva Chanel snuggled up next to him. Arykah lay on her side of the bed and turned to face him. "I'm really sorry, Bishop. I know that there was no excuse for me to behave the way that I did."

"It was bad enough that Monique jumped on Angela, but you are my wife, the first lady of the church, Arykah."

"Well, Lance, I couldn't just stand by and let Monique fight my battles."

"Neither of you should have been fighting. What are you, teenagers?"

Arykah became defensive. "Wait a minute, Bishop. You ain't gonna put this all on me. Part of this is *your* fault. You let me walk into the fellowship hall blind. Had you been honest with me and told me about *Ho Angela*, I would have dealt with her a long time ago."

"What are you talking about? I *did* tell you about her."

"All you said was that she was your *ex* -girlfriend, but you didn't tell me that she was pushing up on you."

"Because there was no need."

"What do you mean 'there was no need'?"

"I know how you are, Arykah. You have a short fuse, and you don't always deal with situations the way you should. You have zero patience. You have zero filter. And I don't need you poppin' off every time someone pisses you off. I can handle Angela. She ain't got nothing coming from me."

"Lance, she shouldn't be flirting with you. I don't like that. And it shows that she has no respect for me. I'm your wife. I don't understand why you can't see my point of view. That stank broad stood in my face and asked me how she should go about getting you back. What did you think my reaction should have been?"

"Certainly not to push her and certainly not for you and Monique to jump her. I'm not defending Angela. What she did was wrong. I just wished you hadn't allowed your emotions to get the best of you, Arykah. It was embarrassing."

"Are you worried about the deacons?"

"After that funeral fiasco last month, heck, yeah, I'm worried about the deacons."

A month ago Lance went against the church's rules. He chose to have the funeral of a non-member at Freedom Temple.

"First, I go against the church's rules and eulogize a non-member and because of that, cross-dressers, transgenders, and homosexuals tore up the sanctuary. And tonight my wife and her thug friend beat up a woman in the fellowship hall. So, yes, I'm worried."

Lance turned his back to Arykah and switched off his lamp on the nightstand.

Arykah lay silent for a minute. "Did you just call Monique a thug?"

"You're a thug too. Both of y'all are thugs."

Arykah didn't argue. For once Lance was correct.

She lay still for fifteen seconds, then reached over and caressed Lance's behind.

"After what you did tonight, don't even think about it."

Arykah knew it would probably be a long shot trying to arouse Lance. She turned over and went to sleep.

Five

At approximately 8:30 the next morning, Adonis answered a knock on the front door. He looked through the peephole and saw two African American female police officers, dressed in blue uniforms, standing on his porch.

"Monique !"

She had just gotten out of the shower. Monique walked into the living room wrapped in a terry cloth robe and wearing a shower cap on her head. She saw Adonis standing at the front door. His hand was on the doorknob. Monique frowned at the horrid expression on his face. "Who's at the door?"

"Two cops."

Monique's expression matched her husband's. *"What?"* She went to Adonis, removed his hand from the doorknob, and opened the front door herself.

"Monique Cortland?" the taller of the two officers asked.

Monique became nervous. "Yes. Can I help you?"

The same officer who confirmed Monique's identity extended her a sheet of paper. "We have a warrant for your arrest."

Adonis's eyes grew wide. "What is this about?"

The shorter officer entered the home and addressed Adonis. "Sir, please step aside."

Monique read the warrant. Her heart started to race.

"Why are you arresting her?" Adonis asked.

The taller officer entered the home and spoke to Adonis. "She's under arrest for the assault and battery against a Miss Angela Moore."

"Oh my God," Monique cried out.

The taller officer read Monique the Miranda Rights. "Monique Cortland, you have the right to remain silent. Anything you say can and will be used against you in the court of law."

Monique looked at Adonis as tears spilled from her eyes.

"You have the right to an attorney," the officer continued. "If you can't afford an attorney, the court will provide an attorney for you. Do you understand these rights?"

Monique didn't answer.

"Can she get dressed before you take her away?" Adonis asked.

"That'll be fine," the shorter officer said.

Adonis attempted to take Monique by the hand and lead her to the bedroom.

"Sir, you stay here," the shorter officer demanded. "I'll go with her."

Ten minutes later Monique emerged from the bedroom dressed in blue jeans and a red tank top with blue flip-flops on her feet. Her knees buckled when the taller officer handcuffed her.

"Where are you taking her?" Adonis asked.

"The Cook County Correctional Facility on twenty-sixth and California," the shorter officer answered.

Adonis needed every bit of strength he had to not break down. Seeing his wife in handcuffs broke his heart. He walked to Monique and kissed her cheek. "Don't worry, Baby. I'll be right there to post your bail."

Monique remained silent. Tears dripped from her chin onto her tank top as she was led away. Adonis stood in the doorway and watched the officers place Monique in the rear of the cruiser.

***

As he did every Saturday morning, Lance opened the front door to retrieve his newspaper from the front porch. His heart stopped momentarily when he saw a Caucasian policeman walking up his driveway. Lance's body froze. He heard the telephone ringing.

The officer climbed the five steps. "Does Arykah Miles-Howell reside here?"

Lance and the officer heard Arykah scream out. She came running from the bedroom with the cordless telephone in her hand. *"Lance , Adonis is on the—"* Arykah words were cut short when she saw the police officer standing in her living room. She dropped the telephone, and it made a loud sound when it landed on the hardwood floor.

The officer walked to her as he reached for his handcuffs on his waist. "Arykah Miles-Howell?"

Arykah placed her face in her hands and cried.

One hour later, at the Cook County Correctional Facility, Arykah and Monique stood in a line with twelve other female offenders. All of the ladies had their mug shots taken and fingerprints recorded. The next step was to be interviewed by a counselor.

Monique stood third in line behind Arykah. Up ahead she saw the door to a room open and the lady ahead of Arykah entered in. "Why do we have to see a counselor?"

Arykah shrugged her shoulders. "I don't know."

"Everybody has to see the counselor," a lady standing behind Monique spoke up.

Monique turned around and looked in the face of a very pregnant lady. "But why?"

"The counselor asks questions about what we did to get here, and she'll ask if we're remorseful. Basically, she picks our brains to see if we're fit to stand trial or if we should be shipped off to the nuthouse."

Arykah looked at her. "How do you know that?"

"Because this is my third time here. I'm kind of a pro at this."

Monique couldn't believe her ears. What was a pregnant woman doing at the jailhouse? "This is your *third* time?"

"Yep. And I'm pretty sure that I won't make bail this time. I'll probably have my baby in here."

"What makes you think that you won't make bail?" Arykah asked her.

Before Arykah knew it, a female guard was at her side. "Hey, Fatso. No talking in line."

Arykah had to throw her head all the way back and look up to see the guard's face. She stood about six foot three, and she towered over every female standing in line. Her aura was very powerful and intimidating. Arykah noticed that she held on tight to her nightstick hoisted on her belt loop.

The guard addressed the entire line. "That goes for all of you hoes," she yelled. "Don't speak unless I tell you to."

Her voice was like thunder, and it made Monique shiver.

"Who is *that*?" Monique asked out of the side of her mouth when the guard walked away.

"That's Jocelyn, the head guard of the women's section of the facility," the pregnant lady answered. "She has a big bark and an even bigger bite. She don't take no crap, and she ain't got no patience."

Arykah silently prayed that God would deliver her out of this situation.

After standing ten minutes in a line of silence the door opened. Arykah saw the woman who stood in line ahead of her exit with a tear-stained face.

"It's your turn, Fatso," Jocelyn yelled from across the room.

Arykah's feet were glued to the ground. She couldn't move. When Monique saw Jocelyn coming their way, she nudged Arykah's back. "Here she comes. Go-ahead."

Jocelyn took Arykah's elbow by force and basically threw her into the counselor's office. "I don't want any trouble out of you, Fatso."

The door slammed behind Arykah.

"Sit down."

Arykah saw a light-skinned woman sitting behind a metal desk. She had pink hair pulled back into a ponytail. A pair of small glasses sat on top of her petite nose. Arykah sat in the chair across from her.

The woman looked down at a sheet of paper as she spoke. "State your name and date of birth."

The room was cold, and the counselor's voice was even colder. She didn't bother to look Arykah in the face.

"Arykah Miles-Howell. November sixteenth, nineteen eighty-five."

"What were you arrested for?"

"Assault."

"Against who?"

Arykah looked at the counselor's name tag that was clipped to the pocket of her white lab coat. *JoAnna Lovejoy.*

"Against Angela Moore," Arykah answered. She didn't see any resemblance to Santana Lovejoy. Arykah wondered if there was any relation between the two women.

"Why did you assault Angela Moore?"

Because she was trying to screw my husband. Remembering what the pregnant woman said, Arykah knew that she'd better not sound crazy. She didn't want to be taken to a psychiatric ward. "She said something to me, and I lost my cool. It was wrong, and I regret what I did."

"You accept responsibility for your actions?"

Arykah wished the counselor would look her in the eyes. "Yes."

The counselor wrote on the paper in front of her. "Okay, you can go for your physical now."

Arykah's head cocked to the side. "Physical?"

"Yes. A physical is required before anyone is placed in the holding pen."

"What kind of physical?"

The counselor looked up at Arykah. "It's basic. A blood sample will be taken. Your mouth will be swabbed. And a doctor will take a look inside your cervix. It's painless."

Arykah became nervous. Even though the room was ice cold, she started to sweat. Visions of the man raping her flashed in her mind. She shook her head from side to side vigorously. "No. I can't lie on a table and spread my legs."

"It's mandatory."

She didn't even ask why Arykah was uncomfortable with having to undergo a pelvic exam. Arykah concluded that the counselor may have felt that she was just another criminal passing through.

"I was raped five weeks ago, and I had a miscarriage because of it. I can't open my legs."

On Sunday Lance and Arykah had made love for the first time since she was attacked. He was loving and gentle. Arykah's assailant was the exact opposite, and based on Jocelyn's and the counselor's coldness toward her, Arykah knew the pelvic exam would be just as cold and maybe painful. She started to cry. "They'll hurt me. I can't do it."

The counselor looked up at Arykah and saw that her entire body shook. She pulled a Kleenex from a box that sat on her desk and gave it to her. That was the first sign of sympathy. "I'm sorry to hear that." She wrote more information on the sheet of paper. She looked up at Arykah again. "Have you sought professional help?"

Arykah blew her nose in the Kleenex and nodded her head. "Yes. I went to see Doctor Santana Lovejoy." She held her breath and waited to see how the counselor would respond.

She looked at Arykah curiously. "Really?"

Arykah nodded her head again. "Just last Saturday."

"Santana is my wife," the counselor revealed.

Arykah gasped. She thought that maybe Santana and JoAnna were sisters or maybe even cousins.

"Oh," was all Arykah could say. She prayed that patient and doctor confidentiality held up in marriages too. *Lord, please don't let her know that I ran out on my session with her wife.*

"You're married?"

"Yes," Arykah answered.

"For how long?"

"Almost six months now."

"Before marriage, how many sexual partners have you had?"

Arykah frowned. She didn't understand why her sexual past needed to be known.

"Mrs. Howell, a pelvic exam checks for sexually transmitted diseases. I'm trying to help you out, but I need you to answer the question truthfully."

Arykah still didn't understand, but she told the truth. "I was celibate for about three years before I married my husband."

The counselor nodded her head. "That's good." She wrote more words on the sheet of paper.

"Okay," she said. "Based on the fact that you were celibate for years before you got married, I will waive the pelvic exam; however, you must have your blood drawn to check for tuberculosis. *That* I cannot waive."

"Thank you so much," Arykah exhaled and said.

With the sheet of paper in her hand, the counselor escorted Arykah to the examining room. Once inside, the counselor whispered to the female doctor and gave her the paper.

"Good luck to you," the counselor said to Arykah, then left.

Arykah's mouth was swabbed. Three vials of blood were withdrawn from the crease of her left arm, then she was dismissed.

The smell of the holding pen almost caused Arykah to vomit. The stench of urine mixed with bodies that hadn't been bathed any time recently penetrated her nostrils. She looked around the pen and saw approximately twenty other women standing against the walls and seated on benches.

"Welcome home, Fatty," Jocelyn said to Arykah, then slammed the bars shut.

To Arykah, the bars coming together sounded like loud cymbals clanging in her ears. All eyes were on her as she stood by the bars.

"Relax. No one is gonna bite ya," a woman standing on Arykah's right said.

Arykah looked at the woman. The creases across her forehead told Arykah that she was probably in her midsixties. She wore a bright stiff red wig. Her black sheer blouse and extremely short yellow skirt and lace pantyhose caught Arykah's eye. She assumed the woman had been arrested for streetwalking.

Arykah looked at a woman in one corner of the cell. Her body was folded in a fetal position. Arykah stood in shock as she watched the woman rock back and forth moaning and crying. She rubbed her hands over her arms as if she was chilled to the bone, but the temperature in the cell was only about sixty-five degrees. Arykah couldn't help but to stare.

"She's a junkie. She needs a fix," the streetwalker said when she saw that Arykah couldn't take her eyes away.

Arykah didn't respond. She scanned the cell and saw a large woman with a shaved head and hard features. Arykah had a hard time distinguishing if the person was male, female, or both.

"That's Roxy. She and I are regulars here. But you may wanna stay out of her way. Roxy is hardcore, and she likes females. If she digs you, she'll let you know but in a not-so-nice way."

Arykah noticed no one sitting on the bench with Roxy. She sat by herself. At the end of Roxy's bench, Arykah noticed a stainless steel toilet with a small stainless steel sink attached to it. The toilet was exposed, and it was nasty. Urine and smeared feces stained the seat. Arykah saw urine puddled around the base of the toilet. She frowned. *Oh my God.* She couldn't believe that she was stuck in a dirty, filthy place. She was in jail.

"That toilet is for everybody? There's no privacy?"

"Yep and nope," the streetwalker confirmed.

Arykah frowned. "But it's nasty. No one cleans it? They really expect for us to use that thing? That's not right."

The streetwalker laughed and so did others who heard Arykah.

"Stupid broad, this ain't the Ritz Carlton," Roxy said. "You're a criminal, you're scum. You ain't got no rights."

Arykah was stunned.

"Uh-oh. You messed up now. You just pissed Roxy off," the streetwalker said.

The bars behind Arykah opened, and Jocelyn shoved Monique inside the cell. They grabbed each other and held on for dear life. "I'm so glad you're here," Arykah said in Monique's ear.

Monique looked all around the cell. The stench hit her nose quickly. "Oh, God, that smell," she frowned.

"Shut up," Arykah scorned. She glanced at Roxy. She was engaging in a conversation with another female. Arykah was glad that Roxy hadn't heard Monique's complaint. "You see that big overgrown girl over there?" Arykah nodded her head in Roxy's direction.

"Yeah."

"Well, she doesn't want to hear your complaints."

Monique looked all around the holding pen. She saw a woman wearing a short black skirt. A stream of blood ran down her leg. She saw the nasty stained toilet. Monique frowned. She was disgusted.

"There's no place to sit," Arykah said.

"Good. I wouldn't sit anywhere in here anyhow. It stinks really bad."

Arykah glanced at Roxy again. She was looking right at her and Monique.

"I told you to keep your comments to yourself. Angela Moore we can handle, but that big broad over there looks like she can go fifteen rounds with Sugar Ray Leonard and come out a winner."

"Adonis and Lance will be here soon," Monique said.

Arykah's body shivered at the thought of coming into contact with any of the women in the cell. "They can't get here soon enough."

As one woman was released from the cell at least two more were thrown in. Four hours after Monique and Arykah were there they were served cold bologna sandwiches on stale bread with a fruit punch juice box. They both rejected the lunch. Neither of them would dare touch the sandwich. But Monique was thirsty. The fruit punch would quench her thirst.

"You better not drink that," Arykah advised.

"Why not?"

"What if you have to go to the bathroom? You see how nasty that thing is?" Arykah looked for toilet paper and didn't see any. "And there's no toilet paper for you to line the seat with."

Monique offered her juice box to another woman in the cell.

The bars opened and Jocelyn shoved a woman inside. Monique couldn't help but to stare at the slashes and cuts on her face. Her nose was bloody and her lip was busted.

Arykah nudged Monique and whispered, "Don't stare."

Monique immediately averted her eyes to the floor.

"I can't believe this is happening. I am a *preacher's* wife, for God's sake."

Monique lay her head on Arykah's shoulder. "I'm so sorry, Sis. This is all my fault."

"No. Don't you dare apologize. You're not at fault for anything."

"I shouldn't have jumped on that chick."

"You were gonna get her, or I was gonna get her. Either way, that tail was gonna get got. Ride or die, remember?"

"Like Thelma and Louise," Monique said. "We always said that we would drive off the cliff together."

"We just may have to go to jail," was what Monique had said to Arykah when the havoc started at Freedom Temple five and a half months ago.

Nine hours later, the jail cell bars opened and Monique and Arykah were allowed to run into their husbands' arms. As soon as the couples exited the correctional facility the ladies were approached by a sheriff. "Arykah Miles-Howell and Monique Cortland?"

Monique exhaled. "What now?"

The sheriff gave each of them a tan eight-by-ten-size sealed envelope. "You have been served."

Inside the envelopes were restraining orders. Neither of them was permitted to go within 500 feet of Angela Moore.

***

"Slow down, Cheeks."

Arykah shoved three french fries into her mouth. "I can't help it. I'm so hungry."

"Sliders with cheese are my favorite," Monique said as she bit into a double cheeseburger.

On the way to taking Arykah and Lance home, Adonis had almost driven past a White Castle hamburger joint when Monique ordered him to stop at the restaurant.

Lance saw how Monique savored her onion rings. "You weren't given anything to eat at the jail?"

"We didn't want that sh—I mean stuff." Arykah rephrased her response. "We didn't want that *stuff.*" Improving her vocabulary was going to be more difficult than she had anticipated.

Adonis laughed. He knew it was a struggle for Arykah not to curse. "Having a hard time adjusting, First Lady?"

Arykah swallowed a sip of a strawberry milkshake. She exhaled. "Adonis, trying to stop myself from cussing is like squeezing a square inside of a circle. It's just not meant to be."

Monique dipped a fried onion ring into a small cup of ketchup. "Well, personally, I don't see a problem with letting one slip from time to time. There are occasions when cussin' is necessary." She inserted the onion ring in her mouth.

Lance was disturbed by Monique's comment. He had finally gotten Arykah to try to curb her taste for the forbidden language. He didn't need Monique encouraging her to backslide. He looked at Arykah. "As the first lady of a church, it's *never* necessary."

"Bishop, let's just agree to disagree, okay?"

"No, it's not okay, Cheeks. Folks are watching and listening to everything you do and say. There are young, impressionable girls at Freedom Temple. What would you do if a woman barged into your office cussing and hollering about an issue that she had?"

"Depends on the situation she's in. If the cussing is justified, I'd probably give her a high five."

Monique and Adonis hollered out.

"See? Like I said, sometimes it's necessary to cuss."

Lance glared at Monique.

Arykah knew how serious it was that she watch her tongue. Being the pastor's wife made her a role model. She saw the disappointed look on Lance's face. "I'm taking baby steps, Bishop. I gotta be weaned. Can you please work with me?"

Lance didn't want to hear Arykah's poor excuse for getting her way. "Whatever, Arykah. I'm ready to go. I have an early doomsday meeting with the deacons before service."

"Uh-oh," Adonis said.

"Uh-oh is right," Lance confirmed. "I see a suspension coming."

"Oh, Babe. I'm sorry." Arykah felt terrible that she was the reason that Lance's position as pastor was in jeopardy.

"Me too, Bishop," Monique added. "I regret what happened last night."

"Well, it's no use crying over spilled milk. I won't know my fate until I get to church in the morning."

"Do you want me to go to the meeting with you? I can explain my actions, and it may smooth things over with the deacons."

"And if that doesn't work, you can always show a little cleavage," Monique offered. "I bet those old men would foam at the mouth for a peek."

"Especially Deacon Jerry Wallace. He's so old he probably ain't seen a boob since the seventies," Arykah added.

Monique laughed at the thought. "Girl, I bet if you walk in that meeting with just a little bit of your triple Ds exposed, the deacons will probably appoint *you* as pastor. And Lance would be the first man."

The two ladies giggled.

"I'm glad the two of you are taking this matter seriously. You really have no idea the extent of the damage you caused. *And* the embarrassment." Lance paused and shook his head from side to side. "Oh my God."

"I'm offering to go with you to meet with the deacons."

"Maybe we both should go with you, Bishop," Monique offered. "We'll apologize. It could help."

Lance didn't address Monique. He looked at his wife. "You ain't going nowhere near Freedom Temple."

"And neither are *you* ," Adonis said to Monique.

Arykah's eyebrows rose in the air. "What do you mean?"

"*Hello?* Do the words 'restraining order' ring a bell?" Adonis asked Arykah. "That envelope you two were served with less than an hour ago is real."

Arykah looked at Lance. "Why can't I go to church?"

"Because Angela may be there."

The look on Arykah's face was cause for alarm. *"What do you mean I can't go to church because Angela may be there? Who in the devil's hell is Angela?"* Her loud voice caught the attention of others in the restaurant.

"Lower your voice," Lance said. "You gotta stay five hundred feet away from her, Arykah. You and Monique assaulted her in the church. The restraining order is to keep both of you away from her. She sees you as a threat."

"And that means . . ." Adonis started as he looked at Monique and Arykah, "neither of you can be anywhere near her, and that includes the church, the nail shop, the weave shop, grocery store, and wherever else Angela may be."

"Oh hell to the no!" Monique yelled out. She couldn't believe what she was hearing. "This is some freakin' bull right here. So, the lady elect can't go to church but the pastor's *ex-girlfriend can?"*

"Where they do that at, Lance?" Arykah asked him with raised eyebrows.

Lance threw his hands in the air. "Hey, I don't make the rules. It is what it is."

"That broad is trying to take your place, Arykah."

Lance scolded Monique with his eyes. "Would you stop trying to get her fired up? No one is trying to take her place." Lance looked at Arykah. "No one could *ever* take your place."

Arykah was way past pissed. She met Lance eyeball for eyeball. "You be sure to tell the *stank ho* that."

"Point-blank and the period," Monique added.

Six

Diva Chanel jumped at Arykah's knees as soon as she entered the foyer.

"There's my beautiful girl," Arykah said. She scooped Diva Chanel up and kissed her wet nose. "Did you miss Mommy? Huh? Did you miss me?"

Diva Chanel's petite tail was wagging hard as she licked Arykah's face.

"I gotta take a shower, Bishop. That jail cell was nasty." She turned to see Lance set the house alarm. "You wanna join me?"

"Nah. I got some thinking to do."

Lance's cellular telephone beeped. He removed the telephone from the holster on his belt loop and checked the text message.

I know your wife is out of jail. She better not be at church tomorrow .

"Who is that?" Arykah asked.

"Nobody," Lance quickly answered. "Um, just an alarm that I set to remind myself of the meeting with the deacons." His lie was effortless. Lance knew that if he revealed the true message of the text, Arykah would be back in jail in no time. He erased the text and headed down to the lower level of the estate. "I'll be in my office."

Arykah stood holding Diva Chanel. She didn't like Lance's body language. He seemed nervous when she asked who had texted him. She watched him walk down the steps until he disappeared from her view. *He could be telling the truth*, Arykah thought to herself. Lance did have a meeting with the deacons in the morning, and he did have reason to be nervous about it. She took Diva Chanel to the master suite.

Downstairs in his office Lance made absolutely sure that Arykah was not in earshot. On his cellular telephone he searched his contact list for the name "Arthur." When he had found the name, Lance touched the telephone number beneath it.

After only one ring Lance heard, "I knew you'd call." Angela purred like a kitten.

"I want you to drop the charges and retract the restraining orders against Arykah and Monique."

"Why would I do that?"

"Because I'm asking you to. Arykah is my wife, Angela. She belongs in church."

"Well, hood rat and hood rat number two should have thought of that before they jumped me."

"You're not innocent. What you did was foul. Asking Arykah, in front of everyone, how to get your ex-lover back. What did you think was gonna happen when you told her who you were?"

Angela didn't answer Lance's question. "She's not the woman for you, Bishop."

Lance didn't want to engage in that topic. He didn't need to explain to Angela, or anyone else, why he married Arykah or why she was perfect for him. "I want the charges dropped."

"What's in it for me?"

Lance exhaled and looked toward the staircase to make sure Arykah wasn't descending. He lowered his voice to a whisper. "What do you want?"

"Come to me right now. I'll open up a bottle of wine and you and I can discuss it."

"Are you nuts?"

"Do you want the charges dropped or not?" Angela shouted. She was no longer purring. She was demanding.

"Angela, I'm not gonna play this game with you."

She chuckled in his ear. "If you want your wife to stay out of jail and back in church, then you *will* play. Naked Twister."

Lance disconnected the call. He erased his call log and powered off his cellular telephone. He placed it on the charger on top of his desk. Then he sat in his chair and logged on to his Desktop computer. Lance searched for the sermon he was set to preach in the morning. He hoped that he would get the chance to grace the pulpit. It depended on what the deacons would do.

After her shower Arykah was on the floor in her closet. "My Lord, I messed up again. I know You're disappointed in me, Jesus. I let You down, and I've embarrassed my husband. I brought shame to the church and because of me, my best friend is facing jail time."

Tears welled up in her eyes. "Father, this first lady thing is too hard for me. I don't think I can do it. I try and I try and I try, but my back is constantly being pressed against a wall. I don't know what You expect of me, Jesus. What do You want me to do?"

The tears spilled onto her cheeks, and Arykah wiped them away. "I apologize, Father. My mouth can get out of control sometimes, and for that I'm deeply sorry. I know I need to learn how to let things roll off my back. But, Lord, I'ma tell You this right here and right now. Angela Moore will *not* take my husband away from me. You better snatch her before I do."

Arykah stopped herself when she realized that she had just threatened God. "Okay, Jesus, I'll make a deal with You. I will stop cussin' and almost cussin' and lashin' out if You'll allow the deacons to be easy on Lance. Please don't let him lose his position as pastor because of my actions. Lance is a good man, Lord. Freedom Temple needs him."

She heard Diva Chanel scratching at her closet door. "Father, I pray that You hear me." She paused. "Please hear me."

Diva Chanel licked Lance's nose. Sunday morning came quick for him. It seemed like as soon as his head hit his pillow, the sun was peeking through the miniblinds.

He stirred. "Good morning, Diva." He looked over his shoulder and saw that Arykah's side of the bed was empty. He grabbed Diva and snuggled with her. "Where's your mom?"

Lance got out of bed and carried Diva Chanel with him to the master bath to search for Arykah. When he didn't find her there, he went to the kitchen. No Arykah. "Where is she?" he wondered out loud. He set Diva Chanel down on the floor, and she took off running back to the master suite. Lance followed and saw her jumping and scratching at Arykah's closet door. He scooped Diva Chanel up, then opened Arykah's closet door by pressing his thumbprint against a black magnetic pad on the wall. The door opened, and Lance saw Arykah on the floor praying.

Before Lance had gone to bed the night before, he saw Arykah in that same position on the floor of her closet. He wondered if she had come to bed at all.

"Cheeks?"

Arykah looked up at him. "Hey, Babe."

"Have you been in here all night?"

Arykah exhaled. "Yeah, I had some serious repenting to do and some serious pleading to do." Arykah tried to get up, but her legs were numb. "Oh, Bishop, I can't move," she moaned.

With his free hand, Lance extended his arm to Arykah. She grabbed his bicep and pulled herself up from the floor. "Oh my goodness, my legs feel like I have a thousand needles in them." Arykah hobbled out of the closet, sat on the end of the bed, and stretched her legs forward. "I'm exhausted, Bishop."

Lance set Diva Chanel on the bed next to his wife. "Well, you'll have all morning to get some rest since you can't go to church."

"Oh yeah . . . that," Arykah sighed.

Lance proceeded to his closet to select his attire for church.

"What time is your meeting with the deacons?" she asked.

"Nine o'clock." He searched through all of his tailor-made suits. "Maybe I should wear black. This could be the death and funeral of my pastorship at Freedom Temple."

Arykah rose from the bed and went into Lance's closet. "Listen, God and I talked for hours. We met at a crossroads, and He and I came to an understanding. You don't have anything to worry about."

"If only that was true," he chuckled.

Arykah stepped to Lance and kissed his lips softly. "It *is* true. Trust your wife. I have your back."

Lance wrapped his arm around Arykah's waist and pulled her closer to him. "I know you do, Cheeks." He looked into her eyes. "You are an amazing wife."

She smiled. "I try to be, Bishop. I really do."

"You're psychotic. You're a hothead. You're a loose cannon. Sometimes you need to be buckled in a straitjacket. And I honestly believe that you'll shoot somebody. But you know what? There ain't a better woman on this earth for me." Lance meant those words wholeheartedly. As crazy as Arykah was, he could not have found a better wife.

Arykah chuckled. "Well, heck, I don't know if I should be offended or flattered."

"You should be flattered, Cheeks. It's your love that gives me fuel."

Arykah took Lance by the hand and led him out of the closet. "In that case, Pastor, follow me over to the bed. The first lady is gonna send you off to church feeling mighty good."

Lance didn't enter the main church doors. Instead, he had driven his car to the rear of the church and entered the back door. He didn't want to deal with anyone asking questions about what happened on Friday night or Arykah's whereabouts. He had only one thing on his mind, and that was facing the deacons. Lance knew that by Sunday morning the entire congregation would know about Arykah and Monique fighting. He would make a formal statement to the church if the deacons didn't dismiss him.

He ascended the rear stairs up to his office. When he saw his office door ajar, he knew the deacons were already waiting for him. The closer Lance got to his office the more nervous he became. His heart beat out of his chest when he entered. He saw all five deacons sitting around his desk.

"Praise the Lord, Deacons," he greeted.

No one returned Lance's greeting. He became even more nervous. He took his seat behind his desk. "How's everybody doing this morning?"

Still no response from the deacons. They silently stared at him.

Lance leaned back in his chair and loosened his tie. What he really wanted to do was start packing his personal belongings. He was sure the deacons were giving him his walking papers.

"Okay, I'll start," Lance said. His palms were sweaty. "Um," he paused. "Well . . . first . . . um." Lance extended his long legs beneath his desk, then folded them beneath his chair. "I'd like to apologize for what happened in the fellowship hall on Friday evening. And also Lady Arykah sends her deepest regrets. And . . . um . . . the truth of the matter, Deacons, is—"

"Where's Lady Arykah?" Deacon Lloyd Turner asked.

He cut Lance's words off, and it worried him. "She's at home this morning."

"She should be here with you," Deacon Bronson Marshall said.

Lance concluded that they wanted to fire him and Arykah together. "Well, she can't be here because—"

"That's too bad," Deacon L. C. Woodard said.

Lance was confused. He cocked his head to the side and looked at each of them. "I'm sorry?"

"It's too bad Lady Arykah isn't here. We wanted to let you both know what a wonderful job you're doing here at Freedom Temple. Since the day we appointed you as the pastor of this church, you have done an outstanding job, Bishop," Deacon Jerry Wallace said.

Lance was totally thrown for a loop. He was dumb-founded. That wasn't at all what he was expecting to hear.

"We think Lady Arykah is doing a fine job. She's rough around the edges, and we didn't know what to expect when you brought her here. But the love and support she's shown to the ladies and young girls hasn't gone unnoticed," Deacon Bartholomew Tidwell added.

When Lance realized his mouth was hanging open he quickly covered it with his hand.

"Bishop, we were very impressed with the way Lady Arykah conducted herself on Friday night," Deacon Jerry Wallace commented.

Lance frowned. *Are they talking about the same Lady Arykah and the same Friday night that she and Monique beat Angela Moore down?*

"She answered every question with grace, truthfulness, and dignity," Deacon Lloyd Turner added.

The frown lines across Lance's forehead became deeper. *"Did y'all see the fight?"* he asked in a high-pitched tone.

"Yeah, we saw it, Bishop. You know we don't approve of fighting in the church."

Lance looked at Deacon Bronson Marshall. "Of course, Deacon. And again, Lady Arykah and I are both ashamed, and we assure all of you that it will never happen again."

"You ain't still messing around with Angela, are you?"

Lance's eyebrows rose at Deacon L. C. Woodard's question. *"Still* messing around with her? Deacon, Angela and I were over when I was called to preach."

"But does *she* know that?" Deacon L. C. Woodard asked.

Lance looked at all of the deacons. "I'm gonna make sure of it."

The deacons called the meeting to a close. They stood, shook Lance's hand, and blessed him.

"Let the Lord use you this morning," Deacon Jerry Wallace encouraged Lance before leaving his office.

Lance sat in his chair and exhaled a huge sigh of relief. He pinched himself to make sure he wasn't dreaming. "Did that really just happen?" he asked himself.

He wondered why the deacons had given him another pass. And the endorsement they gave Arykah came out of left field. Before Lance arrived he was as nervous as a hooker sitting in church. Now he could preach.

He leaned back in his chair and thought about what had just taken place in his office. The more Lance pondered the clearer things became.

At one time Deacon Bartholomew Tidwell faced eviction from his home. A retired Chicago firefighter, Bartholomew had confided in Lance that he couldn't afford the taxes on his home. He had only three days to pay before his home would be up for auction. His ailing wife was unable to work, and Bartholomew's fixed income hadn't been enough to make ends meet. Lance wrote a check covering the cost of the taxes, gave it to the deacon, and wished him well.

Three years ago, on a Sunday night, Deacon Jerry Wallace had called Lance to say that he had been arrested for soliciting prostitutes. Too embarrassed and ashamed to call his children or wife, Deacon Wallace had to face his pastor and confess what he had done. After posting his bail, Lance prayed with Deacon Jerry Wallace and laid holy hands on him. The deacon was delivered from his sexual addiction, and Lance had kept his secret.

It was during Lance's first year as pastor of Freedom Temple Church of God in Christ when Deacon Lloyd Turner was stricken with prostate cancer. A widower at only sixty-two years old, Deacon Turner had no children. It was Lance who drove him to the hospital and waited until the operation was over. And it was Lance who drove Deacon Lloyd Turner home. Every morning before he went to work, Lance stopped by the deacon's house to prepare his breakfast, assist him to the bathroom, and made sure the good deacon took his medicine.

Deacon L. C. Woodard's lust for alcohol had cost him his driver's license when he was charged with his second DUI. Four times Lance got out of his bed extra early on Sunday mornings and drove twenty-five miles past the church to get him, just to make sure that Deacon Woodard could attend Sunday morning service. With his personal money Lance bought a van and hired a driver to chauffeur Deacon Woodard, and others without transportation, to and from church.

Like Lance, Deacon Bronson Marshall was an avid golf player. When he received a set of tailor-made golf clubs for Christmas from Lance, Deacon Marshall couldn't thank Lance enough. *"I would have never been able to afford these clubs, Bishop. Thanks so much."* Deacon Marshall was always the first to say how wonderful and selfless his pastor was.

Lance couldn't think of any other reason why the deacons had spared his job as pastor. But whether it was because Lance had helped them in their time of need or not, he was grateful that he could still grace the pulpit at Freedom Temple.

Lance answered a knock on his office door. "Come in."

The door opened and Myrtle, Darlita, Chelsea, and Gladys walked in.

"Team Arykah," Lance smiled and said.

"Praise the Lord, Bishop," Myrtle greeted.

The ladies sat in four of the chairs that the deacons had just vacated.

"Bishop, Lady Arykah just called me," Myrtle said. She sighed. "I'm not happy about this situation."

"None of us are," Chelsea added. "I couldn't believe my ears when Mother Myrtle informed us that Lady Arykah and Monique had been arrested and were banned from this church."

"Well, they haven't been banned from the church. Angela Moore has a restraining order against them. They can't be within five-hundred feet of her."

"But Lady Arykah is the first lady of this church, Bishop. *Not* Angela," Darlita complained.

Lance nodded his head in agreement.

"We're feeling some type of way about this. Something needs to be done," Gladys added.

"I don't want any of you getting involved," Lance said. "I'm going to speak with Angela today to see if I can get her to drop the charges against Arykah and Monique."

"But what if she doesn't?" Myrtle asked.

"Then we finish where Lady Arykah and Monique left off," Darlita responded.

All but Myrtle nodded their heads at what Darlita had just said.

Lance held up his palms. "Whoa, hold on now, Sister Darlita. There's no need for that kind of talk. And I don't wanna take another trip to the jailhouse."

It seemed that the more time Arykah's team spent in her presence the more they behaved just like her.

"If I'm gonna get Angela to drop the charges, I need all of you to behave. If she comes to church today, don't look at her crazy, don't roll your eyes, and don't point your fingers in her direction. We don't wanna give her any reason to not drop the charges."

Team Arykah sat in Lance's presence with their lips pursed.

"Agreed?" he asked them.

No one responded.

He raised his eyebrows and looked each of the ladies in their eyes. "Agreed?" he asked again.

"Agreed," they mumbled.

Lance dismissed the ladies, then dialed his home from his desk telephone.

"Praise the Lord," Arykah answered.

"Cheeks, you won't believe what the deacons said."

Arykah's heart started to race. "Oh no. They fired you?"

Lance chuckled. "Just the opposite. They praised us."

She frowned. "What?"

He chuckled again. "They told me that you and I were doing a fantastic job at Freedom Temple. They even said that you should have been here so they could tell you themselves that you were great on Friday night."

Arykah shrieked into the telephone. *"What?"*

Lance laughed out loud. "I know, right?"

"What a minute. Hold up, Bishop." Arykah needed to be sure that she was hearing Lance correctly. "The deacons said it was great that I helped beat down Angela?"

"You know what's crazy, Cheeks? I had to remind the deacons about that. They didn't even mention the fight, but I had to because I wanted to make sure that I was on the same page with them. All they did was remind me that fighting was prohibited in the church."

"O . . . M . . . G," Arykah said. "All that stressing you did was for nothing."

Lance shook his head from side to side. "If you hadn't laid before God all night, the meeting probably wouldn't have gone that way. There is power in prayer, Cheeks."

"Humph," Arykah said. "You ain't gotta tell *me*. My legs are still burning."

Lance heard praise and worship beginning. "I gotta go, Cheeks. I just wanted to call and tell you about the meeting."

"Okay, Babe. Have a great service. Diva Chanel and I send kisses."

"I'll see you both when I get home."

Arykah disconnected the call from Lance and dialed Monique's home.

"What's going on, Thelma?" Monique greeted.

Arykah laughed. "Good morning, Louise."

"It feels weird being at home on a Sunday morning, doesn't it?"

Arykah sighed. "Yes. But I called with good news. The deacons didn't fire Lance."

"That's awesome," Monique said. "Adonis and I were so worried. Before he left for church this morning he told me that if Lance was released from Freedom Temple, he'd leave too."

"Really?"

"Adonis was grateful that Lance gave him that job as head musician. He owes Lance."

"No, he doesn't. When Lance does something, he does it from his heart."

"That's true," Monique agreed. "So, what did the deacons say to the bishop?"

Arykah shrugged her shoulders. "According to Lance, the meeting was called to tell him how pleased they were with him as pastor. And apparently the deacons are good with me too. Lance said they didn't even mention the fight. He had to remind them about it."

"Shut the front door!" Monique said. "Are you serious?"

"Ain't that crazy?"

"Well, I'm glad everything worked out."

"So, what are you gonna do this morning?"

Monique sighed. "Girl, try to clean this house, I guess."

Arykah frowned. "Uh-uh. Let's go shopping."

Monique became excited. "For stilettos?"

"Yep."

Monique cheered into the telephone. Whenever Arykah bought stilettos for herself, she bought Monique a pair as well. That method kept Monique out of Arykah's closet. "Where are we going?"

"Neiman Marcus, Honey. Where else? If you fly, I'll buy."

"That works for me. Give me about ten minutes to shower and I'll swing by to get you."

"Sounds good."

The presence of the Holy Spirit was evident at Freedom Temple. Adonis was on the organ. The entire musician staff was on point with the choir. Praise and worship always got the people wound up and ready for Bishop Lance to deliver what thus said the Lord.

Myrtle, Chelsea, Darlita, and Gladys sat on the front pew, opposite the deacons, but were disturbed by Monique and Lady Arykah's absence. However, they did their best to participate in the fellowship.

"I love you, Jesus," the congregation sang. "I worship aaannnnnd adore you. Just want to tell you, Lord, I love yoooouuuuu more than anyyyyythannnggg."

The congregation was on their feet. Hands were in the air and heads were thrown back. Eyes were closed as they gave honor to the Father.

Lance stood in the pulpit giving God His due when he opened his eyes and saw a striking beauty enter the sanctuary doors.

Angela sashayed down the center aisle wearing a wide-brimmed white hat. She was dressed in a starched white two-piece suit with pearls trimming the wrist and collar. The skirt was extremely short. A French manicure adorned her toenails, and they looked pretty in the strappy high-heeled gold sandals.

She demanded the attention of the worshippers. Each pew that Angela passed on her way to the front of the church caused folks to look her way.

Lance had forgotten about praise and worship. He and others watched Angela's boldness as she strutted to the front pew and placed herself in Lady Arykah's spot. She stood right next to Myrtle.

Myrtle was too outdone. She looked at Angela with bulging eyes, then connected her eyes with Lance in the pulpit. Myrtle saw Lance's eyes pleading with her to remain calm and keep her composure. But it was Darlita, Chelsea, and Gladys that stepped to Angela.

"Trick, you got a lot of nerve," Darlita said.

Myrtle grabbed Darlita's elbow and tried to pull her away from Angela's face. Gladys stepped in the spot where Myrtle had pulled Darlita from. She glared at Angela.

"You are *not* gonna sit here."

"That's Lady Arykah's spot," Chelsea added.

Though Team Arykah knew that their first lady wouldn't attend church that morning, they wouldn't allow anyone—especially Angela Moore—to fill the void on the front pew.

The congregation's attention was pulled away from praise and worship. Everyone focused on the drama occuring on the front row. Lance didn't move from the pulpit. His right-hand man, Minister Carlton Weeks, saw the commotion and was headed toward Angela and the ladies, but Lance stopped him because he saw two female ushers coming up the center aisle. He knew they would ask Angela to sit somewhere else.

The ushers were dressed in black suit jackets, black skirts, and wore short white gloves.

"Sister Moore," the tallest usher said to Angela, "this seat is reserved for Lady Arykah."

"We can find you another place to sit," the other usher said to her.

Chelsea, Darlita, Gladys, and Myrtle waited to see what Angela would do. It would be in her best interest to move. Team Arykah was ready to pounce on her if she didn't.

"Lady Arykah isn't here," Angela said. "And she won't be for the foreseeable future."

Chelsea rushed to Angela, "Girl, I will beat the—"

"Chelsea!" Myrtle yelled. She stepped between Chelsea and her target.

The entire congregation watched Lance come from the pulpit and whisper in Myrtle's ear. She glared at Lance before whispering his words in Team Arykah's ears. All four ladies angrily snatched up their Bibles and purses from the front pew and exited the sanctuary.

Angela sat on the pew. Lance instructed the ushers to leave her be. He went back to the pulpit. He knew he had to deal with Angela, but right then wasn't the time. Lance would allow her to have her one hour of fame that she desired more than her next breath.

Lance was disappointed that he had to dismiss Team Arykah from the sanctuary, but he had no other choice. His reputation was on the line. From the unauthorized funeral he permitted at Freedom Temple to Arykah and Monique fighting in the fellowship hall to Angela Moore imitating the first lady, Lance didn't want or need another fiasco. If Angela thought, for one moment, that she was going to replace Arykah, she had another thing coming. He had a surprise for the Arykah-wannabe.

He stood at the podium, then nodded his head to Adonis. Adonis understood and brought the organ's pitch back to where it originally was. Lance did his best to get the people back in praise mode. "I love you, Jesus," he sang. His spirit was jacked up. He hoped that the Lord would restore his mind so that he could preach the Gospel. He continued to worship. "I worship and adore you."

Slowly but surely, the people joined in with Lance.

Angela didn't care that she had just interrupted service. She came to make a point that she—not Arykah—belonged on the front pew, and she would see to it that she remained there. She closed her eyes, raised her hands, and sang along with everyone else. It didn't bother Angela that the church looked at her like she was insane. There were whispers and mumbling all around her. Heads were shaking in disgust. "I worship and adore you," she sang out loud. For that moment *she* was the first lady.

When praise and worship ended, Lance asked the church to be seated. Usually it was during that time, just before Lance addressed the people, that he and Arykah would wink and blow kisses at each other. He refused to look in Angela's direction. Lance figured she'd probably lick her lips seductively or uncross her legs, then cross them again. The skirt she wore that morning hadn't left much for anyone's imagination.

"Praise the Lord, everybody," Lance said.

The people responded, "Praise the Lord."

"Praise the Lord, *everybody*," he said again with his voice an octave higher.

"Praise the Lord!" the congregation shouted back.

"It is truly an honor to be back in the house of the Lord one more time."

There were a bunch of "Amens" to Lance's statement.

Lance looked out at the people. "Y'all look good today." He scanned the audience. "You're wearing that hat, Sister Green."

Delores Green, a widow and a longtime member of Freedom Temple, stood from the fourth pew so that everyone could see her new hat.

It was no secret that Deacon L. C. Woodard was attracted to Sister Delores Green. He had been chasing her for a whole year before Lance tried to make a love connection between the two.

"Sister Delores, why don't you give Deacon Woodard a chance? He's a cool dude, and he has a nice pension."

She shook her head from side to side. "No, Bishop, I can't do that. L. C. is still sucking on that bottle." She shook her head again. "Uh-uh. I can't be bothered with that."

Delores was turned off when Deacon Woodard asked her on a date. He was honest and revealed that he didn't have a driver's license because of his drunken driving charge.

"So, you mean I gotta drive you around all the time?"

By the tone of her voice, Deacon Woodard knew that he'd never have a chance with Sister Green. But he never gave up hope of changing her mind. He continued to flirt with her.

"Ain't she fine this morning, Deacon Woodard?" Lance asked.

The congregation chuckled.

Deacon Woodard looked at Sister Green and winked his eye at her. "She sho is, Bishop."

The congregation chuckled again.

Sister Green waved her hand at Deacon Woodard to dismiss his comment, then she sat down.

The folks at Freedom Temple loved their pastor. Lance often brought smiles to their faces in a comical way on Sunday mornings. But Lance knew the time had come for him to speak about what happened at the "Ask Arykah Anything" session and why she was absent from church that morning.

He scanned the folks and remembered seeing many of them on Friday night.

"I know by now that most of you, and maybe all of you, have heard what took place downstairs, in the fellowship hall, this past Friday evening. First and foremost," he said. "I want to apologize to those of you who were present to witness Lady Arykah, Sister Monique, and Sister Angela fighting."

The people mumbled and many looked at Angela and wondered why she was sitting by herself on the front pew.

"Lady Arykah and Sister Monique regret their actions. Unfortunately, neither of them could be here this morning. They are remorseful and asked that I speak on their behalf. Lady Arykah and Sister Monique send their sincerest apologies and ask for your forgiveness."

More mumbling came from the people. Lance could tell by the expressions on their faces that they were wondering why Arykah and Monique couldn't be there to speak for themselves.

"Hopefully," Lance said, "when enough time has passed, things can get back to normal and Lady Arykah and Sister Monique can attend church. But for now, because of their actions, they can't be here."

Good riddance to both of them, Angela thought to herself. With the restraining orders in place, Angela could show Lance and the entire Freedom Temple Church family that she was more fit to be the first lady.

Lance decided not to preach. His heart wasn't in it, and he didn't want to short-change the people and give them a mediocre sermon. Souls were at stake. He knew today he wouldn't do the Gospel any justice. Instead, he took the morning service in another direction.

"Brother Adonis," Lance looked at him.

Adonis sat behind the organ ready for whatever Lance was going to do. "Bishop?"

"Play something soft," Lance said to him.

Adonis pressed down on the organ's keys, then looked at his staff and nodded his head. The drummer, keyboardist, and trumpet player followed his lead.

"Many of you are afflicted," Lance said to the congregation. "Today is a day of healing."

"Yes, it is, Bishop," someone responded.

"Amen, amen," others said.

Lance turned to his right-hand man. "Weeks, get me my oil."

Moments later, Minister Carlton Weeks was at Lance's side with a small bottle of blessed oil in his hand. Lance moved from behind the podium and exited the pulpit with Minister Weeks in tow. He came and stood before Jasper Sprawlings, an elderly man confined to a wheelchair. Jasper had been stricken with multiple sclerosis ten years ago. In spite of his disease, he attended church every Sunday morning.

"Brother Sprawlings," Lance said to him, "because your faith in God never faltered and because you continue to praise Him, God is gonna do a miraculous thing for you today."

"Amen, Bishop," the people responded.

Those seated near Jasper stood and stretched out their hands in his direction. The congregation knew how Lance flowed. They knew he was going to lay holy hands on and bless Jasper.

Lance held up his palm. Minister Weeks poured a small amount of the blessed oil into his hand.

Some folks started speaking in an unknown tongue as they watched their pastor.

Lance massaged the oil in both of his hands, then knelt before Jasper. He closed his eyes and began to pray for healing on Jasper's behalf. Jasper closed his eyes and lifted his hands in the air to receive the blessing from God. Lance spoke in an unknown tongue as he rubbed the oil up and down Jasper's legs.

The church's prayers got loud. Adonis raised the pitch on the organ.

"Thank ya, Jesus !" a woman shouted out.

With his free hand, Minister Weeks stepped to Jasper and touched his shoulder. He stood in agreement with what Lance was doing.

"Hallelujah!" the folks shouted out. *"Glowraaaaay to God!"*

When he had finished praying for Jasper, Lance stood and looked at him. "Stand up."

Jasper hadn't been on his feet in so many years, he didn't think it was possible.

Lance saw the doubt in his eyes. "Trust the Father. Stand up."

Minister Weeks folded down the silver footrests on Jasper's wheelchair beneath his feet.

The people's prayers were loud, knocking at the door to heaven. Adonis raised the organ's pitch even higher. The mood in the sanctuary of Freedom Temple Church of God in Christ was electric.

With the assistance of two young men that came to Jasper's side, he trusted his faith and began to stand up from the wheelchair. Lance took a step back and allowed him room. Slowly but surely Jasper rose from the wheelchair. He wavered back and forth as the two men held on to his arms.

"Release him and move the chair," Lance instructed the men.

The two men obeyed their bishop. There Jasper stood on his own two feet for the first time in years. He looked up toward heaven and started to cry.

The sanctuary sounded like a football stadium after a home team had just scored a touchdown.

Lance held out his hand toward Jasper. "Walk to me, Brother."

Like a one-year-old child taking his first step, Jasper moved his right leg forward, then dragged his left leg to meet it.

"Ha . . . lle . . . lu . . . jah," the people shouted.

Adonis and the musicians were going crazy.

Jasper moved his left leg forward and dragged his right leg to meet it.

"In the name of the almighty God, Brother Jasper," Lance stated. "You are healed."

Jasper took three more steps and almost collapsed in Lance's arms. Lance held on to Jasper and cried with him. When Lance looked up he saw the people dancing, shouting, and giving God glory.

Move!

Lance heard the voice of God and obeyed. He released Jasper and went to Melesha Thompson, a fourteen-year-old girl with a hole in her heart. Melesha's condition kept her from doing the things a normal teenager would do. She couldn't jump rope, play hopscotch, chase her younger siblings around, or even sing in the choir.

Lance stood before Melesha, then turned to look for Arykah. He needed his wife to be at his side to lay hands on Melesha's chest. He saw Angela standing in Arykah's spot. He knew he couldn't depend on Angela to surrender herself to God's will. At that moment she was only at church for show. She had a personal agenda. Lance told Melesha's mother, who was next to her daughter, to stand.

Folks stretched out their hands in Melesha's direction.

"Pray, church, pray!" Lance shouted out over the music.

The people obeyed and began to pray for Melesha's healing.

Minister Weeks poured blessed oil in Lance's hand and Lance transferred the oil to Melesha's mother's hand. He instructed her to rub her hands together, then place them on her daughter's chest. Lance put both of his hands on top of Melesha's head and closed his eyes. He spoke to God in an unknown tongue. Melesha's mother was praying and crying.

Melesha fainted in the Spirit of God.

"Pick her up," Lance said. He didn't care who did it.

Minister Weeks and Melesha's mother stood her up in front of the pastor.

Lance knew the request he'd made to God hadn't been completed. He couldn't afford to play around. He threw caution to the wind and touched Melesha's chest just above her left breast and shouted out to God.

Melesha fainted again.

When Minister Weeks went to pick Melesha up, Lance stopped him. He got down on the floor and lay holy hands on Melesha and cried out for God to heal her. Melesha's mother jumped and shouted. Those nearby joined her in the praise.

When he had finished praying, Lance stood and pulled Melesha up from the floor. She looked as though she had been in a war. She was drunk in the Spirit. Melesha couldn't keep her balance as she swayed back and forth.

"Raise your hands," Lance said to her.

Melesha was weak, but she did it.

Lance looked in her eyes. "Sister Melesha," he started, "by God's power that is invested in me . . ." he paused. His body shook. *"Good God Almighty,"* he shouted out. His blood was running hot through his veins. "Melesha," he said again. "You are healed in Jesus' name."

Melesha fainted again.

Move!

Lance turned and went to Frances Magazine, a new member to Freedom Temple. Lance stood speechless as he looked in Frances's eyes. He waited for the Holy Spirit to guide him. Frances started to cry. She felt heat radiating from Lance's body, and it gave her a magnetic shock. She reached out and touched his shoulder. *"Bishop,"* Frances cried out.

When she had touched him, Lance hollered out, "Oh, God." He grabbed her right arm and turned it inside out to reveal many small puncture wounds in the crease of her arm. Lance grabbed the bottle of blessed oil from Minister Weeks and poured three drops on the holes in her arm. He gave the bottle back to Minister Weeks, and then massaged the oil into the crease of Frances's arm while speaking in tongues. More tears spilled out of her eyes as she prayed that God would deliver her from drug addiction.

Lance opened his eyes and looked for Arykah and realized, again, that she wasn't there. If there was ever a time when he needed his wife, it was right then. He stepped to Frances and whispered in her ear. "Surrender yourself to the will of God and you will be delivered."

Frances fell down on the pew and began shouting out praises.

Lance was sweating profusely. He went back to the pulpit and stood behind the podium. The Holy Spirit was moving, and the musicians were on point. Lance looked out over the people and stretched out his hands. "By His stripes, you are healed. You are free. You are delivered. And you are healed. Receive it in the name of Jesus."

Not one soul was seated. Every foot was moving in the sanctuary. Every mouth was open. Every hand was shaking.

"God is here, church," Lance shouted out. *"He's here. He's here. Welcome Him."*

Adonis stood up but kept his hands on the keys. *Don don don don.*

The drummer stood but kept banging on the drums. *Pop pop pop pop.*

"Praise Him," Lance said to the people. "Give it to Him, give it to Him." He lost his own self-control.

"Many are the afflictions of the righteous," Lance shouted out, "but the Lord will deliver them out of them all."

The people were caught up in the Spirit and rejoicing all over the sanctuary.

"The Bible says in Romans chapter eight, verse eighteen," Lance started. He pounded the podium four times. "For I reckon that the sufferings of this present time . . ." He pounded the podium four more times, "are not worthy to be compared . . ." Lance pounded the podium a third time. "With the glory which shall be revealed in us."

Folks were lying on the sanctuary floor shouting out praises to God. Others were dancing.

Adonis raised the organ's pitch higher.

"Get ready for your healing! Get ready for your deliverance! Get ready, church! It's coming! It's coming! It's coming!"

Lance couldn't hold it any longer. He made himself happy. He joined the congregation and danced.

In the women's shoe department at Neiman Marcus in Oakbrook Terrace Mall, Arykah and Monique both modeled six-inch tan and black patent leather stilettos by the designer Rock Bottom.

"OMG, these are just too hot," Monique said as she strutted back and forth.

"Yassssss, Honey," Arykah agreed. "They are a must-have." She heard her cellular telephone ringing. She went to her purse and grabbed it just before the caller was sent to her voice mail. Arykah saw Chelsea Childs on the caller ID and wondered why she'd be calling at that time. "It's Chelsea," she said to Monique.

"Why isn't she at church?"

Arykah shrugged her shoulders. "I don't know." She pressed the talk button on her telephone, then brought it to her ear. "Hey, Chelsea."

Moments passed before Monique saw all the blood drain from Arykah's face. "What is it?"

With the telephone pressed against her ear Arykah walked to a chair and sat down.

Monique followed and did the same. "What is it?" she asked again.

"I know you are freakin' kiddin' me, Chelsea," Arykah said into the telephone.

Monique leaned close to Arykah and tried to hear what Chelsea was saying.

"I'm about to catch another case," Arykah said angrily. "Why did he make y'all leave?"

"Who made who leave from where?" Monique asked Arykah.

Arykah didn't answer Monique. She had to focus on what Chelsea was telling her.

"Well, why didn't Lance put that *slut* outta the church?" Arykah was breathing heavy. "Where y'all at now?" She waited for Chelsea to answer.

Arykah nodded her head. "I want you, Darlita, Gladys, and Mother Myrtle to meet me and Monique at Gibson's Steakhouse in Oakbrook Terrace. Do you know where it's at?" Arykah nodded her head again. "Yes, right now." She disconnected the line and glared at Monique.

"You won't believe what that tramp, Angela Moore, did at church this morning."

Monique's eyes were as big as golf balls. "What?"

Arykah stood up. "Let's go. I'll tell you in the car. We gotta meet the team." They took off the stilettos they were modeling and put them back in the boxes. Arykah and Monique left Neiman Marcus with four pairs of stilettos each . . . the heels just high enough to put up somebody's behind if need be!

It only took Monique five minutes to drive herself and Arykah to Gibson's Steakhouse. They decided to go inside the restaurant to wait for the remaining members of Team Arykah to arrive. As soon as their waitress seated them, Arykah said to her, "Can you please bring me an apple martini?"

Monique's eyebrows rose. "Um, First Lady, it's Sunday morning, not quite noon yet."

"Humph, apparently Angela Moore is the first lady today. Do you want one?" Arykah asked her. She didn't care what time of day it was. After the bomb Chelsea dropped on her, Arykah needed a strong drink.

Truth be told, Monique would love to have had a martini but remembered she was driving. "No." She looked at the waitress. "I'll have a Coke, please."

"Absolutely," the waitress said. She gave Arykah and Monique menus, then walked away.

"A martini, huh?" Monique said. "So, you're gonna allow Angela Moore to take you there?"

"I told you what Chelsea said happened at church this morning. Angela's got some balls, but guess what? Mine are bigger."

"What I can't figure out," Monique started, "is why didn't Lance make Angela leave the sanctuary. Why did he ask the team to leave?"

"According to Chelsea, she, Darlita, and Gladys were two seconds off of Angela's behind. Lance thought it best to remove them from the situation."

"And he gave that trick a pass?"

Arykah rolled her eyes and shrugged her shoulders.

The waitress was back with their drinks. "Here you go," she said. She set Arykah's apple martini on the table in front of her, then set Monique's glass of Coke on the table in front of her. She looked at them both. "Are you ladies ready to order?"

"Actually, we're waiting on four more women," Monique said. "They should be here in about ten more minutes."

"Okay. That's fine," the waitress said. "I'll check back with you then."

Before the waitress walked away, Arykah said, "You can bring me another one of these." She was already half finished with her apple martini.

"Of course," the waitress said and walked away.

"Slow down on the vodka. Don't you wanna be coherent when Mother Myrtle gets here?"

"Who do you think introduced me to apple martinis?"

Monique's eyes bucked out of her head. *"Stop lying!"* she shrieked.

"I'm telling the truth and shaming the devil."

Monique's mouth dropped wide open. "No. Not my Gravy." Monique had nicknamed Myrtle "Gravy" the first time she sat at her dinner table. She told Myrtle that she made the best homemade gravy in the world. She looked at Arykah curiously. "Really?"

Arykah waved her hand at Monique. "Girl, Myrtle is an old 'G.' Back in the day when you and Boris was going thru y'alls thang and you didn't wanna listen to reason, me and Mother Myrtle would get us a bottle, sit in her living room, and drink to the wee hours of the morning."

Monique never knew that. "Why didn't y'all call me over? I like martinis."

Arykah shook her head from side to side. "Uh-uh, we couldn't do that because we were talkin' about how stupid you were."

"That is so shady, Arykah."

"Well, you *were* stupid."

The waitress set Arykah's second apple martini on the table in front of her. She picked it up and looked at Monique. "Bottoms up." She swallowed half of the contents in the glass.

"Hey, ladies," Darlita greeted as she, Gladys, Chelsea, and Myrtle approached their table.

Arykah quickly drank the remainder of her apple martini and pushed the empty glass toward the middle of the table. It was one thing to drink alcohol in the presence of Monique and Myrtle, but Arykah was careful to not offend Chelsea, Gladys, and Darlita.

"Y'all made it," Arykah said. She stood and hugged the team.

"Lady Arykah," Gladys started, "now you know I'm on a budget. Why did we have to meet here at Gibson's Steakhouse? My money is funny."

"Gladys, your money is no good here anyway. Order whatever you want. The tab is on me today."

"But the tab is always on you whenever we get together," Darlita said.

What Darlita said was absolutely true. Whenever Team Arykah met to have a feast it was always at an expensive restaurant. And Arykah didn't mind paying for everyone's food.

Myrtle was on a fixed income and barely made ends meet. Darlita had just separated from her husband and was living with her brother, saving every penny she made to pay for a divorce attorney. Chelsea made a nice living as buyer for JCPenney but wasn't able to splurge. Gladys worked two jobs to take care of her daughter and her unborn grandbaby. Monique was doing very well as the executive producer at the WGOD radio station. Monique had money, but she didn't have Arykah's kind of money.

"So, who's keeping a track record of the meals that I pay for?" Arykah asked Darlita. *"I'm* not."

"We don't want to take advantage of your kindness, Lady Arykah," Gladys said.

"You do a lot for us," Chelsea added.

Arykah looked at all of the ladies seated at the round table. "Y'all are my girls. You're the only women that held me down and had my back when the mothers were at my throat. And I appreciate that. Your loyalty means the world to me. So, if I wanna treat all of you to a nice meal, then let me. I honestly don't think that I do more for you than y'all do for me. And if you were with me and Monique about an hour ago, y'all could've gotten some stilettos."

"What?" the ladies, with the exception of Myrtle, shrieked.

"Yep," Monique bragged. "I got me some Kenneth Coles, some Rock Bottoms, some Baby Phats, *and* some Bandolinos. See, that's what you get when you throw down for the first lady."

"Well, it was almost another fight in the sanctuary today," Myrtle confessed. "I had to step between Chelsea and Darlita. They were getting ready to beat that girl down right on the front pew. The bishop told me to get them out of there."

"'Splain that to me, Gravy," Monique said. "Why did the bishop put y'all out and not Angela?"

"That trick wasn't going anywhere," Chelsea answered. "She walked her behind right up to the front row and stood next to Mother Myrtle."

"And we snapped," Darlita added. "We weren't having it."

"Y'all had forgotten that you were in church," Myrtle fussed. "Angela was wrong, yes, she was, but so were all of you when you went after her the way you did. That's why the bishop put us out. Remember what he said to us in his office, before church?"

"What did he say?" Arykah asked Myrtle.

"He said that he was going to try to get Angela to drop the charges and the restraining order against you and Monique."

"But he needed the team to keep our cool," Gladys added. "We did exactly what he asked us not to do. We gave Angela a reason to not drop the charges."

The waitress was at their table with six glasses of water. "I see the rest of your party has arrived," she said to Arykah and Monique. She set their glasses on the table. "Is everyone prepared to order?"

"Does everyone want a steak?" Arykah asked the ladies.

"I do," Myrtle said.

"Me too," Monique added.

Chelsea, Darlita, and Gladys searched the menu for the cheapest steak.

"I'll have the six-ounce rib eye," Gladys ordered.

Darlita looked at the waitress. "Is that the smallest steak you have?"

"We'll all have a porterhouse," Arykah said sternly. She looked at her team. "Now tell her how you want your meat cooked."

When their orders had been placed and the waitress walked away, Arykah spoke. "Please don't ever do that again. That was embarrassing."

"Do what?" the ladies asked in unison.

"If I invite y'all to an expensive restaurant, please know that I'm gonna pick up the tab. I mean, didn't we just have this discussion about two minutes ago?" She looked at all of them. "I know all of your financial situations. I know it's hard out there. I don't expect you to get a burger if I'm eating a steak. So we're *all* gonna have a steak."

"You're way too good to us," Gladys said.

Darlita, Chelsea, Monique, and Myrtle nodded their heads in agreement.

"No more than you are to me, Gladys. I just sold a seven million-dollar estate."

"Oh, wow," Darlita said.

"Yay, way to go, Lady Arykah," Chelsea cheered.

"God has truly blessed me to be in a position to give to others and not expect anything in return. I've never had a problem with paying it forward. That's how I stay blessed," Arykah said.

"Amen," Monique said.

"Yes, I'm a shopaholic, a shoeaholic, and sometimes I can be an alcoholic. But I pay my tithes, I try to live right, and I stay prayed up. So when I call y'all and say, 'Let's roll,' y'all better put those Rollerblades on and roll with me."

"Trust when I tell you," Monique said to the ladies as she thought about the stilettos Arykah just bought her, "y'all don't wanna be left behind."

Gladys picked up her glass of water and held it out over the middle of the table. "To Team Arykah!" she said.

The ladies lifted their glasses and toasted them all together. "To Team Arykah."

The waitress was at their table. "Ladies, your steaks will be ready in about twelve to fifteen minutes."

"Good," Arykah said to her. "We're hungry."

Arykah's cellular telephone rang. She saw the church's name on the caller ID. "I bet this is Lance calling," she said to the ladies. She pressed the talk button and brought the telephone to her ear. "Lady Arykah speaking."

Lance sat behind his desk at the church. "Hey, I've been calling the house and didn't get an answer."

"That's because I'm not there."

"Well, where are you? How about we meet for lunch?"

"I'm eating lunch now."

Lance looked at the time on the clock on his desk. *11:49 a.m.* "Already? Where are you?"

"At Gibson's Steakhouse in Oakbrook Terrace. Is church over?"

"Yeah, it doesn't take the Holy Spirit long to move."

"You didn't preach?"

"No, I didn't need to. A steak sounds good, I'm on my way."

"Uh-uh, I won't be here that long. I'll bring you take-out."

Lance sensed that Arykah was upset. She had never not wanted him to join her for a meal. "Are you okay?"

"Uh-huh."

"Who are you with?"

"My team."

"Oh, so that's where they went. They just couldn't wait to tell you everything."

"They did what they were supposed to do," Arykah said. "Were *you* gonna tell me?"

"Of course, Cheeks. That's why I was calling. I wanted us to grab a bite to eat and discuss this mess."

"I'll be home in about an hour. We can discuss it then." She disconnected the call.

"Whatever you do," Myrtle said to Arykah, "keep in mind that he did what he thought was best."

"He thought it was best to put y'all out of the church and leave Angela on the front pew?"

"You weren't there, Arykah," Myrtle said. "These girls were getting ready to put a hurtin' on Angela."

"Yeah, we were," Chelsea confirmed. "Don't be angry at him, Lady Arykah. Bishop Lance did the right thing by putting us outta the church."

"Humph," was all Arykah said.

Seven

Arykah arrived home from the restaurant at approximately 1:20 p.m. *"Diva Chanel,"* she sang out loud when she entered the front door.

Moments later, Arykah heard little toenails scratching the hardwood floors.

"There's my girl," Arykah cooed when she saw Diva Chanel running toward her from the great room. Arykah walked to the kitchen with Diva Chanel jumping at her legs. She set Lance's takeout, and her bag from Neiman Marcus, on the center island. Then she scooped up Diva Chanel and kissed her wet nose. "Were you a good girl? Huh? Were you a good girl, Diva?"

"No, she wasn't," Lance said when he came into the kitchen. "She got ahold of one of my shoes again."

Arykah set Diva Chanel down on the floor and looked at her husband. "She's a puppy, Lance. Puppies eat shoes. You know that."

"My shoes cost a lot of money," he fussed.

"I pay for them so who knows that more than me? You don't see any of *my* shoes on the floor for Diva Chanel to get at. Why can't you keep your shoes in boxes, in your closet, like I do?"

"Because, sometimes, Cheeks," Lance started, "when a man walks into his home, he just wanna kick his shoes off and relax. He shouldn't have to worry about his shoes getting chewed up."

"He should if there's a puppy in the house," Arykah retorted. "Which pair did she destroy this time?"

"My tan leather loafers designed by Tom Ford."

Arykah's eyes grew wide. "Lance, those were brand-new, and I paid over a grand for them." She was disappointed that Lance was so careless. Three weeks ago, Diva Chanel had gotten ahold of the Alexander McQueen dark blue velvet slippers that cost Arykah $750.

When Arykah married Lance, the most expensive pair of shoes he owned had cost $200. She wasn't only a shoe fanatic for herself, Arykah spent a pretty penny dressing Lance's feet as well. And since it had been her hard earned dollars that funded his expensive shoe collection, Arykah figured he would be more responsible and protect them from a puppy.

She shook her head from side to side. "You can't be careless like that, Babe. Not when you know that Diva Chanel is a shoe lover like her momma. I love to wear them, and she loves to chew them."

"I'm putting her on punishment."

Arykah looked at him. "I don't think so. You're the adult here, Lance. It's not Diva Chanel's fault that you don't care about your shoes." Arykah pointed to the takeout bag she had placed on the center island. "I bought you a porterhouse steak, well done. There's also a loaded baked potato in the bag."

Lance rubbed his empty belly. "You're a woman after my own heart, Cheeks. I'm starving. What's in the other bag?" he asked. Lance knew exactly what was in the white paper bag with the red writing. Neiman Marcus was Arykah's home away from home.

"Therapy," Arykah answered. "I needed to purchase some therapy to help me deal with this Angela Moore situation. And after what Chelsea told me had happened at church this morning, I need to go back and purchase more therapy."

Lance knew his wife, and he knew her very well. Arykah used any excuse to buy shoes. High heels were her addiction. If Arykah had a headache, she shopped for heels. If it stormed outside, she would shop for shoes. If there was a full moon, half moon, or crescent moon, Arykah shopped for shoes. In her world, any excuse, any reason, or any occasion was cause for shoe shopping. Arykah exercised and did squats in stilettos. She vacuumed the rugs in stilettos. And often Arykah made love to her husband in stilettos.

"I'm gonna take Diva Chanel outside in the backyard to play while you're eating. When you're done, Lance, we need to discuss Angela Moore and what we're gonna do about her."

"I can tell you right now that *we* ain't gonna do *anything* about her. *I'm* gonna handle Angela *alone*."

Arykah shifted all of her heavy weight onto one leg and glared at Lance. "What do you mean you're gonna handle her alone? We're in this together, Lance. You and I will handle this as a couple."

"First of all, Cheeks, you can't be within five hundred feet of Angela. Remember?"

"I don't want *you* near that tramp either."

Arykah didn't know that Lance had been keeping a secret from her. It was his intention to use that secret to get Angela to drop all charges against her and Monique. What Lance was about to do would ensure that Lady Arykah would be sitting on the front pew at Freedom Temple Church of God in Christ, with her best friend at her side, come Sunday morning.

Lance nodded his head. "I understand that, Cheeks. Angela may think she has the upper hand, but I'm going to beat her at her own game."

Arykah looked at him curiously. "What are you gonna do, Lance?"

Lance stepped to Arykah and kissed her lips softly. He smiled. "Do you trust me?"

"Of course," Arykah said. "It's Ho Angela that I don't trust. How do you think it made me feel when I heard that she walked her behind to the front pew and sat in my seat? It doesn't feel good to know that she took my place."

"First of all," Lance said, "I already told you that no one can take your place. There is no substitute for Lady Arykah Miles-Howell."

Arykah turned her head. Lance placed two fingers on her chin and softly turned her face back to where it was. "Look at me," he said.

Arykah connected her eyes with her husband's.

"I love you. And no matter what Angela does or says, that will never change."

Arykah exhaled. "I know that, Lance, but—"

"There is no 'but.' Okay? Listen to what I'm telling you, Cheeks. *You* are my wife. We have a great life together, a great marriage, a great ministry, a great house, and a great dog when she's not chewing my shoes."

Arykah chuckled.

"Do you really think that I'll let someone like Angela take all of that from us? You think I'm gonna allow her foolishness to destroy what we have?" He shook his head from side to side. "Nah, Cheeks. I ain't having that."

Arykah loved the way Lance spoke. Everything he said sounded good to her ears.

"Lance, I just gotta ask this because it's bugging me."

He stepped back and folded his arms. "What?"

"Why did you put my team outta the church and let Angela stay?"

"Angela needs attention. She's full of drama, and she would have caused the biggest scene had she been asked to leave the church or the front pew. The sanctuary was not the place for Angela to act a fool. That's not what the congregation came to church for. Folks were there for healing, for deliverance, and to receive the Word of God. I wasn't gonna give Angela that shining moment that she wanted so badly. I refused to do it."

Arykah nodded her head. She wished Lance had put Angela out and allowed her team to stay, but she understood his decision. "Yeah, I guess you're right."

"And if I hadn't dismissed your girls, I would have had to make another trip to the jailhouse. And my bail money fund has been depleted."

Arykah chuckled again. "Mother Myrtle told me all about that."

"I needed you today," Lance admitted. "I kept looking for you because I wanted you to stand with me and pray for the people. The Holy Spirit moved through Freedom Temple this morning. I was missing my other half. Every time I looked toward the front of the church, I saw that you weren't there. You know when I'm ministering, Cheeks? When I lay hands on the people and I turn and give you that look?"

"Yeah," Arykah said nodding her head. She knew exactly the look Lance was talking about. Whenever he stood before someone, especially a female, he'd turn and look at Arykah with a certain glare in his eye. That was his signal for her to come to him. Arykah loved ministering with Lance. It kept her adrenaline flowing. "I hate that I couldn't be there this morning."

"Angela was standing up front, and when I looked for you, I saw in her eyes that she was pleading for me to ask her to minister with me."

"Humph," Arykah said. "She wants to be me so bad. It's so shameful."

"Well, she's out of luck. God only made one Arykah." Lance saw Diva Chanel sniffing at the kitchen sliding doors. That was how he and Arykah knew she needed a potty break. "Go ahead and take Diva Chanel outside," Lance said. "Let *me* worry about Angela Moore."

Arykah believed in her husband. If Lance said he would handle his ex, then Arykah would relax and trust that he would.

The next morning when Arykah turned over in bed, she saw that Lance was already gone. She glanced at the clock on her nightstand. She lay her head back on the pillow and sighed. "Nine thirty-nine."

She remembered last night. Lance had lit candles around their Jacuzzi tub, drawn Arykah a bath, and joined her. The events that took place after that had caused Arykah to oversleep. She threw the covers from her body and got out of bed. Her inner thighs were sore. "You worked me good, Bishop," she mumbled on the way to the master bath.

Arykah went to her sink and brushed her teeth. She heard Diva Chanel scratching at the master bedroom door. "Coming, Diva," Arykah said. She opened the bedroom door and Diva Chanel shot inside. She ran past Arykah and jumped on the bed with her tail wagging.

"Time to go outside," Arykah said to Diva Chanel.

Because Lance was always up before Arykah, he had taken on the responsibility of letting Diva Chanel out in the backyard to relieve herself and play. Lance always brought the Yorkie back into the house before he left for work.

Arykah disarmed the house alarm on the panel in the laundry room that separated the garage and the kitchen. She then unlocked and slid open the kitchen patio door and watched Diva Chanel run out. The telephone rang. Arykah picked up the receiver from the kitchen wall next to the refrigerator. She saw Dr. Santana Lovejoy on the caller ID and sighed.

Arykah didn't want to answer the call but knew she had to. She wouldn't be able to avoid Doctor Lovejoy forever. She pressed the talk button and brought the receiver to her ear. "Hello?"

"Good morning. Is this Arykah?"

"Yes, this is she," Arykah confirmed as she watched Diva Chanel run from one side of the fence to the other.

"This is Doctor Santana Lovejoy. How are you?"

"I'm very good, Doctor Lovejoy. You?"

"I'm well, thank you. I wanted to give you some time before I reached out. I'm just calling to check on you and see how things are progressing. I'd also like to schedule another session with you and your husband if you're up to it."

Arykah thought about it. She didn't want to see a therapist. She only agreed to sit down with Dr. Santana Lovejoy because everyone was pressuring her to do so. "Well, since my first session didn't go so well, I think I'll pass."

"Are you sure?" Doctor Lovejoy asked. "It couldn't hurt to open up and get your emotions out. Perhaps a session alone, without your husband, would work better for you. And we don't have to meet at my office, Mrs. Howell. We can get together at a café, or a park, or anywhere that you may feel comfortable. I understand that a stuffy office isn't the most relaxing place."

Arykah tried to tell Dr. Santana Lovejoy, in a nice way, that she didn't want to be bothered. She wasn't getting the hint. "I appreciate you for checking on me, but really, I'm fine. And if I decide that I need to speak to someone, I'll be sure to call you."

"Well, okay then," Doctor Lovejoy said. "If and whenever you want to talk, just call."

"Thanks again, Doctor Lovejoy," Arykah responded. "Good-bye."

"Take care." With that being said, Dr. Santana Lovejoy disconnected the line.

Arykah placed the receiver on its base and wondered if Doctor Lovejoy had only called because her partner may have told her that she had been arrested the day before. Arykah would bet the topic of her time spent at the Cook County Correctional Facility was pillow talk for the female couple.

She glanced through the patio doors and saw that Diva Chanel was sniffing a little too closely to the tomatoes that Lance had planted two months ago. She opened the door and called Diva inside. Then Arykah set the house alarm and went to the master bedroom to take a shower.

At approximately 1:15 p.m., on the north side of Chicago, Lance sat behind his desk at Howell Construction ending a lunch meeting with two contractors. He put the last of an Italian beef sandwich in his mouth when his secretary, Vivian, pressed the intercom button.

"Mr. Howell, Miss Angela Moore is here to see you."

"Thanks, Vivian. Send her in and hold all calls until further notice," Lance responded. "We're done here, guys," he said to the contractors.

Both men stood, gathered their empty lunch containers, and proceeded to leave Lance's office when the door opened.

Angela entered wearing a cherry-colored corset that laced up the front. Her C cup-size breasts stood at attention. The black tight jeans she wore were extremely tight. Black strappy high-heel sandals were on her feet. Angela's makeup was done to perfection, her body was extremely pleasing on the eye, and her perfume was alluring.

The two contractors stopped in their tracks to get a good look at her. Angela smiled at the men. Without saying a word she knew she demanded their complete attention. They couldn't take their eyes off of her. When Angela walked past them, they turned to glance at her outstanding butt.

Then they shook their heads in disbelief at the perfect figure eight walking by.

"That'll be all, guys," Lance said to dismiss them though he understood why the men were in awe of Angela. She had the body of a goddess.

The men gathered themselves and left Lance's office.

Angela chuckled as she sat in a chair on the opposite side of Lance's desk.

"You always gotta have all of the attention, don't you?"

Angela crossed her right leg over her left knee. "Not all of the attention, Bishop. Just yours," she answered seductively.

Her perfume smelled heavenly, but Lance dared not tell her. Angela was strikingly beautiful, but Lance knew it would be best if he kept his comments to himself.

"Thanks for coming." He had been expecting her.

Angela looked at the empty container that had held Lance's Italian beef sandwich, the half-empty fruit punch bottle, and the remaining five french fries on his desk. "You asked me to meet you at your office for lunch. Well, here I am, and it looks like you've already eaten."

Lance picked up a french fry and put it in his mouth. "You were mistaken. I said to meet me in my office *after* lunch." He'd never break bread with Angela again.

That didn't please Angela. She had hoped that she and Lance would have a romantic lunch in his office, then lock the door and make wild passionate love on top of his desk like they used to do. She had come prepared. Angela was without panties or a bra. "Why am I here?"

"Why do you think?"

Angela rolled her eyes. "Look, Bishop, if you're gonna try to get me to drop the charges against your wife and her friend, it ain't happenin'. Okay? Court is tomorrow, and I plan to tell the judge that I fear for my life. Oh, and just so you know, Sharonda heard your wife tell you that she was gonna kill me. I got my witness in place."

Sharonda witnessing what Arykah had said to him behind closed doors was news to Lance. But at that point, it didn't matter. When Lance got out of bed that morning he knew what needed to be done with Angela and Sharonda. They both had some not-so-pleasant surprises coming their way. He had already informed Vivian what role she needed to play.

Lance leaned back in his chair and crossed his ankles beneath his desk. "Are you sure this is what you want to do?"

"I kinda like sitting on the front pew. I could get used to that."

"Angela, you could never take Arykah's place. Not as my wife or as the first lady of Freedom Temple."

"Humph," Angela commented sarcastically. "Never say 'never.'"

Lance smiled at her. He opened the top right drawer of his desk, retrieved an eight-by-ten letter-size envelope, and placed it on his desk in front of her. "I thought you may wanna read this letter before Vivian puts it in the outgoing mail."

Angela glanced at the envelope, then looked up at Lance. "What's that?"

Lance didn't answer her. He just kept his smile in place.

Angela opened the envelope and pulled out a sheet of paper. She saw Howell Construction's letterhead across the top. She read it silently.

> *To the Brainerd Park Rehabilitation Center,*
> *This letter is to inform the center that, effective immediately, Howell Construction will no longer cover the cost of the care for Reginald Moore. . . .*

Angela's dark skin turned as white as snow. She looked up at Lance. Her eyes were the size of Ping-Pong balls. "You can't do this."

"It's done," Lance confirmed.

Her world was suddenly turned upside down. "But you promised."

Lance shrugged his shoulders. "Oops," he said nonchalantly.

She panicked. "But . . . but . . . What am I supposed to do?"

"Drop the charges against Arykah and Monique and the letter doesn't get mailed."

Tears welled up in Angela's eyes. "This is blackmail," she whined.

"Call it what you want, Angela. The ball is in your court. The choice is yours."

She wiped the tears that had fallen on her cheeks. "But you said you'd always take care of him. You promised, Lance."

Her tears didn't move him at all. Arykah's freedom was at stake. "And you promised to never hurt me. Well, when you hurt my wife, you hurt me."

Angela sobbed loudly. "What do you mean, 'hurt your wife'? She and her friend jumped *me.*"

"You provoked Arykah, and you know it. That was your reason for coming to the 'Ask Arykah Anything' session. And I warned you to stay away from her and not do anything crazy. Now, as far as her best friend goes, you can't insult one without the other taking offense as well. Arykah and Monique are connected together like Siamese twins."

Angela's sobbing got louder.

Lance exhaled. The crocodile tears and moaning were annoying him. "Save the waterfall, Angela." He glanced at his wristwatch. "I need to get to a construction site. What's it gonna be?"

Six years ago, Angela's then twenty-four-year-old brother, Reginald, had been sideswiped on his motorcycle. His left leg was amputated, and the accident had left him paralyzed. Angela's parents were divorced. She and Reginald hadn't seen or heard from their father since they were children. Angela and her mother, together, couldn't cover the cost of Reginald's medical bills and his lifetime therapy. Lance was so in love with Angela at the time, that he volunteered to pay all of Reginald's medical expenses. Back then, he had assumed that he and Angela would be together forever.

Shortly after Reginald's accident God had called Lance to preach the Gospel. When he told Angela that he had chosen to live a celibate lifestyle, she ended their relationship. But because Lance was a man of his word, he never stopped paying for Reginald's care. Lance hated that he had to resort to extreme measures, but he would do whatever he needed to do to save Arykah. She was his first priority.

Angela sat at Lance's desk crying. A box of Kleenex tissue sat on top of the desk, but he didn't offer any to Angela. He wanted her out of his office. "The clock is ticking."

She sat in silence for a few moments. *Sniff, sniff.* "Okay," she mumbled. *Sniff, sniff.*

"Okay, what?" he asked.

"I'll drop the assault charges against them."

"*And* the restraining orders."

Angela was angry, but Lance had her in handcuffs. She was powerless. "And the restraining orders." She stood to leave. *Sniff, sniff.*

"There's one more thing," Lance said.

Angela looked at him. "What?" she asked angrily.

"Lady Arykah doesn't wanna see you at Freedom Temple ever again. Your face irritates her. And I will not have her feeling uncomfortable."

Angela lost her balance and had to lean on Lance's desk for support.

He saw her breaking down emotionally. He didn't care. "Is that understood?"

She looked at him with contempt in her eyes. "Yes."

There was no strut in Angela's walk when she left Lance's office. Her head hung low. Gone was the wide grin her face held when she had entered. Her cockiness had vanished. Lance had burst her bubble with a very large pin. Angela Moore was defeated.

When she had closed the door behind her, Lance pressed the intercom on his desk.

"Yes, Mr. Howell," Vivian said.

"Make the call, Vivian."

"Yes, sir."

As Vivian made one call, Lance made another using his cellular telephone. He called Brian Lewis, the church's custodian. Brian was mowing the church's lawn when he felt his cellular telephone vibrate in his back pocket. He shut the lawn mower off, then answered the call.

"Hello, Bishop."

"Brian, my man. What's happening?" Lance asked.

"Doing some yard work."

Lance glanced at his wristwatch again. He knew Sharonda's schedule. "Sharonda is at lunch, right?"

"She just left, Bishop. She should be back in about an hour or so."

"Brian, listen to me. My secretary is sending over a locksmith to the church. He'll be there in about ten minutes and will change the locks on the front and back doors. When he's done, lock up the church and leave. I will pick up the new set of keys from you later today. And don't worry, you'll be paid for the entire day."

"Okay, but what about Sharonda? How is she gonna get in the church?"

"As of right now, Brian, she no longer works there."

When Lance woke up that morning he had decided that he was going to clean house. Too many folks were running amok at Freedom Temple. He felt it was time to make things decent and put stuff in order. Sharonda's employment was already on the chopping block, and the information that Angela had just shared with him confirmed to him that firing Sharonda was inevitable and a necessity.

Exactly one hour later, Lance was touring a construction site. He and four other men, wearing white hard hats with shirts and ties, were walking and talking when he saw Sharonda's name appeared on the caller ID on his cellular telephone.

"Excuse me for just one second," Lance said to the men as he stepped about five feet away from them. "Yes, Sharonda?" he answered. He had been expecting her call.

"Bishop, I got back from lunch and couldn't get inside the church. I called Brian, and he said that you had given him the rest of the day off. He also said that I should give you a call."

"Sharonda, you have been relieved of all your duties. I will see to it that a check for two weeks severance pay is sent to your home."

On the other end of the telephone line, Sharonda was stunned and speechless. "But . . . but . . ."

"That'll be all, Sharonda." Lance disconnected the call and rejoined the tour.

Sharonda and her grandmother, Gussie Hughes, were thorns in Arykah's side. And since Sharonda was willing to be a witness for Angela, Lance hadn't felt the need to give her a reason for why she was fired.

Eight

"All rise," the bailiff shouted when the judge entered the courtroom. "The Honorable Judge Clarence McIntire is presiding."

On one side of the courtroom, Lance, Arykah, Adonis, Monique, and Team Arykah stood. Myrtle, Gladys, Chelsea, and Darlita had rearranged their schedules to be at court to support their first lady and Monique.

Angela Moore stood alone on the opposite side of the courtroom. She had no supporters.

The Caucasian male judge sat in his seat.

"Be seated," the bailiff shouted.

Everyone watched the judge turn to his right and whisper words to the court clerk who sat next to him. She nodded her head and stood. "The court calls the case of Moore versus Cortland. Please come forth."

Monique and Angela stood and came to the front of the courtroom. Both appeared before the judge.

Judge McIntire looked at Angela. "State your name for the court."

"Angela Moore," she mumbled.

"Speak up!" the judge ordered.

She cleared her throat. "Angela Moore."

He looked at Monique. "And you are?"

"Monique Cortland, Your Honor."

The judge looked at the file before him. "Miss Moore, you're accusing Mrs. Cortland of assault and battery. Do you wish to continue on with this case?"

"No, Your Honor."

The judge looked at her. "I beg your pardon?"

"I'm dropping all charges against Mrs. Cortland."

The judge wrote down words in Angela's file. "Has anyone threatened you to drop the charges?"

"No."

"Are you sure?"

"Yes, Your Honor. And I want to recall the restraining order against her as well."

The judge looked at Angela, then at Monique, then at Angela again. "It is noted," he said. He wrote down more words, then looked at Monique. "Mrs. Cortland, all charges against you have been dropped. You are free to go." He banged his gavel, then looked at the clerk. "Call the next case."

Monique went and sat next to Adonis, but Angela remained where she was. She knew she had to do it all over again.

The clerk stood. "The court calls the case of Moore versus Howell. Please come forth."

Arykah stood and took Monique's place at the front of the courtroom.

"State your name for the court," the judge said to Arykah.

"Arykah Miles-Howell."

He looked at Angela. "Miss Moore, you're accusing Mrs. Howell of assault and battery. Do you wish to continue on with this case?"

Angela turned and looked past Arykah at Lance. He glared at her. She turned back around. "No, Your Honor. I'm dropping all charges against Mrs. Howell, and I wish to recall the restraining order that I have filed against her."

The judge wrote down words in Angela's file, then looked at her. "Has anyone threatened you to drop the charges?"

Angela paused. She gritted her teeth. "No, sir."

"Are you sure?" the judge asked her.

"Yes, Your Honor."

The judge wrote down more words. "It is noted," he said. He looked at Arykah. "Mrs. Howell, all charges against you have been dropped. You are free to go." He banged his gavel, then instructed the clerk to call the next case.

Outside the courthouse Team Arykah rejoiced with Arykah and Monique.

"Wow, that was fast," Darlita said.

Arykah hugged all of the ladies. "I'm so happy y'all came."

"You know we love you and Monique," Chelsea stated.

"We had to come and support," Gladys added.

Adonis pulled Lance to the side. "How did you do it?"

Lance smiled. "Do what?"

"You know," Adonis said looking over his shoulder to make sure that his words couldn't be heard by anyone else. "What did you do to get Angela to drop the charges and recant the restraining orders?"

Lance chuckled. "Well, I could tell you, but then I'd have to kill you." He patted Adonis on his back and walked away.

"It's still morning," Lance said when he rejoined the ladies. He wrapped his arm around Arykah's waist. "How about I treat everyone to a victory breakfast?"

Arykah kissed Lance's cheek. "That's nice of you, Bishop." She looked at everyone. "Wishbone?"

"Ooh, yeah," Monique said. "Wishbone has the best pancakes."

"Sounds good to me," Darlita chimed in.

"Let's do the darn thing," Adonis added. He rubbed his belly. "A brother is hungry."

As the group walked toward the parking lot Angela stood on the front steps of the courthouse watching them.

It was a quick drive from the courthouse to Wishbone Restaurant on Washington Boulevard. Lance asked for a table for eight, and the waitress seated them immediately. She gave each of them a menu, took their drink orders, and walked away.

Myrtle laid her menu on the table. "I'm glad all of this Angela drama is over."

"Me too, Gravy," Monique said.

"Nobody more than me," Arykah confirmed. "Not being at church is like being a fish out of water. I was miserable last Sunday."

Lance looked at her. "Really? I thought Mr. Neiman Marcus did a great job of cheering you up."

The table laughed out loud.

Arykah glared at him. "You're not cute, okay?"

Monique looked at Arykah. "Why do you think Angela dropped all charges against us? I was not expecting for that to happen."

"Yeah, *Bishop*," Adonis said before Arykah could speak. "Why do *you* think all charges were dropped?"

Lance looked at him. "I've learned that everything that God does isn't meant to be questioned. Sometimes blessings come for no reason." Lance winked his eye at Adonis. He knew Adonis had tried to put him on the spot.

"Amen to that," Arykah said. She accepted Lance's reasoning temporarily. Later, she would demand to know how he had gotten her and Monique out of trouble with such ease.

The waitress was back with their drinks. After she placed the drinks on the table, she took their orders.

"This will all be on one bill," Lance said to the waitress. He pointed to Adonis. "Except for that man sitting there."

Adonis chuckled. "Come on, Bishop. You're gonna do a brother like that?"

Lance returned the chuckle. "I could ask *you* the same thing."

Monique and Arykah looked from Adonis to Lance. The ladies didn't understand the words they exchanged.

"What's going on between you two?" Myrtle asked the men.

"Adonis tried to be slick," Lance answered. "So, now he gotta buy his own breakfast."

"The two of you look so good together," Chelsea said admiring her pastor and first lady.

"Yeah, I'm his better half," Arykah joked.

"I'll give you that," Lance said to her. "I am much better now that you're in my life."

Arykah leaned over and kissed his lips.

"Yuck, get a room," Monique said.

"Maybe we will," Arykah chuckled.

Gladys, Darlita, and Chelsea had never seen their bishop so relaxed. The only encounters they'd had with Lance was at church when he was strict and in pastor mode. Before Arykah came into their lives the ladies only saw Lance dressed in suits and robes on Sunday mornings. It was different to see him dressed down in jeans and a button-down shirt. They enjoyed watching the chemistry between him and his wife.

"I fired Sharonda," Lance announced.

"What?" everyone asked at the same time.

Arykah was happy but very surprised. She had been begging Lance to get rid of Mother Gussie's granddaughter for over a month. "Why?"

"It needed to be done," Lance answered. "And you won't be seeing Angela Moore at Freedom Temple anymore. I told you that I would handle her. You got your wish."

Arykah hollered out and stood up. She started praise dancing. Everyone in the restaurant gave her their full, undivided attention, but Arykah didn't care. She danced and danced and danced. Monique, Chelsea, Myrtle, Gladys, Darlita, and Adonis all laughed out loud.

"Cut it out, Cheeks," Lance said as he pulled Arykah's arm toward him. "I can't take you nowhere," he fussed.

Arykah sat down in her chair out of breath. She grabbed her napkin off the table and fanned herself with it. "Whew, I had to get that out, Bishop."

Monique chuckled. "Girl, you are crazy."

Arykah rocked back and forth in her chair. "All my life I had to fight. I had to fight temptation, I had to fight against sin, but I never thought I had to fight in my own church."

Team Arykah screamed out and Adonis hollered. They laughed at Arykah's imitation of Oprah Winfrey's line in the movie *The Color Purple*.

The ladies were laughing so loud that every customer in the restaurant was eyeballing them.

Lance was extremely embarrassed. "Cheeks, please. You're causing a scene."

Arykah didn't care who was watching her. "Bishop, sometimes you gotta throw caution to the wind and bless God right where you are. I ain't ashamed at all. Glowraaaaay," she shouted out.

Lance glanced over his shoulder and looked at everyone with an apologetic look in his eyes.

Arykah sang, "God is tryin' to tell me somethin'."

Team Arykah couldn't stop laughing at their first lady. Even Myrtle and Adonis couldn't hold it in. Arykah tickled them.

"So now the church is without a secretary," Adonis said.

"I'm available," Myrtle offered.

The entire table looked at her.

"You are?" Lance asked her.

She nodded her head. "Yeah. I ain't doing nothin' but sittin' at home. Oprah don't come on anymore, and all these reality shows give me the heebie-jeebies. I could come to the church and answer the phone."

"Well, the job is a little more than just answering the phone, Gravy," Monique said.

Myrtle looked at Monique. "What else I gotta do?"

"The church secretary keeps the pastor's schedule, Mother Myrtle, and my schedule too," Arykah offered.

"That shouldn't be too hard," Myrtle said to Arykah.

"It's an eight-hour-a-day job. You gotta make my coffee, update the church's calendar, set up appointments for premarital counseling, prepare the announcements for Sunday morning, and just be my eyes and ears," Lance said. "And there's one important thing, Mother Myrtle. No one gets to me unless they go through you first. That's one good thing I can say about Mother Gussie," Lance said. "She knew how to handle crazy folks. I don't wanna be bothered with any foolishness, Mother Myrtle. I need you to handle certain situations *before* I hear about them. You understand what I'm saying?"

Myrtle nodded her head. "Yep. Like if a woman calls and says that she's lonely and needs the bishop to come to her house and pray for her."

"You can pass *that* call to me," Arykah said pointing to herself. "I'm serious, Mother Myrtle."

Myrtle looked at Lance. "Bishop, if you'll have me, I'm willing to give it a shot. But you know I don't drive. How will I get to church every day?"

"Don't you worry about that," he said. "We'll get you there."

The waitress brought their breakfast to the table. Once everyone was served, Lance blessed the food. Everyone ate until their hearts were content.

"I expect to see all of you at Bible class tonight," Lance said.

"I don't drive," Myrtle spoke up.

"I gotta babysit my sister's kids," Chelsea said.

"It's me and Monique's date night," Adonis offered.

"I'm taking Miranda to register for her baby shower," Gladys added.

"I'm going Christmas shopping," Darlita revealed.

Lance looked at her. "In May?"

She nodded her head. "Now's the time to buy while everything is on sale."

Lance just shook his head from side to side. He looked at Arykah. "Don't you even try it."

"I'll be there, Bishop," Arykah said to him, smiling. "Oh, I forgot to tell you that Doctor Lovejoy called me yesterday."

Lance looked at her. "Really?"

"Yeah, she wanted to set up another appointment with me, but I turned her down."

"Why?" Myrtle asked Arykah.

Arykah shrugged her shoulders. "I just don't feel that I need to talk about what's in the past."

No one at the table commented on what Arykah had just said. They ate their food and chose to stay out of that sensitive conversation.

Arykah inserted a forkful of strawberry crepes into her mouth. "Though, I gotta admit, I was surprised to find out that she's married to a woman. Doctor Santana Lovejoy is a beautiful chick and could probably have any man she wants. I don't understand what attracts a woman to another woman."

"You'll find that some lesbians have been hurt by more than one man," Chelsea said. "They may feel that a woman can give them what a man can't."

Arykah nodded her head. "Probably. Then again, Doctor Santana Lovejoy could have that Almond Joy and Mounds mentality."

"What do you mean, Cheeks?"

"Sometimes she may feel like she wants a nut, and sometimes she don't."

Everyone at the table spat their food out.

Lance raised his hand and called for the waitress. "Check, please."

Later that evening at the church, Lance sat in his office, behind closed doors, putting the finishing touches on his Bible study lesson. Across the hall in Arykah's office, Diva Chanel ran and fetched a small pink ball, then brought it back to Arykah. She dropped the ball at Arykah's feet, then moved back and hunched down. She was ready to run again.

"Don't your little legs ever get tired of running, Diva Chanel?" Arykah picked up the pink ball and tossed it across the room. Diva took off running after it.

Arykah answered a knock on her office door. "Come in."

The door opened and she saw a familiar face peek inside.

"Hi, Lady Arykah. You have a minute? Is this a bad time?"

"Hey, Stephanie," Arykah stood from her desk and greeted her. "Come on in, girl."

Stephanie entered the office and shut the door behind her.

"You here on church announcement business?"

"No," Stephanie answered. "I wanted to speak with you about a personal matter before Bible class begins."

Arykah sensed uneasiness about Stephanie. "Okay. Let's sit on the sofa."

The ladies sat on the sofa in the corner of Arykah's office. Diva Chanel held the small pink ball in her mouth. As soon as Stephanie sat, Diva Chanel dropped the ball at her feet.

"She's so cute," Stephanie said.

"She's cute and full of energy. She never gets tired of running after that ball." Arykah picked up the ball and threw it across the room. "So, what's going on with you?"

Stephanie exhaled. She hesitated before she spoke. She opened her mouth, then closed it.

Arykah could tell that Stephanie was struggling to keep tears from falling from her eyes. She grabbed Stephanie's hand and squeezed it. "It's okay. Let it out."

Stephanie took Arykah's advice and released her emotions. She put her face in her hands and cried openly. Arykah pulled Stephanie in her arms and consoled her. "Oh, Stephanie. What happened? Is it your mother? Has she gotten worse?"

Two Sundays ago, Stephanie had announced to the church that her mother had been diagnosed with stage four ovarian cancer. She had requested the church's prayers. Stephanie shook her head and pulled away from Arykah. "No. Mom hasn't gotten any worse."

Arykah stood from the sofa. She went to her desk and retrieved a box of tissue and brought it back to Stephanie. "Then what has you so upset?" she asked when she sat down.

Stephanie pulled a tissue from the box and blew her nose. She looked at Arykah. "Three nights ago, I walked in on my husband and my sister. They were in my bed."

Arykah's eyes grew wide, and she gasped. *"What? Stacy and Kenneth?"*

Sniff, sniff. Stephanie nodded her head. *Sniff, sniff.*

"No way, Stephanie. I can't believe it." Stephanie's sister, Stacy, sang in the adult sanctuary choir. Kenneth played the drums. Adonis often spoke highly of Kenneth and said that he was the best drummer he had ever worked with.

"It ain't the first time," Stephanie revealed.

Arykah's eyebrows rose. "You mean it ain't the first time you caught Kenneth cheating?"

"I mean it ain't the first time I caught him and Stacy together."

If Arykah had been standing, she would've fallen to the floor. *"Girl , you're kidding me.* Please tell me you're joking with me right now."

More tears fell onto Stephanie's face. *Sniff, sniff.* "I wish I could, Lady Arykah."

"When was the first time?"

Stephanie wiped the tears. "It was last summer. My entire family took a cruise vacation. During dinner, Stacy said that she had a headache. She said she was going back to her cabin to rest. Not long after, Kenneth said that he had gotten seasick. I believed him because that night the tides were high and the boat was rocking. The captain had announced that everyone should take Dramamine. So when Kenneth said that his stomach was queasy, I didn't have reason to doubt him. He told me that he was going back to our cabin to relax.

"When I had finished eating dinner, I headed back to our cabin. That's when I met Kenneth coming out of Stacy's cabin. He told me that he was just checking on her, but I knew something was up. Her perfume was all over him. I didn't confront Stacy, because I couldn't fathom the thought of my own sister messing around with my husband. But for the remainder of the cruise Stacy and Kenneth avoided each other like the plague."

A dead giveaway, Arykah thought. "So, here we are, a whole year later, and you caught them again. You know what that means, don't you?"

Stephanie nodded her head. "Yes. That my suspicions on the cruise were correct, and that they've been screwing around ever since, and possibly even before the cruise."

Arykah didn't comment, but Stephanie hit the nail on the head. "What happened when you walked in on them three nights ago?"

"I had just come from the grocery store. I put the bags on the kitchen table and heard moaning coming from my bedroom. My heart dropped because I heard my sister call out my husband's name."

"Oh my God," Arykah said.

"I burst in the bedroom and saw Kenneth pleasuring her."

Arykah placed her hand on her heart. "Oh my God," she said again. "What did you do, Stephanie?"

"I screamed, and they both jumped from the bed. I lost it. I ran to Kenneth and started hitting him and calling him all types of names. When I saw Stacy try to run past me, I turned and grabbed her by her hair and pulled her back. She and I started fighting, and Kenneth pulled us apart. He told Stacy to leave. She grabbed her clothes and ran into the bathroom and slammed the door shut. She kept calling my name and apologizing over and over again. I got a suitcase from the closet and threw some clothes and underwear inside. I left that night and went to stay at my mother's house. I ain't going back. Both Stacy and Kenneth have been blowing up my cell leaving messages that they wanna talk, but I haven't returned any of their calls."

Arykah exhaled. "Oh, Jesus. So what are you gonna do?"

Stephanie looked at Arykah. "That's why I'm here. I want a divorce."

Other than console Stephanie and pray for her, Arykah didn't know what advice to give her. Though had it been Arykah who walked in on Lance having sex in her bed with her sister, the outcome would have been very different. Arykah would have stopped both of their hearts that day. As the first lady of Freedom Temple Church of God in Christ, Arykah knew she couldn't reveal to Stephanie what her own actions would have been. "Is your marriage over?"

Sniff, sniff. "Yes." *Sniff, sniff.*

"Don't you wanna speak with Kenneth to get his side of the story?"

"He has no side of the story, Lady Arykah. I caught him in my bed with my sister."

Arykah nodded her head. She agreed with Stephanie, but she had to make sure that she encouraged Stephanie to reconcile with her husband. That's what God and Lance would want Arykah to do, even if she felt differently. In Arykah's world, there was never an excuse for infidelity. "How about you and Kenneth sit with me and the bishop? We can try to get to the bottom of why he cheated."

Stephanie shook her head from side to side. "I don't care *why* Kenneth cheated. The reason he cheated is not my concern. But he *did* cheat, twice that I know of, with my own blood. There's no turning back from that. I can't stay with him. Not after I've seen it with my own eyes."

Arykah nodded her head again. She understood. "What about Stacy? She's your sister, your family. You can certainly divorce Kenneth, but you can't divorce your sister. With everything that's going on with your mother's health, you and Stacy need each other."

"I know. But I'm not ready to deal with her just yet. She betrayed me, Lady Arykah."

Arykah reached out and rubbed Stephanie's arm. "I know, Sweetie."

"Once I'm done with Kenneth, maybe Stacy and I can reconcile, but for now, I got only one thing on my mind, and that's getting his trifling behind out of my life."

"Whatever you decide, I'll support you, but I wanna give you some advice. Your mother is in the hospital fighting for her life. Don't burden her with this news of Kenneth and Stacy. She doesn't need to worry about anything else but beating the cancer."

"I could never put this on my mother. It wouldn't be fair."

"You know I'm always here for you. Whenever you need to talk," Arykah said.

"Thanks, Lady Arykah." Stephanie stood. "You won't tell the bishop about this, will you?"

"Not if you don't want me to."

"I don't want him to know about my plans to divorce Kenneth. Bishop Lance will try to get me to change my mind, and I don't want to. I'm done with Kenneth and this marriage. There is no going back."

"I understand. I won't say a word."

Arykah hugged Stephanie tight. She prayed with her and wished her well. "Remember, you don't have to go through this alone. Call me anytime, day or night."

"I will."

When Arykah was alone, she sat in the chair behind her desk and thought about what she really wanted to advise Stephanie to do. *Cut off a pant leg from each of his suits and throw out one shoe from each pair he got. I could call Monique's cousin, Amaryllis. She's a witch and will put a root on both Kenneth and Stacy. Both of them would be cross-eyed and tongued-tied for the rest of their lives.*

"See, God," Arykah said out loud. "I kept my personal thoughts to myself. I'm growing."

***

Outside, on their patio that night, Arykah and Lance were enjoying ice-cold lemonade with chips and salsa. They watched Diva Chanel run around the backyard.

"It's a beautiful night, ain't it, Cheeks?"

Arykah looked up toward the pitch-black sky. The stars were shining bright. The temperature was about seventy-five degrees. "It feels good. It's nights like this one that I wish we had a hammock out here. It would be so nice and romantic to lie in your arms and watch the stars."

"Mmm," Lance commented.

"Lance, I'm gonna ask you a question, and I want you to be totally honest with me."

He looked at her. "I'm always honest with you, Cheeks."

"It's about Angela Moore."

Lance shrugged his shoulders. "What about her?"

"On Sunday you told me that you would handle her. Today in court she dropped all charges against me and Monique. Even the restraining orders were thrown out. I wanna know how you got her to do that."

It was time for Lance to confess the secret he had been keeping from Arykah. Two things could happen. Arykah could flip the table over and spray salsa and lemonade everywhere, or she could stab Lance in his sleep.

God, please let her understand. He exhaled. "I black-mailed her."

Arykah frowned. "With what?"

"Years ago when Angela and I were dating, her brother Reginald was hit while riding his motorcycle. His leg was amputated, and it left him paralyzed. Reginald didn't have medical insurance. Angela and her mother couldn't afford to pay for the therapy and care that Reginald needed. I was in love with her, Cheeks. I had a very good relationship with her mother and Reginald, so I offered to pay his medical bills and therapy."

"Okay. Well, that was good of you to do that for them, but what has that got to do with blackmailing Angela?"

"I'm *still* paying Reginald's medical bills *and* for his physical therapy."

Arykah's face got heated. *"What ?"*

"It was a promise that I had made to Angela back then. I told her that I would always take care of Reginald's bills and make sure he had the best care. I'm a man of my word, Cheeks. You know that. I made a promise, and I intend to keep it. And that's what I used to blackmail Angela with. I told her that I would no longer pay for Reginald's care if she didn't drop all charges against you and Monique." Lance sat and waited to see how Arykah would react. His heart beat out of his chest.

"So, I can assume that if you hadn't had that card to play against Angela, Monique and I would be facing assault charges and possible jail time."

"It would have been a great possibility, Cheeks. Yes."

Arykah dipped a tortilla chip in the salsa and ate it. "Okay." She drank her lemonade.

Lance was stunned. That was way too easy. He was dealing with an atomic bomb, a hothead. Arykah was a stick of dynamite, C-4. There was no way she was okay with what he had just told her.

"Okay?"

Arykah looked at him. "Mmm-hmm." She swallowed more lemonade.

"Just like that?"

She chuckled. "What do you want me to say, Bishop? You are a man of your word. That's one of the things that I love about you. When you say you're gonna do something, you mean it. You made that promise to Angela and her family when you were in love with her. I can respect that. I'm thankful that you were able to get her to dismiss all charges. I'm happy to be back at church, I'm happy that Angela won't be there, and I'm happy that you fired Sharonda. I'm one happy fat chick. So you go ahead and pay those medical bills. It's not taking anything away from me and how I live my life."

Lance pinched himself to make sure that he wasn't dreaming. He was so sure that an ambulance would need to be called to their home. He just knew that Arykah was going to blow her top. But she had thrown Lance for a loop. "You are way too calm, cool, and collected about this. What you got in that lemonade you're sippin' on?"

Arykah chuckled.

Lance reached across the table and picked up Arykah's glass and looked at it. He brought it to his nose and sniffed the contents. *"I knew it!"* he hollered out.

She laughed out loud.

Lance sipped the lemonade. *"I knew it!"* he hollered out again. "What's in here?"

"Bacardi rum," she confessed.

He looked at her. "You got liquor in the house?"

Arykah nodded her head. "And a bag of weed too," she said nonchalantly. "When was the last time you took two puffs and passed? You wanna smoke a joint and have a drink with me?"

"Wha . . . you . . . ha . . . wha . . ."

Arykah laughed at Lance's loss of words. She wished she had her camera on hand to capture the look on his face. "I'm just joking with you, Bishop. I ain't got no weed." Truth be told, Arykah wouldn't mind smoking a joint right then. "You want some rum in your lemonade?"

Lance didn't answer. He took a big swallow of Arykah's drink. "That's pretty good."

"Oh, heck no," she said. "You can't drink mine. That's what you *ain't* gon' do." Arykah stood. "I'm going to get the bottle."

She left and came back to the patio moments later. She poured rum in Lance's lemonade, then she freshened her own drink. The two of them moved to lounge chairs. They watched the stars and drank until the wee hours of the morning.

Nine

Bright and early Wednesday morning Lance and Arykah were in the rear of a limousine as they waited for Myrtle.

"Is your head okay now?" Arykah asked Lance. He seemed to be a little woozy when they woke up that morning.

He nodded his head. "Yeah, I'm cool. How much rum did we drink?"

"The whole bottle."

Lance shook his head from side to side. "Remind me to never do that again."

"Next time I'll give you two Excedrin capsules to take before you drink alcohol. That's how you cheat a hangover."

"Spoken like a professional drinker."

"I is what I is, Bishop."

The driver opened the passenger-rear door and Myrtle got inside the limousine. "Morning. I wasn't expecting this. I was looking for a taxicab. This is fancy-shmancy."

"Morning, Mother Myrtle. Ready for your first day at work?" Arykah asked her.

"Ready as I'll ever be. Morning, Bishop."

"Good morning, Mother Myrtle. This is your car service." Lance introduced Myrtle to her personal driver who stood outside the car. He hadn't yet closed the door. "Your driver's name is Cliff, and he will be here every morning at eight to drive you to the church."

Cliff tipped his hat to Myrtle. "It's a pleasure to meet you, ma'am."

Myrtle was too outdone. "Wow, all of this for li'l ole me? I can already hear my neighbors gossiping."

"The bishop and I figured that hiring a personal driver for you would be much better and safer for you than calling a cab every morning."

Lance and Arykah could've sent the limousine for Myrtle, but Arykah thought it would be best if they rode with her on her first day of work.

"Did Mother Gussie get the red-carpet treatment too?" Myrtle asked.

"Hel—I mean heck, no," Arykah answered.

"We're ready to go, Cliff," Lance said to the driver.

Cliff closed the rear door, got behind the wheel, and pulled away from the curb.

Myrtle noticed that Arykah didn't have her baby in her purse. "Where's the brat?"

"Diva Chanel is in doggie day camp where she belongs," Lance said.

Arykah rolled her eyes.

"You know, Bishop," Myrtle started, "we never discussed my pay."

"Yes, I know."

"Well, don't you think we should?"

"Mother, Myrtle, you volunteered for the job; now you expect to get paid?" Arykah teased.

Myrtle's eyebrows rose. Lance chuckled at the expression on her face. He knew she wanted to curse Arykah.

"Chile, don't play with me, okay? Y'all gon' pay me."

"Of course, Freedom Temple will pay you, Mother Myrtle. You'll have health and dental insurance coverage as well," Lance said. "We'll fill out the forms when we get to church."

That news excited Myrtle. "Really? So, this is a real job, huh?"

"Yep," Arykah answered. "Get ready for Uncle Sam because he's coming after you."

"How much will I make as the church secretary?"

"The secretary position pays fifteen dollars an hour," Lance responded.

"Okay," Myrtle said nodding her head. "Fifteen dollars an hour, plus health and dental. And all I gotta do is answer the phone, take messages, and keep the kray krays away from the bishop. I can work with that."

Arykah laughed out loud. "Kray krays? Where did you hear that kind of talk?"

"From all the young folks at church. They keep me in the loop."

After thirty minutes of driving, Cliff drove the limousine up to the front door of the church. He opened the rear door. Lance, Arykah, and Myrtle got out.

"Thanks, Cliff," Lance said. "We'll see you at five."

Upstairs, on the second floor of the church, Lance and Arykah showed Myrtle her desk. It was the same desk that Mother Gussie and Sharonda sat at, right outside of Lance's office.

"Do you know how to work a computer?" Arykah asked her.

"Not really."

"You've never used Excel?" Lance asked.

Myrtle looked at him. "What's that?"

"Oh boy," Arykah sighed. "Let's make the Bishop's coffee. That has to be the first thing you do every morning. Then you and I will go over everything you need to know."

"Have fun, ladies," Lance said as he unlocked the door to his office and went inside.

Myrtle and Arykah went across the hall to the kitchenette. Arykah instructed Myrtle how to make Lance's white mocha chocolate-flavored coffee and sweeten it to his taste.

Myrtle brought the mug into Lance's office and set it on his desk. "Here you go, Bishop. Light and sweet, just the way you like it."

"Thank you, Mother. Lady Arykah is gonna show you how to use Excel. When you're comfortable with the program, I'll need you to categorize all the members' names in alphabetical order. Then you'll need to send the list to the photographer that's gonna take pictures of the entire congregation. We're putting together a book that will have the members' photos, names, and phone numbers. After that list is compiled, I'll need for you to call everyone who is on the sick and shut-in list and ask if they need anything. Once that's completed, Mother Myrtle, please call Holy Trinity Church and confirm that Pastor Jackson Montgomery will be our guest speaker in two weeks. The church's information is in the rolodex on your desk."

"Yes, Bishop." Myrtle turned to walk away.

"One more thing, Mother."

She stopped and turned around.

"I will need the names of all of the parents that are having their babies dedicated next month. Lady Arykah can help you with that."

Myrtle didn't say a word. She left Lance's office in a hurry. She got back to her desk and saw Arykah sitting in her chair typing on the keyboard.

"You ready for your Excel lesson?" Arykah asked her.

"You can stay right where you are. Call Cliff back here so he can take me home."

Arykah looked up at Myrtle and frowned. "Why?"

Myrtle lowered her voice so that Lance couldn't hear what she was saying. She pointed toward his office. "He's crazy."

"What's the problem?"

"He wants me to make a list of the members for some kind of photo book. Then he wants me to check on the sick folks. Then he wants me to call Holy Unity to confirm that Michael Jackson is coming next week and—"

"It's Holy *Trinity* ," Arykah interrupted. "His name is *Pastor Jackson Montgomery,* and he's coming in *two* weeks."

"Whatever," Myrtle said. "He also wants every baby and their momma's names. *And* he wants me to learn the excellent computer program."

"It's Excel."

"Whatever," Myrtle said again. The fear of failure was evident on her face. *"Chile , I can't do all of that."*

Arykah laughed at the creases on Myrtle's forehead. "It sounds overwhelming because you haven't done it before. This really is a simple job once you get the hang of it. It's all computer work." Arykah stood up. "Come on and sit. It'll be okay. I'll be here with you all day and tomorrow."

"Not Friday?"

"Friday morning, my client is closing on his house, but as soon as I'm done with that, I'll come straight here."

As soon as Myrtle sat down at the computer, the telephone rang. She looked up at Arykah. "Should I answer it?"

"Well, it ain't gonna answer itself."

Myrtle picked up the receiver and brought it to her ear. "Good morning, Freedom Temple."

"Um, yes, um, I'm calling to see if Bishop Howell can come to my house and pray for me. I need some sexual healing," a woman said in a seductive voice.

Myrtle's mouth dropped wide open. Stunned, she looked up at Arykah and mouthed the words, "It's a crazy woman."

"What does she want?" Arykah mouthed the words back.

Myrtle shrugged her shoulders and spoke into the receiver. "What's your name, Miss?"

"Baby Girl."

Myrtle frowned and repeated the name. "Baby Girl?" Myrtle looked at the caller ID and recognized Monique's cellular telephone number. "Wait a minute. Is that you, Monique?"

Both Monique and Arykah hollered out laughing.

"You ain't got nothin' else better to do than call my job and harass me?"

Arykah took the telephone from Myrtle. "Girl, we got her good. You should've seen her face."

Myrtle stood and went to Lance's door. She saw that he was laughing too. He must've been in on the prank. "I quit," she said. "I ain't gotta deal with this foolishness."

Lance jumped up from his chair, came to Myrtle, and hugged her. "We're sorry. It was a bad joke." He looked at Arykah. "Aren't we sorry, Cheeks?"

Arykah was still laughing on the telephone with Monique. "I gotta go, girl. She just quit." Arykah put the receiver on its base and came to hug Myrtle. "We're sorry. Lance made us do it."

Lance quickly shook his head from side to side. "Uh-uh. You ain't putting this on me. Cheeks, you are in the church so tell the truth," he said. "You told me that there wouldn't be any hanky-panky for a week if I told Mother Myrtle what you and Monique were up to."

Myrtle went back to her desk and sat down. "Y'all are evil kids. All of ya. Evil, evil kids."

By noontime, with Arykah's help, Myrtle was in full swing of the secretarial position at Freedom Temple. Pastor Jackson Montgomery's visit to the church was confirmed. Myrtle had contacted every member who was on the sick and shut-in list. She and Arykah had compiled the list of every member and telephone numbers. Arykah showed Myrtle how to fax the list to the church's photographer.

Myrtle went to Arykah's office and saw her typing on her computer keys. "Where do I find the name of all the babies and parents for next month's dedication service?"

"Sharonda has the names in a folder on the desktop."

Myrtle nodded her head, then went back to her desk and sat down. She searched the desk for a folder with the babies' names. After removing everything and putting it back, Myrtle went to Arykah's office again. "There is no folder with baby's names on top of the desk."

Arykah looked at Myrtle and chuckled. "I really gotta fast-forward your computer skills to the twenty-first century. The desktop is your computer. When you look at the screen, you'll see a folder that says 'July Baby Dedication.' Just click on it, print the page, and give it to Lance."

"Why didn't you say that in the first place?"

"I did."

Myrtle exhaled out of frustration. "You said the names were in a folder on top of the desk."

Arykah knew that Myrtle was fit to be tied and she'd never win an argument with her. "I'm sorry, Mother. I should have explained myself better. When someone says 'desktop,' they're referring to the computer that sits on top of a desk. Just like a laptop is a smaller computer that people set on their laps."

"I don't know why everything has to be so difficult."

"It's only your first day. You'll get the hang of it. Patience is a virtue. That's the word."

"Yeah, well, I wasn't born with any patience, and I'm too old to get it now," Myrtle said as she walked away.

"Ain't that the truth," Arykah mumbled.

"I heard that."

Myrtle went back to her desk and found the folder on the desktop that she was looking for. She printed the list of the names of the newborns and their parents and took it to Lance's office. "Bishop, here's the list you wanted."

Lance looked up from writing on a notepad. He took the list from Myrtle. "Great. Thanks, Mother. By the way," Lance started. He opened his top right desk drawer and pulled out three keys on a ring. He extended them to Myrtle. "Here are your keys. The large gold key is for the front and rear doors of the church."

Myrtle took the keys and looked at them. "The same key for both doors?"

Lance nodded his head. "Mmm-hmm. The pink key is to Lady Arykah's office, and the blue key is to my office. The only other folks that have copies of the keys to the church are Brian, the deacons, and Minister Weeks."

"Why do *I* need keys to the church?"

"Because sometimes you'll be here alone."

Myrtle's breath caught in her throat. "In this big ole church?"

"Well, yes," Lance said. "You know I own a construction company on the north side of the city. I divide my time between there and here at the church. And Lady Arykah rarely comes here in the mornings because she sells real estate. The custodian, Brian, will be here most of the time. He cleans the church and takes care of the landscape. Are you okay with being alone sometime?"

Myrtle shrugged her shoulders. "I guess I'll have to be, won't I?"

"I don't want you to worry. The church is in a pretty decent neighborhood. Cliff will bring you right to the front door. Brian works the same hours as you, nine to five, but often he's here as early as eight. Once you're inside, lock the door behind you and don't open it for anyone. I overheard you and Cheeks talking earlier. She pointed out where all of the emergency contact numbers are, right?"

"Yes, she did. She also programmed yours and Minister Carlton Weeks cell numbers in my phone."

Lance smiled. He pointed to an empty chair across his desk. "Have a seat."

"Should I get my notepad and pen?"

"No," he chuckled. "Not for this."

Myrtle sat across from Lance.

"I'm really glad you're here, Mother."

"Why is that, Bishop?"

"I know I can trust you. You left your church where you've been for most of your life to come here and rescue Arykah from Mother Pansie Bowak and Mother Gussie Hughes."

"I was furious when Monique told me what they were doing over here. I had to come. I love Arykah so much," Myrtle said. "Both of them are the daughters I never had."

Lance nodded. "I know you love them, and it shows. You have Arykah's back, and you're exactly who we need working at this church."

"I love you too, Bishop. You are an awesome pastor, an amazing husband to Arykah, and you're just an all-around cool dude."

Lance smiled at Myrtle's words. "I never thanked you for what you did for me when I felt like I was losing a grip on things when Arykah was attacked. Do you remember what you said to me in my kitchen the night I brought Arykah home from the hospital?"

Myrtle nodded her head. "Yep, Monique and Adonis had left, and I was washing the dinner dishes when you walked into the kitchen."

"Thanks for staying over tonight, Mother Myrtle. I can't do this on my own."

Myrtle dried her hands with the dish towel. "Come and sit at the table, son."

They both pulled out chairs and sat down.

"Trust me when I tell you that the devil has peeked into your future, and he doesn't like what he sees," Myrtle said. "He's so angry at you for conquering the role as a husband and a pastor. He doesn't wanna see you and Arykah blessed. Arykah's rape was a setback, but she's gonna be all right. Both of you will get through this."

Myrtle grabbed Lance's hands and squeezed them inside her own. "I know she has distanced herself from you. Just be patient and love her. Hold on to God's unchanging hand. Be still and know that He is God. There is glory after this."

"I'll never forget that," Lance said.

"And wasn't I correct? Didn't God bring y'all out?"

"He sure did."

Arykah poked her head inside Lance's office. "What's going on in here?"

"Mother Myrtle and I were just going over a few things."

"It's lunchtime," Arykah said.

"Neither of us have our cars; we'll have to order in."

"Chinese?" Arykah asked.

"Yeah, that sounds good. Mongolian beef with fried rice," Lance said to Myrtle.

Arykah looked at her. "Chicken with broccoli for me."

Myrtle sat and looked from Arykah to Lance. She wondered what the heck they were gaping at her for. "I gotta order y'alls lunch too?"

"Oh, didn't I tell you?" Lance asked Myrtle.

"Tell me what?"

"Not only does my secretary make my coffee, she fetches my lunch too."

Arykah chuckled.

Myrtle stood from her chair and headed to her own desk. "You better be glad I like you," she said to Lance. "And don't think I ain't getting myself lunch on *your* dime."

On Friday, late morning, at Bowen Realty Offices, Arykah and Randy Brown finalized all of the paperwork. After he autographed his name for what seemed like one hundred times, Randy received the keys to his new estate in North Barrington.

"Congratulations," Arykah said. She extended her hand to him.

Randy shook her hand. "Thank you."

"So, how will you surprise your wife? Tamara, right?"

"Tamara, yes. I haven't quite figured that out yet."

The wheels in Arykah's head turned. She recalled the day she sold Lance their home before they were married. He had invited Arykah over for dinner that very night he closed on the home. She thought that was very romantic. "Can I make a suggestion?"

"Absolutely." Randy folded his arms across his chest.

"Ask Tamara to meet you at the estate. Make up an excuse that your colleague or one of the baller's are away on vacation and asked you to check on their house or feed their dog. When she gets there, have a picnic basket on the floor of the living room, filled with all of her favorite foods. The estate has built-in speakers all throughout. So, do it up with jazz music and let candles be the only light in the room. As soon as Tamara walks in the front door, you know what to say, right?"

Randy smiled and nodded his head. He was impressed. "Welcome home," he said. "I like that."

"It wouldn't hurt to have a birthday gift as well. A Fendi bag, perhaps?"

Randy's eyebrows rose. "The *house* is Tamara's gift."

"And what a beautiful gift it is, but she needs something to unwrap."

Randy chuckled. Arykah was over the top. "How about I hang a bow on the front door?"

"Make it a big one."

"Aw, sooky, sooky now."

Myrtle turned from the computer and saw Deacon Bronson Marshall smiling at her. His two front teeth where surrounded in gold. The sparkling metal was a turnoff for her. "Morning, Deacon."

"How you be today?"

Myrtle was about to ask Deacon Marshall how he gained entry into the church but remembered that Lance had told her that all of the deacons were given a set of keys. Myrtle didn't like the fact that Deacon Marshall was able to walk right up to her. She had no idea he was even in the building.

"I'm all right, Deacon. You?"

As soon as she inquired about his well-being, Myrtle wished that she hadn't. Deacon Marshall liked to talk. Myrtle was the exact opposite. She was still learning her new job and didn't feel like entertaining the sixty-nine-year-old Southerner.

"Somebody told me that there was a new pretty thang workin' at the choch house. I had to come on down here and see for maself, and hot dog, they was right. Myrtle, you sho is a pretty thang."

Myrtle looked at the black shirt Deacon Marshall had on. It was the first week in June and eighty-seven degrees outside. *Why is he wearing a long sleeve shirt?* Myrtle noticed the shirt buttoned all the way to Deacon Marshall's neck. *Ain't you hot?* She moved her eyes down to Deacon Marshall's wide white belt he wore with light blue polyester pants. She couldn't see his shoes from where she sat, but had she made a bet that Deacon Marshall completed his ensemble with white patent leather shoes, Myrtle would've won. The black shirt, white belt, and light blue pants put a chuckle in her throat.

"You like what ya see?" he asked when he saw Myrtle eyeing his clothes.

Are you kiddin' me? "Um, not so much, Deacon. It's a bit warm outside for a long sleeve black shirt and polyester pants, don't you think?"

He glanced down at his attire, then looked at Myrtle. "Whatcha mean?"

"I *mean* it's too hot to be wearing something like that. Don't you have any short sleeve cotton shirts? Or pants with a thinner material?" Myrtle felt kind of sorry for Deacon Marshall. He didn't have a wife to show him how to dress for the seasons or for the current time. The seersucker suits he wore to church on Sunday mornings were shameful and should have been burned four decades ago.

"I got good ah in ma cah," he said.

"That's good, Deacon," Myrtle responded. He wasn't her husband, so she didn't feel the need to spend another second talking about his wardrobe. "Are you here to see the bishop?"

"I told you I come to see you."

Myrtle's eyebrows rose. *"Me?"*

He smiled at her. The gold in his mouth sparkled.

"Okay, well, now you see me."

"Did you get sumtin' ta eat?"

She didn't understand his question. "Huh?"

"It's time to eat. You wanna get some food?"

Myrtle looked at the digital clock on her desk and saw that it was twelve thirteen. She hadn't realized that it was noontime already. She wondered why Lance hadn't mentioned that he was hungry. Myrtle stood from her chair. "Excuse me, Deacon." She went to Lance's office door and peeked inside. She saw that he was on a call.

Lance looked at Myrtle and raised his eyebrows. Myrtle knew that signal was asking her what she wanted. "You want some lunch?"

He shook his head from side to side. Myrtle nodded her head and went back to her desk and sat down. "Thanks for coming by, Deacon Marshall, but the bishop is pretty busy, and so am I."

"You don't want to grab a bite to eat wit' meh?"

Myrtle hoped that Deacon Marshall would get the hint that she didn't want to be bothered with him. He wasn't her type, and Myrtle would die if someone recognized her out in public with him dressed like that.

"I brought a tuna sandwich from home."

"Tuna? You can't eat a tuna sammich on a day lak tuday. The sun is out, and the bards is sangin'. Why don't you let me take you to a nas restauroont? Anyweyah you wanna go."

"Aw, shucks," Arykah said smiling as she walked up on them. "What's going on here?" she asked Myrtle and Deacon Marshall. She heard him practically begging Myrtle to go to lunch with him.

"Hey, there, Lady Eerkah," he greeted.

"Good afternoon, Deacon Marshall," she responded, smiling at them both.

"I'm glad you're here," Myrtle said. She was thankful for the interruption.

"I'm tryin' to get this pretty yun thang to go get some lunch wit' meh."

"Really?" Arykah asked. She smiled at Myrtle. "I think that's a wonderful invitation."

Myrtle scowled at her. "I'm not hungry, and I got way too much work to do." Myrtle prayed Arykah would get her hint and help her out of that situation.

"Well, you gotta eat sometime," Arykah said.

"Yeh, you gotsta eat sumtime," Deacon Marshall confirmed.

Myrtle gave Arykah a look to let her know that she was in trouble.

Arykah chuckled.

"Look, Deacon," Myrtle started, "asking me to lunch is nice of you, but this is only my third day on the job. I have a lot of things that I need to figure out, and I really don't wanna go out for lunch right now."

"Then why don't both of you order some food in?" Arykah suggested.

Myrtle was so aggravated with Arykah by now that her face started to twitch.

"Yeh, we can do dat," Deacon Marshall said.

"You know what, Deacon? I had forgotten that I was on a diet," Myrtle said. "So I won't be eating anything today or tomorrow or the next day."

Arykah hollered out.

"Gal, you ain't big as nothin'," Deacon Marshall said to her. "What you talkin' 'bout you's on a dat?"

"It's the first I've heard of it," Arykah said.

Myrtle snapped her head at Arykah.

The look Myrtle gave her was frightening, and she knew that Myrtle was serious. "Oh, yeah, the diet," Arykah said tapping the side of her head. "I had forgotten that we're both on diets."

Myrtle nodded her head. "That's right. Sorry, Deacon. I can't break my diet."

"Well, okay," he said pitifully. "But I ain't givin' up on ya, Myrtle."

Myrtle faked a smile at him. *You may as well.*

Arykah couldn't resist. "She likes fruit and salads."

Myrtle stood from her chair and walked past both of them.

"Weyah you goin'?" Deacon Marshall asked her.

"To get a switch."

"Uh-oh," Arykah said to Deacon Marshall. "One of us is in trouble."

"Well, I ain't fixin' to stick round 'n' fine out which one." He immediately left the church.

Arykah opened the door to her office, entered, and then locked herself inside.

Five minutes later Myrtle turned her pink key in the lock on Arykah's door. "You thought you could lock me out?" she asked when she opened the door.

Arykah sat behind her desk. She laughed out loud when she saw a long skinny twig in Myrtle's hand. "What are you gonna do with that?"

Myrtle held up the switch. "I'ma put you over my knee and whack your backside with it if you do that again."

"Do what?"

"You know full well what you did. I ain't interested in that man whatsoever."

"Maybe that's your problem."

Myrtle walked farther into Arykah's office and put her free hand on her hip. "What are you talking about? I ain't a got a problem."

"You ain't got a man either," Arykah said matter-of-factly.

"And that's *my* choice, li'l girl, not that it's any of *your* business."

Arykah shrugged her shoulders. "Okay. If you like being alone all the time and not having warm arms to hold you at night, then good for you."

Myrtle came and stood directly across from Arykah's desk and looked down at her. "I ain't one of them women that *need* a man."

"I don't *need* a man either," Arykah retorted. "I don't need Lance. I can take care of myself. But I sure am glad that I have a husband. It's a blessing having someone to share my life with. Someone that I know loves me and wants to be with me."

"Listen," Myrtle started, "I've been there and done that. I had a husband, and he turned out to be the biggest creep on this earth. I put up with his lying behind for as long as I could. Divorcing him was the best thing for me."

Arykah nodded her head. She knew all of the details of Myrtle's failed marriage. But Myrtle had been single for many years. Every man that smiled her way, she brushed them off. "Every man is not your ex-husband. Deacon Marshall was only inviting you out to lunch. He didn't ask for your hand in marriage."

"Did you see what that fool had on?"

"Mother Myrtle, you are much too old to be picky."

"Humph, when it comes to a man, Honey, I gotta be picky. And I ain't picking a gold tooth-wearing, musty-smelling man."

"Wait a minute now, that ain't fair," Arykah said. "You weren't even close to Deacon Marshall. How do you know he was musty?"

"Anybody wearing a long sleeve black shirt and polyester pants in June is musty."

Arykah hollered out and laughed. "You ain't right."

Lance appeared at Arykah's office door. "I thought I heard you cackling," he said to her. "What are you screaming about?"

"You're gonna have to lay some hands on this woman, Lance. She just broke Deacon Marshall's heart."

Myrtle turned and walked past Lance and out Arykah's office. "Ain't nobody gotta lay hands on me," she said over her shoulder.

"The temperature is gonna drop tonight," Arykah yelled after Myrtle. "Don't you want some arms wrapped around you to keep you warm?"

"Not no musty arms," Myrtle yelled back.

Lance sat down in a chair opposite of Arykah's desk. "What is she wound up about?"

Arykah waved her hand in Myrtle's direction. "She's playing hard to get. Deacon Bronson Marshall was just here, and he asked her to go to lunch. She turned him down flat."

"Really? I heard her talking to someone. I didn't know it was Deacon Marshall."

"He seems to be really sweet on Myrtle. I felt bad for him. She claims it's his wardrobe that's turning her off."

Lance laughed. "Myrtle can't get with the old-man attire?"

"I got an idea, Babe. Aren't you playing golf with him tomorrow?"

"Yeah, we tee off at nine a.m."

"How about taking Deacon Marshall on a shopping spree after golf? Pick out some nice shirts, slacks, and shoes that's up-to-date."

Lance thought about it. "I guess I can do that."

"The next time he approaches Mother Myrtle, her reaction may be different if he's dressed appropriately."

"Are you trying to make a love connection?"

She smiled. "Maybe."

"How did your closing go this morning?"

"It was fabulous. I tell you, Randy Brown is a charmer. Any man that buys a house for his wife is all right with me."

When Arykah sold Lance his estate, he hadn't anticipated falling in love with and marrying her. However, God brought them together. Now they shared his home as man and wife, and Arykah wasn't required to pay one single bill in the home.

Lance cleared his throat.

"You're all right with me too, Bishop."

"Listen, I wanna talk to you about something. I saw on the church's calendar that you're planning a baby shower for Miranda in two weeks, here at the church."

"That's right," Arykah said. "She asked me to be the baby's godmother."

"Yes, I know. But Miranda is an unwed single mother, Cheeks."

Arykah shrugged her shoulders. She didn't understand what Lance was getting at.

"It's highly inappropriate for the pastor's wife to throw a baby shower for an unwed mother, *especially* at the church."

Arykah exhaled. "Before I flip out on you, I need to know if you're seriously saying this to me. Are we *really* going down this road again, Lance?"

It wasn't long ago that Arykah and Lance argued over Miranda's pregnancy. Mother Pansie had talked Lance into agreeing that Miranda should be dismissed from the young adult choir because she was pregnant. Arykah had to convince Lance that it wasn't the church's responsibility to punish unwed mothers. Even though fornication had been committed and a baby was conceived, Miranda was still a child of God and keeping her from singing praises to Him wasn't Lance's or Mother Pansie's decision to make.

"Cheeks, please try to understand that it doesn't look good, and it sends the wrong message."

"What message does my throwing Miranda a shower, here at the church, send?"

"Well, first of all," Lance started, "there are other impressionable girls at Freedom Temple who may look at what you're doing for Miranda and think it's okay to get pregnant because the church supports it. It's like you're rewarding the sin Miranda committed."

Arykah leaned back in her chair and exhaled. "You know, it amazes me how you so easily omit Titus, the young boy Miranda had sex with."

"I'm not omitting anyone, Cheeks."

"Sure, you are. You just said that I am rewarding *Miranda's* sin. And it wasn't that long ago when you and Mother Pansie took her out of the choir. You didn't remove her child's father from the choir. You're only focusing on Miranda, and that's not right, Lance."

"Because boys are viewed differently."

"And why is that? I'll tell you why. In today's society, males are considered players if they date numerous women. Men can get a whole bunch of women pregnant, and they just get a pat on the back. But when a woman dates more than one man, she's called a floozy or a jezebel. And if she ends up pregnant, then she's shunned or frowned upon."

As much as Lance didn't want to agree with what Arykah had just said, he had to because it was the truth. "Cheeks, I get what you're saying, but didn't I get Miranda and put her back in the choir myself?"

"Only after I threw a fit, Lance."

"You throwing a shower for Miranda, at the church, is giving the green light for girls to have sex and get pregnant."

"No, it's not. Don't put that on me. It's up to the parents of girls to raise them and teach them right from wrong. That's not *my* responsibility."

"As the first lady of this church, it's *absolutely* your responsibility to steer young girls in the right direction."

"Listen, I didn't get up on Sunday morning and make an announcement to young girls to have sex and get pregnant, then I'll give them a baby shower. I'm not a fan of adultery or fornication. Gladys is a single mother working two jobs just to support herself and Miranda. Now she has a grandson coming in three weeks. Miranda isn't working; she's in school. I'm just trying to help Gladys as much as I can. The baby will need everything. A crib, diapers, formula, clothes, a changing table, a bassinette, a playpen, bottles, everything. Gladys can't afford to buy all of that stuff, Lance."

"But the godmother can certainly afford them."

Arykah cocked her head to the side. "What do you mean?"

"I'm saying that Miranda doesn't need for you to throw her a baby shower. Why not just buy the things the boy will need?"

Arykah thought about it. "I suppose I could do that."

"No one will have to know. And I won't have to worry about sending the message that you and I condone unwed pregnancy."

"But folks, *and you*, need to understand that baby showers are for the baby, not the mother of the baby. Miranda can't fit in a crib, high chair, or a swing. She doesn't wear bibs and diapers. Miranda doesn't suck on bottles. Showers don't glorify the sin. They are thrown for the support of the baby. Can't you understand that?"

Lance didn't say a word. He believed what he believed.

Arykah was disappointed that she couldn't throw Miranda's baby a party like she wanted. "I was looking forward to a cake, decorations, and all of the bells and whistles."

"How about this," Lance started. "Have your shower for Miranda. But not here at the church."

Arykah became excited. "Really? You don't mind?"

"I know you love spending money, especially on other folks. And because you are the boy's godmother, I really think you *should* do something special for Miranda."

Arykah sat up in her chair with more excitement. "I know what to do. I could buy everything on Miranda's registry and have Team Arykah come to Gladys apartment and watch Miranda open the gifts. I can have my cake, and I could decorate Gladys's apartment."

"See, problem solved," Lance said. "The baby will have everything he needs, you get to have cake, and the church stays out of it."

"How do you feel about Miranda not asking you to be the baby's godfather?"

Lance shrugged his shoulders. "I don't feel any sort of way about it."

"Miranda hasn't said this to me, but I think she feels that you're disappointed in her for getting pregnant."

"That wouldn't be far from the truth," he admitted. "Miranda is a straight-A student, and she's always had a good head on her shoulders. Gladys joined Freedom Temple when Miranda was just five years old. When she got around thirteen I can remember Miranda coming up to my office every Sunday after church. She would always say, 'Bishop, you preached me happy today.' I've watched her grow into a smart young lady. So, of course, I was disappointed to learn that she was pregnant. It broke my heart."

"And she senses that, Lance. You know you're gonna have to speak with Miranda eventually."

"Yeah, I know. There's no use in crying over spilled milk. The baby is coming, so we may as well get ready for it. Who did she choose as the godfather?"

"No one. I guess I'll be standing at the altar alone when you dedicate him. Oh, that reminds me. I need Mother Myrtle to add Miranda's name to the baby dedication list for next month."

"I'll have to dedicate Miranda's baby in my office, Cheeks. Because she's a single mother, it can't be done in the sanctuary."

Arykah shook her head from side to side vigorously. She needed to dismiss the words Lance had just spoken to her. "What?"

"That's a tradition in the Church of God in Christ. Only babies whose parents are married are allowed to be dedicated in the sanctuary."

"Lance, that has got to be the most dumbest, most ignorant, most craziest crap I've ever heard. That's some Mother Pansie and Mother Gussie bull right there."

"It's been that way for as long as I can remember."

"Lance, *you* are the pastor of this church. Why do you allow such foolishness to go on?"

"What foolishness, Cheeks? It's tradition."

"It's a stupid tradition. Just because Miranda isn't married to her baby's father doesn't make the baby any less important than all of the other babies that are getting dedicated. He's still God's creation, he's still God's child. Why punish the baby because he was born out of wedlock?"

"No one is punishing the baby. He'll still be dedicated; just not in the sanctuary."

"Why? Isn't every baby pure when they come out of the womb? Babies can't commit sins, Lance. There is absolutely no reason at all why Miranda's baby shouldn't be dedicated in the sanctuary with all of the other babies. If you can dedicate him in private, then you can dedicate him openly. There was a time when the Church of God in Christ didn't allow women to wear pants in the sanctuary. Now I see women preaching in the pulpit wearing pants. What happened to *that* tradition?"

Lance didn't respond.

"God says that no sin is greater than the next. You got folks smoking weed and shooting up dope, but they are still allowed to partake in holy communion—*in the sanctuary*. I don't see you trotting upstairs to give out crackers and an ounce of grape juice in your office to the folks that are sprung out on dope. And what about Sister TiQuandria Sprawls? Everybody knows she moonlights as a stripper at night. Swinging on that pole keeps food on the table for her six kids. Why is she allowed to take holy communion *in the sanctuary?*"

He still didn't respond.

"Romans, chapter five, verse twelve says, 'Therefore, just as sin came into the world through one man, and death through sin, and so death spread to all men because all sinned.' And moving on up to Romans chapter three, verse twenty-three, 'For all have sinned and fallen short of the glory of God.' And Ezekiel chapter twenty-eight, verse fifteen says, 'You were blameless in your ways from the day you were created until unrighteousness was found in you.'"

If Arykah had a microphone in her hand, she would have dropped it and exited the stage.

Lance sat in the presence of his wife in awe of her. He had no reply. She just preached to the preacher. Arykah stood up and grabbed her purse. "There is no way I'm gonna allow this church to treat Miranda's baby, *my godson*, like he's an outcast. Now I caved in with the baby shower thing. I'm not gonna host Miranda's baby shower in the fellowship hall. But I'm *not* caving in on this, Bishop. Right is right, and wrong is wrong. You need to research these traditions and find out who started them and where they came from. You're gonna mess around and lose souls trying to hold on to traditions that ain't about nothin'." Arykah put her purse on her shoulder. "I don't know what you're gonna do about this baby dedication thing, but you need to figure it out, Bishop. I'm going to pick up Diva Chanel from doggie day camp. She and I will see you at home."

Arykah left Lance sitting alone. When she walked out of her office she looked at Myrtle sitting at her desk. Myrtle nodded her head, winked at Arykah, and gave her two thumbs-up. She had heard their entire conversation.

Lance exited Arykah's office and walked past Myrtle. "You sure you don't want any lunch, Bishop?"

"Not right now," he said. "I need to figure something out." Lance went into his office and shut the door. Myrtle clicked on the icon on her desktop to open the list of parents for the baby dedication ceremony. She added Miranda Blackmon to the list. There was no doubt in her mind that Miranda, her baby boy, and Arykah would be standing at the altar with all of the other parents.

From her cellular telephone Myrtle sent Arykah a text.

U go, girl. I'm very proud of u.

Seconds later Arykah responded with a smiley face.

When Lance arrived home that evening, he found Arykah and Diva Chanel snuggled up on the sectional in the great room. He sat down next to them and kissed Arykah's cheek. "I listened to everything you said about dedicating Miranda's baby boy in the sanctuary."

Arykah looked at him. "And?"

"And I've decided to do away with that tradition. You were right. Babies are innocent and pure no matter how they're conceived. They shouldn't be judged by the actions of their parents."

Arykah leaned over and kissed Lance's lips gently. "Thank you, Bishop."

"That tradition should've been cancelled a long time ago."

"That one and all of the other stupid traditions as well."

"I'm looking into every tradition Freedom Temple has."

"That's good. After I left the church, I called Gladys and explained why I wasn't gonna give Miranda a baby shower at the church. She understood and thought it was a great idea that we do something small at her house tomorrow."

"Tomorrow?"

Arykah nodded her head. "Mmm-hmm. I called Babies 'R' Us and set it up to have everything on Miranda's registry delivered to Gladys's apartment in the morning. I've also called the team, and all the ladies will be there."

"Did you order the cake?"

"Yep. I had to pay extra because it was short notice, but I didn't mind that at all."

"What about food?"

"Don't worry, Bishop. I'm not gonna ask you to cater the shower. Since it'll just be the team, we're gonna order pizza."

Lance nodded his head. "Sounds like you have everything under control."

"I called Sister Saminta Williams."

"That's Titus's mother," Lance said.

"Uh-huh. Well, she won't be at the shower. She said that neither she, nor her husband, want anything to do with Miranda or the baby their son fathered."

That news shocked Lance. Saminta, and her husband, Douglas, had been members of Freedom Temple for as long as Lance could remember. They were upstanding members, they tithed faithfully, and seemed to be the all-American family. "Wow."

"Wow is right," Arykah said. "Saminta says Titus will be graduating high school next year. He's the captain of the football team, and she says she will not let a careless girl like Miranda interfere with her son going to college with a promising career in the NFL. Can you believe that, Lance? I really wanted to tear into Saminta for calling Miranda careless. It's obvious that Titus didn't mind screwing without a condom. Wasn't *he* careless as well?"

Lance knew Arykah held a special place in her heart for Miranda. She defended the girl at all costs. "Well, I'm glad you didn't get into an argument with her. You can't make folks do right, Cheeks. If the Williams's don't wanna know their grandson, and if they want to keep Titus away from his son, there's nothing we can do about it. But it's terrible. With no support from Titus or his parents, Gladys and Miranda will need all the help they can get. It's a good thing they have us, right?"

"Mm-hmm," Arykah said again. "We appreciate those that wish Miranda well and those that don't can go to hell."

Lance frowned and looked at her. *"Cheeks,"* he shrieked. "Really? Was that necessary?"

"I'm just saying. Church folks make me sick. My operative words were 'church folks,' not 'Christians.' Although some of them get on my nerve too."

Ten

Saturday morning was chaotic in the Howell home.

Arykah lay on her stomach. She moaned and complained. "You act like this is the first time you've done this. What's wrong with you?"

Lance straddled Arykah on the bed. He was sweating. "Pull your meat in, Cheeks."

Arykah inhaled and held her breath as Lance tried to stuff her back fat in the Spanx. He pulled the nylon material up as far as it would go, just above Arykah's waistline. "It ain't going no higher, Cheeks."

"The heck it ain't," she fussed. "I gotta get into that dress, Lance. Stop being weak and pull this thing up higher. We go through this all the time." Arykah inhaled and held on for dear life.

Lance pulled and tucked, then tucked and pulled. Finally the Spanx was pulled all the way up until it reached beneath Arykah's breasts. Lance fell over onto the bed panting for air. "That was a workout."

Arykah rolled over onto her back and sat up. "Why do you gotta put on a show?"

Lance's eyebrows rose. "Do you see the sweat on my forehead? I can't fake the sweat, Cheeks."

"Whatever," Arykah said. She stood and went toward her closet. "Now you gotta zip me into this dress." She returned with an ivory-colored knee-length cocktail dress. Arykah slipped into the dress, and Lance was able to zip it with no problem. "My stilettos have ankle straps,

Lance. I need you to buckle them for me." Lance exhaled. "Arykah, I can't be late. I told you we tee off at nine."

"Well, you know I can't bend over in this Spanx."

Lance thought of an easy solution. "Then take off the Spanx."

"Then I wouldn't fit into this dress."

"Well, put on another dress," he fussed.

"All of my dresses require Spanx."

"How are you gonna go to the bathroom?"

"Women don't eat or drink when we have to wear Spanx. We know what to do. *What's the problem?*" she yelled. Lance was being inconsiderate, and it irritated her.

"The problem is that I still have to pick up Deacon Marshall and get to the golf course before nine, and you got me stuck here with you. I gotta get dressed myself."

Arykah didn't care what Lance had to do or who he had to pick up. He could complain and fuss all he wanted. He was her husband, and Arykah needed Lance to help her look her best. She slipped on her ivory-colored six-inch platform stilettos. "Just buckle my straps, please."

Lance knelt before Arykah and honored her request. She knew he was fit to be tied with her.

"You know I love you, right?"

Lance stood, exhaled, and looked at her. "You look beautiful."

"Then why all the fussin' and moanin'?"

"Because, you're so extra, Cheeks. You're not a normal chick, and it drives me nuts."

Arykah kissed his lips. "You wouldn't have it any other way."

She was right, but he wasn't going to admit it.

"Give Natasha my love and let her know that her pastor is very proud of her."

Arykah put the envelope she prepared for Natasha in her purse. "Yes, I will. And don't forget, after Natasha's graduation, I'm going straight to Gladys's."

"Okay," Lance said. "Is Diva Chanel ready?"

As soon as Lance said her name, Diva Chanel came to the doorway of their bedroom dressed in an ivory lace dress with two ivory satin bows on the top of her head.

"I need one more favor," Arykah said to Lance. "Scoop her up and put her in my bag."

"Are you kiddin' me?" he asked.

"Just do it."

Three hours later, Arykah sat with Natasha's parents, Regina and Keith Browning, and her younger brother, Keith Jr. They all cheered for Natasha. When the principal called her name, Arykah stood and screamed, *"Yay, Natasha. Woo-hoo!"*

She completely ignored the request that was made to friends and family of the graduates. The program director had pleaded with everyone to wait until after every graduate's name was called before any cheering took place. But Arykah, being Arykah, was one to never follow any rules. *"Yeah, Natasha!"* she screamed as Natasha walked across the stage and received her high school diploma. When Natasha moved her tassel from the left to the right, Arykah went crazy. *"Go, Natasha. You did it!"*

After the graduates tossed their caps in the air, the entire audience cheered. When Natasha had finally made her way through the crowd to her family and Arykah, she ran straight to her mother's arms.

"I did it, Ma. I did it."

Regina was overly excited. "Yes, you did."

"Congratulations, daughter," Keith said to Natasha. He gave her the dozen roses he held in his hand. "Daddy is very proud of you."

"Thanks, Daddy," Natasha said.

Keith Jr. stepped to Natasha and wrapped his arms around his big sister's waist. "I guess you'll be going to college, huh?"

Natasha chuckled. "Yep, but you still can't have my room."

"Aw, man," Keith Jr. whined.

Natasha saw Arykah standing next to her parents. "I'm so glad you came, Lady Arykah, and you brought Diva Chanel." Natasha took the Yorkie from Arykah's arms and cooed her nose. "Oh, her dress is so pretty."

"I told you I'd be here with bells on."

"Yeah, I heard you screaming for me."

"Bishop Lance sends his love. He wanted me to be sure to tell you that he is super proud of you." Arykah reached in her purse and pulled out the envelope she had for Natasha. "This is a token of my and the Bishop's love."

Natasha was happy to receive anything from Arykah. She knew her first lady gave great gifts. Natasha gave Diva Chanel back to Arykah and tore open the envelope.

"You don't have to open it now," Arykah said.

Natasha ignored her and pulled out a card and read it out loud. "It's Your Graduation Day." She opened the card and saw cash. "Ooh," Natasha cheered. She took the money out of the card and read the words inside. *"The easy part is behind you, now the hard time begins. But as long as you stay with God, you'll forever win."*

"That's nice," Regina said.

Natasha counted five one hundred dollar bills and became excited. She wrapped her arms around Arykah. "Oh, thank you, Lady Arykah. I thank you and Bishop Lance so much."

"You know where half of that is going, right?" Keith Sr. asked his daughter.

She frowned and sighed. "Yeah, I know. I gotta put half in my savings account for college."

"Don't be so sad about that," Arykah said to her. "Do you know how many kids can't afford college? Learn to count your blessings and appreciate them."

"That was so nice of you and Bishop Lance," Regina said to Arykah. "And we're so sorry that we didn't have a ticket for him to be here, but we left it up to Natasha to choose which of the two of you she wanted here more."

"She made the right choice," Arykah said smiling. "But the bishop understands."

"I'll give him a great big hug at church tomorrow," Natasha said.

"We're gonna take Natasha out for lunch," Keith Sr. said to Arykah. "Come with us."

Arykah looked at her wristwatch. "I'd love to, but it's Miranda's baby shower this afternoon, and I need to get over to Sister Gladys's house right away."

"Ooh, can I go with you, Lady Arykah?" Natasha asked excitedly.

"We made reservations at your favorite restaurant," Regina said to Natasha.

"But I didn't know Miranda's baby shower was today. Can I go with Lady Arykah? Pleeease?"

Arykah was uncomfortable. She knew Natasha's parents really wanted to celebrate their daughter's graduation. "Why don't you go ahead with your folks? Miranda's shower was planned at the last minute. I'm sure she'll understand."

"No," Natasha whined. "I gotta be there." She looked at her parents. "Please can I go?"

Regina and Keith knew that Miranda and Natasha were close friends. The girls did everything together. Natasha was one of the few girls at church that hadn't shied away from Miranda when her pregnancy was discovered.

"Well, okay," Regina said. "If you really wanna go—"

"Yes," Miranda cut her mother's words off. "I really, really, *really* wanna go."

"We can celebrate your graduation after church tomorrow," her father said.

Natasha hugged him. "Thanks, Daddy."

"We better get going," Arykah said to Natasha.

"Thanks again for coming, Lady Arykah."

Arykah hugged Regina. "It was my pleasure. And I'll be sure to bring Natasha home after the shower."

When Arykah and Natasha arrived at Gladys's apartment a half hour later, the entire team was already there.

"Natasha!" Miranda screamed when she saw her friend walk through the front door. She rushed to Natasha. "You came." Miranda saw that Natasha wore her blue graduation gown. "Congratulations."

Natasha hugged Miranda. "I just found out about your shower. I had to come."

"Hey, li'l momma," Arykah greeted when she closed the door behind her. She set Diva Chanel down and watched her roam through the living room, exploring every corner.

"Hey, Lady A," Miranda responded. "Thanks for everything."

Arykah looked around the living room and saw a light blue car seat, a light blue swing, an oak wood crib with light blue bedding with brown teddy bears. "You like what you got?"

"Yes. It's everything I picked out at Babies 'R' Us." Miranda brought Arykah and Natasha into the dining room where Team Arykah was gathered.

"All right, First Lady," Gladys greeted Arykah. "You're looking as good as you wanna look."

"What's going on, Team?"

"Loving that dress, Lady A," Chelsea said.

"And the stilettos," Monique added.

"Why, thank ya kindly," Arykah said in her Southern belle voice. "I brought Natasha with me."

The team saw Natasha in her graduation gown.

"Congratulations, Natasha," they all yelled.

Natasha mimicked Arykah and said, "Why, thank ya kindly."

Everyone chuckled.

"So, how was your graduation?" Darlita asked her.

Natasha looked at her. "It was awesome. Mom and Dad wanted to take me out to lunch to celebrate, but when Lady Arykah said she was coming here for Miranda's shower, I wanted to come too."

"Now *that's* a real friend," Monique said.

Diva Chanel made her way into the dining room and everyone made a fuss over her ivory lace dress and satin hair bows.

"So, was everything delivered, Gladys?" Arykah asked.

"Lady A," Gladys started, "I just don't know what to say about you. Yes, everything was delivered. Did you see my living room?"

"Monique, Chelsea, Darlita, and Myrtle brought gifts for the baby too," Miranda said.

"Speaking of Mother Myrtle," Monique said, "she just rolled up in a limo."

"Yeah," Gladys said. "I was looking out of the front window for Darlita and saw this long stretch limousine pull up right in front of my building. I didn't know who was gonna get out. When the driver opened the back door and I saw Mother Myrtle, my mouth hit the floor."

"Mother Myrtle, you're making Cliff work on a Saturday?" Arykah asked.

Myrtle shrugged her shoulders. "He told me to call him whenever I needed him."

"Never in my life have I seen a church's secretary get chauffeured to the church," Chelsea said.

"Well, there's a first time for everything now, ain't it?" Myrtle asked her. "This morning, Cliff drove me to the bank, then to the grocery store."

"Hold on now, Mother Myrtle," Arykah said. "Lance offered to pay for your transportation to the church, but I don't know about—"

"I've already talked to the bishop," Myrtle snapped. "And he ain't got a problem with it. And what's between me and my bishop is between me and my bishop."

That shut the conversation down.

"Well, all right then," Arykah surrendered. "I ain't got nothin' else to say about it." She sat down at the dining-room table. "I'm hungry."

"The pizza will be here soon," Gladys said. "Let's all go into the living room and see all the baby things."

There was hardly any room for the ladies to sit. The living room was completely filled with everything a newborn would ever need.

"Lady Arykah, look at what Darlita bought me," Miranda said pointing to baby diapers stacked and shaped into a three-tier cake.

"Oh, wow, look at that," Arykah said admiring it.

"And Mother Myrtle brought me this gift basket." Miranda held up a large brown basket filled with baby wash, washcloths, baby powder, Q-Tips, baby ointment, baby Orajel, and a blue syringe used to remove mucous from a baby's nose. The entire basket was wrapped in light blue cellophane.

"That's beautiful," Arykah said.

Miranda pointed to the chair. "And Chelsea brought all of those small light blue plastic hangers and the little blue baby shoes. Monique and Adonis bought all of those baby clothes on the couch."

Arykah saw so many onesies and bibs and socks and blue pajamas and receiving blankets.

"And, Lady A," Miranda started with tears in her eyes, "I wanna thank you for the crib, high chair, the car seat, and the changing table, and the diaper genie, and the bassinette, and the playpen, and all of the bottles."

"You're very welcome," Arykah said.

"And I want you to know that I put the whole thousand dollars you gave me in the bank."

Everybody's eyebrows rose up as if on cue.

"I didn't spend any of it on myself. I'm going to use it all for the baby."

Arykah felt uncomfortable. She told Gladys that she didn't want the money she'd given Miranda to be made known.

Gladys looked at Arykah with guilty, bulging eyes. She forgot to tell Miranda to keep Arykah's monetary gift a secret.

"That was from me and the bishop," Arykah said. "Did the cake come?"

"Oh, yes," Miranda said excitedly. "It's in the kitchen. I love it. It's light blue and has monkeys all over it just like the bedding in the crib."

The doorbell rang. "That's the pizza," Gladys said. When she opened the door she was shocked to see Lance and Deacon Bronson Marshall. "Look who's here."

"Bishop," Natasha and Miranda shouted and ran to the front door. They both hugged Lance.

Lance hugged Natasha and congratulated her on her graduation. "I'm proud of you." He turned to Miranda and saw her huge belly. "Ooh wee. You sure you ain't got two babies in there?"

"Nope, just one," Miranda responded. If Lance was upset with her, he didn't show it, and Miranda was glad about that.

"Come on in, Deacon," Gladys said. "I'm surprised to see you here."

Deacon Marshall followed Lance inside. "I'm here for the pizza the bishop say y'all is havin'."

Lance and Deacon Marshall walked farther into the living room.

"Hey, Bishop. Hey, Deacon," the ladies greeted.

"Are we too late for the cake?" Lance asked.

"We haven't cut the cake yet, Bishop," Miranda said. "We're waiting for the pizza."

"All right now," Chelsea said when she noticed Deacon Marshall's attire. "Look at how fly Deacon Marshall is."

Myrtle's eyes were drawn to his khaki-colored linen pants. Deacon Marshall wore a white short sleeved cotton shirt with a khaki-colored collar. He had a white Kangol cap on his head. It was golf attire, but Myrtle thought he looked good. He looked younger. She was impressed.

"I ain't recognize you, Deacon," Arykah teased. "You look nice." She looked at Myrtle and smiled.

Myrtle rolled her eyes at Arykah.

The doorbell rang again. "Now *that* better be the pizza," Gladys said. She opened the front door and accepted four pizza boxes from the deliveryman. Gladys gave the boxes to Lance.

"Bishop, will you carry these into the dining room?"

"Of course," Lance said. He took the pizza boxes from her and followed her into the dining room, then set them on the table. Once everyone was assembled around the table, Lance blessed the pizza.

Gladys brought paper plates, napkins, and paper cups from the kitchen. Natasha and Miranda placed two-liter bottles of Pepsi, Hawaiian Punch, and 7-UP on the table. Gladys's dinette only seated four people so she, along with Darlita, Chelsea, and Monique, ate their pizza at the kitchen table. Miranda and Natasha took their pizza and beverages into the living room.

"You and Deacon Marshall finished golf pretty early today," Arykah said to Lance. "Normally, you don't come off the greens until after sunset."

Lance bit into a slice of pepperoni pizza. "It's really hot outside today, Cheeks."

"Darn near a hunnid," Deacon Marshall added. "It's all sun out theya. Ain't safe fa nobaddy."

"It's a wonder you ain't have a heat stroke," Myrtle said to Deacon Marshall.

"Dat's what I know," he chuckled. "Ole man like me ain't got no bidness in nat kinda heat."

Myrtle saw Deacon Marshall's cup of Hawaiian Punch was almost empty. "You want me to pour you some more punch?"

Lance, Arykah, and even Deacon Marshall shot their heads in Myrtle's direction.

"Sho, sho," he said.

Myrtle stood and refilled his cup. "You want more pizza?"

Arykah kicked Lance beneath the table. When he looked at her she motioned for him to follow her. They both stood and took their plates and drinks into the living room.

"All of this is for just one baby?" Lance asked when he and Arykah entered the living room. He allowed Arykah to sit on the only empty chair. He sat on the floor next to her legs.

"Yep," Natasha said. "That boy ain't gonna need nothing."

Lance looked at the crib, bassinette, swing, and high chair. He saw the gift basket, the clothes, and diaper cake. "Do you have everything you need?" he asked Miranda.

She looked all around the living room at her gifts, rubbed her swollen belly, smiled, and nodded her head. "Mmm-hmm. I think so."

"You ready? Your life will forever change when the baby is born," he said. "You know that?"

Miranda nodded her head again. "Yep. I can't change nothin' now. He'll be here in less than two weeks."

"Why aren't the Williams's here?"

Lance already knew the answer to his own question. The night before Arykah had shared with him the conversation she had with Saminta. Lance wanted to see how Miranda felt about her child's father being absent from her life.

Miranda shrugged her shoulders. "I mean, I guess they don't wanna be here. Titus don't even look at me when we're at church. Ever since I told him that I was pregnant, his parents won't let him come anywhere near me. I left him so many messages on his cell, but he won't call me back. My mom says she tried to reach out to Sister Saminta and Brother Doug, but they won't talk to her."

The more Miranda talked, the more irritated with the Williamses Arykah became.

"And how does that make you feel?" Lance asked her.

"I mean, it's cool, Bishop. I can't make Titus be here. I can't make him talk to me, I can't make him call me, and I can't make him be a father. It is what it is."

It broke Lance's heart to hear Miranda explain why her son won't have a father in his life. It was at that moment that Lance decided that he'd do all that he could to make sure that Miranda's baby boy would be loved and cared for. "I'm gonna give you my personal number. If you need anything—anything at all—call me. You understand?"

"Yes. Thank you, Bishop." Miranda came and sat next to Lance on the floor. She reached over and hugged him tight.

Lanced pulled away from Miranda and looked her in the eyes. "I mean it. Don't let me find out that you or the baby were in need of something and you didn't call me. You understand?"

"I understand," she said.

Arykah's eyebrows shot up in the air. Only the deacons, Minister Weeks, Myrtle, Brian the church's custodian, and herself, had Lance's cellular number. It touched Arykah deeply that Lance was falling in love with Miranda and her baby, just as she had fallen in love with them.

"Who wants cake and frappé?" Gladys yelled from the kitchen.

"I do," Natasha yelled back. She rushed from the living room.

Lance stood from the floor and saw Miranda struggling to get up. She turned on her right hip, then turned on her left hip, but couldn't gain the leverage she needed to stand.

Lance stood in front of her. "Give me your hands."

She stretched out her arms toward him. Lance gripped Miranda's wrists and gently pulled her up from the floor.

In the kitchen Gladys cut the cake and served frappé to everyone. Arykah noticed that Myrtle and Deacon Marshall were eating their dessert at the dining-room table. She also noticed that they shared a slice of cake and one cup of frappé. "Hey, now . . ." Arykah said to herself.

Later that night, Lance wrapped his arm around Arykah's waist as they lay in a spoon position. She was drifting off to sleep when he called her name.

"Cheeks, you asleep?"

"Almost."

"Did you notice how small Gladys's apartment was?"

"Mmm-hmm," she moaned with her eyes closed.

"The living room is small, the dining room is smaller, and the kitchen has standing room only."

"It's a galley kitchen, Babe."

"I can only imagine how tiny the two bedrooms are."

Arykah opened her eyes and turned to face him. "That's why the baby's crib was set up in the living room. Miranda's bedroom is small with a full-size bed. There's no space in there for the crib. Gladys's queen-sized bed takes up all of the space in her room so the crib can't fit in there either."

Lance frowned. "So, the baby will have to sleep in the living room?"

"Not right now. For the first few months, he'll sleep in a bassinette next to Miranda's bed. But eventually, I guess he will have to be in the living room."

That didn't sit well with Lance. "That's crazy, Cheeks."

"I know. Gladys is working two full-time jobs. She works afternoon and nights."

"What?"

"Yeah, she chose those shifts so that she could be home during the day for when school starts in the fall. Gladys has to be home with the baby when Miranda goes to school."

"So, Miranda and the baby will be left alone overnight?"

"That's the way it has to be for now, Lance. Gladys has no family. She's doing the best she can."

Lance lay silently for a few minutes. "I think we should help Gladys."

"We *do* help, more than you know. I just gave Miranda one thousand dollars to use toward the baby's needs. I had to beg Gladys to allow Miranda to accept it. And even though Miranda needed everything she received at her shower today, I could tell that Gladys felt some type of way about me purchasing most of it all. Whenever I try to help Gladys, she shies away from me. I think she feels that she and Miranda are a burden."

"That's ridiculous."

"I know. I feel the same way you do."

Lance exhaled and said, "I am not at all comfortable with the baby's crib being stuck in the living room, so close to the front door."

"And it doesn't sit well with me that Miranda will eventually be left alone, overnight, while Gladys works. I mean, how can she be alert and productive at school if she's up all night with a fussy baby? And what if he has colic at three in the morning? A sixteen-year-old girl won't know what to do."

"There are five bedrooms in this house. We share a bedroom and Diva Chanel has a bedroom. The other three bedrooms are furnished, but no one sleeps in them."

Arykah clapped her hands twice, and their bedroom lit up. She sat up on the bed and looked at Lance. "Uh-uh. No way." She knew where he was going.

Lance looked at her. "Why?"

"I wanna stay married—That's why. I'm not sharing my home with another woman. It won't work."

"Cheeks, this house is massive; we'll never see them. Our master is on the first level. The guest bedrooms are on the second level."

Arykah vigourously shook her head from side to side. "I don't care if we had *ten* levels. Ain't no other woman coming up in here. Now if you're *that* worried about Gladys, Miranda, and the baby, then maybe we can consider buying them a condo or a single-family home."

"You would agree to do that?"

"Of course. And if Gladys doesn't have to worry about a mortgage payment, she won't need to work a second job."

Lance nodded his head. "Then she can be home at night."

"But you know Gladys is proud, Lance. If she has a hard time accepting baby donations and money, what makes you think she'll accept a house?"

He shrugged his shoulders. "I don't know, but we gotta do something quick. The baby is coming real soon. We can't let Miranda and the baby be alone in that apartment overnight."

"When I get to the office on Monday morning, I'll look for a condo near the South Shore area near Miranda's high school and Gladys's primary job."

"That's great, Cheeks. Buying Gladys a home is easy. Now convincing her to move in it will be difficult."

"We'll leave it in God's hand," Arykah said. "He'll work it all out."

Eleven

Arykah stepped from her closet dressed in a tangerine-colored sheath made of Georgette material. It stopped just above her knee. It was the first outfit she modeled for Lance. Her platform gladiator stilettos were made of metallic gold. Rhinestones and crystals lined the straps of the heels, and they circled Arykah's thick calves all the way up to her knees.

She was watching an episode of *The Real Housewives of Atlanta* when she saw a scene where Porsha Stewart shopped in a shoe store in Atlanta. When she saw the salesclerk slip Porsha's feet into a pair of stilettos and wrap metallic gold and crystals around her calves, Arykah instantly came close to an orgasm. Her blood pressure escalated. Her temperature rose. Her legs shook. Her body convulsed, and her heartbeat raced. The only other times Arykah's body exploded like that was when Lance touched her the right way.

"Ohhh, Gawwwd," Arykah practically sang. Drool leaked from the side of her mouth as she watched Porsha strut in the gladiator stilettos. Never in her life had Arykah seen a stiletto as elegant as the ones Porsha modeled on television.

When Arykah heard the salesclerk tell Porsha how much the gladiator metallic stilettos cost, she immediately logged on to her laptop and searched the Internet for the website of the shoe store Porsha Stewart was in. She found what she was looking for, then searched for the stiletto. Arykah found them and ordered them in a size eight. She authorized sixty dollars for express delivery through UPS next-day air. Arykah only had to wait twenty-four hours for the seventy-five hundred-dollar heels to arrive at her front door. She never allowed a price tag to prevent her from having exactly what she wanted. It was the luxury Arykah enjoyed from selling million-dollar homes.

"Oh oh oh," Lance said. He was lying on the bed in his usual position, with his arms stretched behind his head. He had been waiting for Arykah to start her weekly Sunday morning fashion show. He placed his right hand on his chest. "Be still, my heart."

Arykah turned from Lance and strutted to their bedroom door so that he could get a full view of her entire outfit.

He sat up on the bed. "Beautiful," he said. "Now take it off."

"What?"

"Take off the dress but leave the heels on and come to bed."

Arykah chuckled. Lance had that look in his eye. "What?" she asked him again.

He stood from the bed, walked over to Arykah, raised the dress over her head, and let it drop to the floor. She stood naked with just the gladiator platform stilettos on.

"Get in the bed," he ordered.

Arykah obeyed her husband and walked past him to their California king-sized bed. When Lance saw Arykah's backside jiggle as she moved, her nickname escaped from his lips. "Cheeks," he moaned.

Arykah lay down. Lance came to the foot of the bed and lifted her left leg high in the air. He ran his tongue from the tip of the stiletto heel, to the metallic and diamond strap, all the way up to Arykah's knee, where the strap ended. Lance had licked the entire length of the stiletto.

Arykah looked down at her husband's face. The passion in his eyes heated her inner core. She was ready to explode. "Why did you stop the tongue action? Come on up a little higher," she said seductively.

He was breathing heavy. "You ready?"

The butterflies in her stomach were fluttering. "Let's go."

The next move Lance made caused Arykah's back to arch. Her eyes rolled to the back of her head. "Oh, Bishop," she moaned.

Arykah rushed into her office, at the church, at ten fifteen a.m. She saw Team Arykah sitting around her desk. "I'm so sorry that I'm late."

"Oooooooh," Chelsea shrieked when she saw Arykah's gladiator metallic gold and diamond platform stilettos. "You are doing the most, Lady Arykah."

"Too freakin' fierce," Monique added. She hoped and prayed that Arykah bought her a pair.

"Okaaaay," Darlita said. "You're about to get jacked for real. Those are *too* sharp."

Arykah chuckled and sat down behind her desk with Diva Chanel in the crease of her arm.

"Girl, we didn't think you and the bishop were gonna make it on time," Monique said.

"Service starts in fifteen minutes," Myrtle fussed. "Minister Weeks is going crazy."

"Why isn't your cell phone on?" Chelsea asked Arykah. "We were all calling you."

"Minister Weeks said that all of his calls had gone straight to the bishop's voice mail," Darlita added.

Arykah looked at Gladys. "Your turn."

Gladys chuckled. "I think they pretty much covered it all."

Arykah set Diva Chanel down on the floor and looked at her team. "I already apologized for being late. I know we meet in here every Sunday for girl chat, but I got distracted this morning."

"Distracted by what?" Myrtle asked her.

Arykah looked at Myrtle. "My husband," she answered matter-of-factly.

Gladys and Chelsea gasped.

"Well, all right, now," Darlita said smiling.

Monique eyed Arykah shamefully. "*Really*, First Lady? On a *Sunday* morning?"

"*Especially* on a Sunday morning," she replied rotating her neck.

Myrtle shook her head from side to side. "Ump ump ump," she mumbled. "You just fast."

Gladys laughed. "I know what that means, Mother Myrtle. When I was growing up, girls were called 'fast' when they were chasing boys."

"Just fast," Myrtle said eyeing Arykah.

"First of all," Arykah started, "I don't do no chasing." She looked at Myrtle specifically and said, "I gets chased." She raised her eyebrows. "Okay?"

"Keep it up, hear?" Myrtle warned Arykah. "I still got that switch."

Lance knocked on Arykah's door, then opened it and poked his head inside. "Morning," he greeted the team.

All the ladies gave Lance a sheepish grin. No one responded to him verbally.

"It's time to head down to the sanctuary," he said to Arykah.

She stood. "Come on, Diva Chanel."

Diva Chanel came to Arykah's feet. Arykah scooped her up and put her in the tangerine leather bucket-shaped Dooney & Bourke bag she carried. "Y'all coming?" Arykah asked her team when she noticed that none of them were preparing to go down to the sanctuary.

"Yeah, we'll be down soon," Monique answered. "We're gonna stay behind and talk about you."

Praise and worship was in full effect, and the congregation was on their feet when Lance and Arykah appeared at the doors to the sanctuary.

"Please receive Bishop Lance and Lady Arykah Howell," the praise and worship leader announced.

With his hand pressed against the small of Arykah's back, Lance escorted her to the front pew. Literally, every eye, belonging to every female, was drawn to Arykah's feet and legs as she walked down the center aisle.

"Look at those heels . . . Wow . . . Beautiful shoes . . . You see her feet?"

When they arrived at the front pew, Lance kissed Arykah's left cheek, as he did every Sunday morning before entering the pulpit. Arykah set her bag on the pew, pulled Diva Chanel out, and held her in the crease of her arm. Diva Chanel's satin orange dress and metallic hair bows matched Arykah's outfit perfectly.

The beat of the drums caused Arykah's eyes to look at the musicians. She saw Stephanie's husband, Kenneth, banging wooden sticks on the drums. Arykah looked at the adult choir singing and saw Stacy in the alto section with her eyes closed and hands lifted in the air. *Are they serious?*

It disgusted Arykah that the two of them could come to church and get in God's face like they weren't living foul. Arykah looked around the sanctuary for Stephanie and saw her standing three pews behind the deacons. Though Stephanie participated in praise and worship, Arykah saw the pain and hurt on her face. She knew it pained Stephanie to have to stare in the faces of her sister and husband, knowing that they were sleeping together.

Arykah's eyes were drawn to Saminta Williams who stood one row behind Stephanie. She was scowling at Arykah. She felt the heat of Saminta's eyes burning on her skin.

Myrtle, Darlita, Monique, Gladys, and Chelsea appeared and sat next to Arykah.

Praise and worship ended, and Lance took to the podium. "You may be seated," he said to the congregation.

When she sat down on the pew, Arykah looked at Saminta again. Arykah wasn't exaggerating about the look this woman was giving her. Saminta looked at her with anger in her eyes. Arykah leaned into Myrtle who sat next to her. "Look three rows behind the deacons toward the middle and tell me if Saminta Williams is staring at me."

Myrtle looked for Saminta and found her. She leaned into Arykah. "Yep. She doesn't look happy. What's her problem?"

Arykah shrugged her shoulders. "Beats me." She set Diva Chanel on the pew between herself and Myrtle and listened to what Lance was saying.

"Church," he addressed, "I don't feel a hoop or a holla in my spirit this morning. Today, I'm gonna talk about traditions."

Arykah sat straight up. Her back came away from the pew.

"Here we go," Myrtle said remembering Arykah's and Lance's conversation that she overheard on Friday.

"All right, Bishop," a few members said.

"Come on and talk about it," others encouraged him.

"The *Merriam-Webster Dictionary*," Lance started, then paused, "defines the word *tradition* as 'a way of thinking, behaving, or doing something that has been used by the people in a particular group, family, society, etc., for a long time.'"

"Teach this morning, Bishop," Myrtle said out loud.

Lance looked down and read his notes, then looked out at the people again. "And it further describes the word *tradition* as 'an inherited, established, or customary pattern of thought, action, or behavior as a religious practice or a social custom. The handing down of information by word of mouth or by example from one generation to another without written instruction.'"

"All right, all right," the people said.

"Tradition," Lance said. "Tradition, tradition. Why do we follow tradition? Who created them and why?"

"That's what *I* wanna know," Arykah mumbled.

"It's a tradition in this church that if a man or woman has been divorced, they can't be remarried in the sanctuary. It's a tradition in this church that an unwed pregnant female must come before the church, confess her sin, and ask for forgiveness. And if, by chance, she's active in the church, she must be pulled, or as Mother Myrtle says, 'sat down.'"

The people mumbled. "Come on, Bishop. You're going somewhere. Teach."

"It's a tradition in this church that babies of unwed parents can't be baptized, christened, or dedicated to God in the sanctuary."

"Welllll," someone sang.

Lance looked at the audience. "I recently had a discussion with my wife about traditions. She and I differ in our opinions on traditions. I was born and raised in the Church of God in Christ where traditions rule the church. Lady Arykah was brought up in the Baptist faith where traditions are almost unheard of."

"Come on, Bishop," Arykah said.

"In speaking with my wife about traditions, she challenged me to research some of them and find out who started them, and *why* they were started. One of the traditions Lady Arykah and I discussed was babies being dedicated in the sanctuary. I can tell it struck a nerve with my wife because her bottom lip was trembling. Her lips tremble when I leave dirty dishes in the sink instead of loading them into the dishwasher."

The congregation laughed, and so did Arykah.

"Her lips tremble," Lance continued, "when I'm the last to rise and don't make the bed."

More laughter came from the people.

"And her lips *really* trembled when she came home and found that I had eaten the last slice of the lemon pound cake that she was saving for the Lifetime movie."

Arykah laughed out loud. "You're right about that."

"So when I saw her lips tremble when we were discussing traditions, I knew I needed to find out why Freedom Temple follows them. And in doing so, I didn't come across one reason why babies from unwed parents can't be dedicated in the sanctuary."

"Preach, Bishop," someone said.

"It took my beautiful, lip-trembling wife to show me that *alllll* babies are pure, no matter how they were conceived."

"Come on now," Gladys yelled out.

"Who started that tradition?" Lance asked the people. "Was it God?"

The congregation mumbled.

"Was it Moses?" Lance asked. "Hmm?"

Darlita rocked back and forth. "Say that, say that."

"It's not written in Freedom Temple's by-laws. It's not there," Lance said. "I checked. Who says that divorcees can't remarry at this altar? Who says that women must humiliate themselves and confess their unwed pregnancies to the church?" Lance shrugged his shoulders. "Who?"

He looked at his flock. "Was it you, Deacon Marshall?"

Deacon Marshall shook his head from side to side. "Nah, sa. It wadden me."

Lance looked at the musicians. "Was it you, Brother Adonis, who said that folks who sin can't work in the church?"

"No, sir," Adonis answered.

"Can anybody tell me why we follow such foolishness?"

Half of the congregation stood to their feet. "You better preach."

"Had I followed tradition . . ." Lance started. He looked at Arykah. "I would've missed out on God's greatest blessing that He had for me."

Darlita stood from the pew and shrieked. *"Preeeaach."*

"Was it you, Mother Myrtle, that said folks couldn't marry outside the C.O.G.I.C.?"

Myrtle waved her hand at Lance. "Boy, gon somewhere. You know I ain't said no mess like that."

Lance laughed, and so did everyone else within earshot of Myrtle.

Arykah placed Diva Chanel in the crease of her arm and stood.

Lance pulled the microphone from its holder and walked to the edge of the pulpit. "As pastor of this church, I declare that every baby will be dedicated in the sanctuary."

"Come on, Bishop . . . Say that," the people responded.

"This sanctuary welcomes all couples who want to be married. This is a new day at Freedom Temple, and I know I got some old schoolers in here that don't agree with me. And I'm sure I'll hear from you, but this is the decision that I've made. You can either be with me or against me. As of today, I declare that Freedom Temple Church of God in Christ has been set free from bondage, we are free from restrictions. The chains are broken. We are no longer bound by tradition."

The people were on their feet. "All right, all right. Amen, Bishop."

"It's time that we are about the work of the Lord," Lance said. "Some of you have been here a long time. Most of you are set in your ways. But I stand before you, as the pastor of this church, as your leader, and as your head shepherd, and say that you can either be with me or go against me. If you choose to go against me, save yourselves the energy and find another church."

The church roared.

"Ha!" Gladys hollered out.

"That's it? That's all, Bishop?" Monique yelled out at Lance.

Chelsea looked at Darlita. "Girl, did he just *Pow, Bang, Boom* us?"

Darlita laughed out loud. "Yes, he did. In our faces."

Lance looked at Team Arykah. "Sister Monique, Sister Gladys, Sister Chelsea, and Sister Darlita, y'all bring my wife to me."

Arykah's heart started to race. She didn't know what Lance was getting ready to do. She put Diva Chanel on Myrtle's lap.

Monique and Chelsea grabbed Arykah's left and right hand and guided her to the pulpit. Gladys and Darlita walked behind them.

Lance called Minister Carlton Weeks to him and whispered words in his ear. Carlton nodded his head and retrieved the bottle of blessed oil from beneath the podium.

Lance reached for Arykah's hand. "Come close to me, Babe."

With her team standing closely behind her, Arykah met Lance at the podium.

He stared into her eyes. "Almost six months ago you came into this church like a raging bull. Folks didn't know what to think as they watched you turn this place upside down. You certainly have shaken things up. What I love about you, Arykah, is your passion to help others."

"Amen," Gladys, Chelsea, and Darlita responded.

"You are just what Freedom Temple needs. A first lady who cares and desires to see others achieve. A first lady who is trustworthy. A first lady that fights for the souls of God's kingdom."

Tears flooded Arykah's eyes.

"A first lady that truly has her husband's back. And I praise God for you. I honestly believe that He couldn't have chosen a better woman for me. You are good to me, and you are good for me."

The tears dripped from her eyes.

"Your steps, Lady Arykah, have been ordered. Thank you for being obedient and walking down the path that God has placed you on because it led you to me and to Freedom Temple."

Sniff, sniff. "Thank you, Jesus," Arykah said. *Sniff, sniff.*

Lance laid the microphone on the podium, then held out his palm. Minister Weeks poured the blessed oil in his hand. He pressed his palm against Arykah's forehead and spoke in an unknown tongue. Arykah closed her eyes and raised her hands toward heaven and surrendered herself to God. In just moments her knees weakened and she fell back into Team Arykah's arms. A female usher quickly came and threw what looked like a bedsheet over Arykah's legs when the team laid her on the floor of the pulpit.

Myrtle sat on the front row crying at what was taking place.

Lance looked at Arykah's team standing next to one another. He stepped to Monique and blew in her face. Monique fell into Darlita, who fell into Chelsea, who then fell into Gladys. The ladies hit the floor in a domino effect.

The congregation was on their feet shouting out praises.

Lance stepped over the fallen ladies and exited the pulpit. He went and stood in front of Myrtle. She looked up at him with tears in her eyes. He pressed his hand against Myrtle's forehead and spoke in an unknown tongue. Myrtle raised her hands and received the Holy Spirit. She shouted out praises. Diva Chanel didn't move from Myrtle's lap.

Lance went back to the podium and picked up the microphone. "The doors of the church are open."

After the benediction, Lance and Arykah stood at the entrance of the sanctuary and shook the members' hands as they left the church. Some members told Lance that they agreed with the decision he made to do away with traditions. Others hugged Arykah and said that she was a positive influence on the church and they were glad she was there. Many women just stood in line waiting to compliment Arykah on her metallic gladiator stilettos.

After Lance and Arykah had shaken the last hand, they started to ascend the stairs. Team Arykah and Diva Chanel were in Arykah's office waiting on her.

"I need a word with you, Lady Arykah."

The strong voice startled Arykah. She and Lance turned around and saw Saminta Williams standing at the bottom of the steps. She had come out of nowhere. Saminta's eyes were still as angry as they were when Arykah saw them during praise and worship.

Arykah tapped Lance's shoulder. "You go ahead, Babe."

Lance kissed Arykah's cheek, then left the ladies alone.

Arykah descended the three steps she had climbed and stood before Saminta. She didn't appreciate Saminta's tone of voice. "You *need* a word with me? How about,

'*Lady Arykah, may I please have a word with you*'? *That* sounds much better."

Saminta gave off a sarcastic chuckle. "Really?"

Arykah's eyebrows rose and her neck danced. *"Really."* She didn't know what Saminta's problem was, but she wasn't going to tolerate any disrespect.

Saminta chuckled again and gave in. "May I *please* have a word with you?"

"Absolutely," Arykah answered. She pointed toward the sanctuary doors. "Let's go in and sit."

Saminta followed Arykah, and the ladies sat down on a pew at the rear of the sanctuary. They were the only two people in the room.

"What's on your mind?" Arykah asked her not really caring. Saminta's attitude had turned her off. But as the first lady of the church, Arykah obliged her.

"I don't appreciate being the source of your gossip."

Arykah was taken aback. "What?"

"Why are you spreading rumors about my family?"

Arykah frowned. "First of all, Saminta, I don't start rumors *or* spread gossip. I'm clueless as to what you're talking about."

"Seriously?" Saminta asked in a high-pitched, disbelieving tone. "Well, then, why have several people approached me with negative comments about my decision to not attend Miranda's baby shower? When you called and invited me, I told you that I wanted nothing to do with that girl or that baby."

"*Miranda* is *that girl's* name, and she is carrying *your* grandson."

"I ain't too sure about that," Saminta fired back. "It could be *anybody's* baby."

Arykah felt herself becoming unraveled. She mentally calmed herself.

"Look, Saminta, I haven't spread any gossip about you. I couldn't care any less about your decision to skip Miranda's shower. We had a great time without you. And if folks are coming to you with negative talk about your absence, then you deal with those folks. Don't assume that I put your business out there. I don't care that much about you."

Saminta was caught off guard by Arykah's boldness. "Is that so?"

It was obvious that Saminta had assumed that she could come hard at Arykah and get away with it. She was thrown for a loop when Arykah came back at her even harder.

"That's *absolutely* so," Arykah confirmed. "If you and your husband choose to not acknowledge that your son is going to be a father, then that's on you. And in my opinion, Saminta, teaching Titus to not take responsibility for the child that he made is disgusting, and it's doing him a great injustice. But that's yours and Doug's little red wagon; I'ma let y'all pull it anyway you want to."

"It really ain't your business what Doug and I do with Titus."

"You made it my business when you told me about Titus's promising football career and how you're not gonna allow a baby to get in the way of that."

"Miranda should have protected herself."

That statement angered Arykah. Her neck really danced. "And Titus should have protected *himself*. Why should the responsibility of birth control only be placed on Miranda?"

"Because men can't carry babies."

"But they can certainly be taken to court and sued for child support." Arykah needed to let Saminta know that she couldn't hide Titus forever. Sooner or later, life will catch up to him and he'll be held responsible for the child he helped to make.

"Lady Arykah, I know that you married rich but—"

Arykah sat straight up on the pew and turned her entire upper torso toward Saminta. "Uh, hold up, Chick. First of all, *I* was rich before I even met the bishop. Okay? I don't *need* his money. You really need to get your facts straight before you shoot off your mouth and come off looking stupid." Arykah dismissed the fact that she was a pastor's wife. At that moment, she was too heated to care.

"Oh, so I'm *stupid* ?" Saminta asked.

"What you *said* was stupid. You don't know where I came from. You're looking at me now, but what you don't know, Saminta, is that my mother gave me away when I was just nine years old. I was passed around from foster home to foster home until the age of sixteen. After I graduated high school, I put myself through college working three jobs. Okay? I come from nothing. No one has ever given me anything. Every penny that's in my bank account, *I've* earned. Yes, I married a rich man, but he also married a rich woman."

"Well, I'm just telling you what I heard."

"I don't give a rat's behind what you heard. I'm giving you truth right here. Now take *that* back to your source."

Saminta shrugged her shoulders. "I don't care anymore 'cause this is our last Sunday here at Freedom Temple."

Bye, Bitch. Arykah immediately silently repented for that thought.

"Doug and I feel it's best for Titus if we found another church."

"I feel that very same way," Arykah responded. *Get the devil's hell out.* Arykah wasn't going to repent for that thought, though. She wished she could have expressed herself verbally.

Without saying another word, Saminta stood and exited the sanctuary.

Twelve

The floor-to-ceiling windows on the thirty-ninth floor provided a majestic panoramic view of Navy Pier. Arykah and Lance saw the largest Ferris wheel in the world spinning.

"This view is awesome, Cheeks."

"Especially at nighttime. The lights from the Willis Tower and the entire city skyline is breathtaking."

"You think Gladys will invite us over to watch the July Fourth fireworks?"

"She'll be here soon. You can ask her yourself."

"What excuse did you use to get her here?" Lance asked.

"I told her that I wanted her to meet me at my seamstress's condominium so she and I can look at patterns and material for the baby's christening outfit."

"I really hope Gladys likes this place."

"How can she not?" Arykah asked. "The three bedrooms are massive with floor-to-ceiling windows. All three have walk-in closets. The master bath is to die for. Gladys has her own washer and dryer. I know she'll appreciate not having to load the car with duffel bags of clothes and driving to a Laundromat anymore. The hardwood floors throughout this unit are gorgeous. The kitchen is updated with granite countertops and top-of-the-line stainless steel appliances. Gladys will have to share this entire floor with only one other tenant. There's underground parking, a doorman, a drycleaners, and a gym on the premises. I'm sure Miranda and her friends will enjoy the rooftop deck and swimming pool. The security here is tight as heck. No one gets past the doorman without identification. Gladys can even send out for groceries if she wants to. She, Miranda, and the baby are minutes from downtown, and the views are spectacular. Plus, this condo is fully furnished. Who *wouldn't* want to live here?"

"You know Gladys," Lance said. "She doesn't like to take handouts."

Arykah shrugged her shoulders. "Hopefully, the fireplace in the master bedroom will influence her. And Miranda's school is only fifteen minutes away. There isn't one reason why Gladys shouldn't be happy here."

The doorbell rang. Arykah walked to the intercom next to the front door and pressed the TALK button. "Yes?"

"Ms. Blackmon is here to see you," the doorman announced.

"Send her up, please." Arykah released the button and looked at Lance. "Okay. Here we go."

"Why are my palms sweaty like I'm interviewing for a job?"

Arykah chuckled. "Because you know with Gladys we may have a fight on our hands."

Five minutes later Arykah answered a knock on the front door. She opened it and welcomed Gladys inside. "Hey, Gladys. Come on in."

"Hey, First Lady," Gladys greeted. She stepped into the foyer and was impressed. "Wow. This is beautiful. Did you see Starbucks inside the lobby?"

Arykah chuckled. "Yep, I sure did. It must be nice to wake up and just go right downstairs for a mocha, huh?"

"Chile, I sure could get used to it. I wouldn't mind that at all."

That's what I wanted to hear. "Come in to the living room," Arykah said.

Gladys didn't even notice Lance sitting on the sofa. Her eyes were drawn to the panoramic views of Lake Michigan. The water and waves were a beautiful sight to see. "Oh my God," she said walking straight to the windows. "Gurrrllll, this is spectacular. Look at this scenery."

Arykah winked and smiled at Lance, then went and stood next to Gladys. "Isn't this to die for?"

"Honey, yes," Gladys responded. "Your seamstress is living off the chain." She gasped when she saw the large Ferris wheel. "OMG."

"I know," Arykah said.

Gladys turned around and was surprised to see Lance sitting there. *"Bishop?"*

He smiled and stood. "You like the view?"

"Um, yeah, um." Clearly, Gladys wasn't expecting to see her pastor. She didn't know why he'd be interested in choosing material and patterns. "What are *you* doing here?" Gladys looked over her shoulder at Arykah. "Where is your seamstress?"

"At home working on your grandson's outfit that I've already designed. We're just waiting on him to be born."

Gladys frowned. "What?"

"Gladys . . ." Arykah started, "the bishop and I leased this condominium this morning."

"This isn't your seamstress's place?"

"No. It's yours," Lance stated.

Arykah and Lance held their collective breaths and waited to see how Gladys would react.

Gladys was confused. She heard what Lance had just said to her, but the words didn't penetrate through her ears to her brain. "What do you mean?" she asked Lance.

"Lady Arykah and I wanted to do something special for you, Miranda, and the baby. We saw how small your apartment was, and honestly, Gladys, I was uncomfortable with the baby's crib in the living room."

Gladys looked from Lance to Arykah, then from Arykah to Lance.

"And I understand that you're working two full-time jobs to keep a roof over your family's head. As your pastor, I'm concerned about Miranda being left alone overnight while you work."

"Gladys," Arykah started, "the bishop and I want to help you. Will you let us?"

Tears flooded Gladys's eyes. She had never experienced so much love. Miranda's father had walked out on them when Miranda was just seven years old. Gladys hadn't heard from or seen him since. For years she had struggled to make ends meet. She looked around and saw the hardwood floors and the fireplace with the oversized mantle. "Why are you doing this for us?" she asked Arykah.

Arykah approached Gladys and wiped her tears away with her hand. She looked into Gladys's glazed eyes. "Because we love you and we care."

"Lady Arykah and I know you're more than capable of taking care of your family. We just wanna lighten the load a little. That's all."

"Don't you love it here?" Arykah asked Gladys.

More tears dripped onto her face. "Yes, but this must cost a fortune."

"The cost of this place is not for you to be concerned about," Lance said. "It's close to Miranda's school. You have secured underground parking. And without a mortgage payment to worry about, you can be home with Miranda and the baby at night."

"Except for water the only utilities you'll have to pay are cable and electricity," Arykah said to her.

Gladys placed her face in her hands and cried openly. Lance went to her and pulled her in his arms. "I hope that's a happy cry," he chuckled.

"Let's have a look around," Arykah suggested. She knew that once Gladys had seen the entire unit, she'd accept their offer.

She and Lance led Gladys to the gourmet kitchen. "Oh my goodness," Gladys said. The stainless steel appliances and granite sparkled. "What am I gonna do in here?"

Arykah laughed. "Bake me a cake."

Lance took Gladys to the master bedroom. "Look at the view from in here. Can you imagine waking up to this every morning?"

"The sun rises in the east, Gladys," Arykah said. "Natural sunlight comes through these floor-to-ceiling windows for much of the day."

Gladys saw the fireplace. "A fireplace in the master? Who has that?"

"You can," Arykah answered. "Check out your private bathroom."

Gladys gasped when she went and stood at the bathroom door. "My own toilet? For real?"

"Your very own toilet," Lance confirmed.

Gladys was impressed with the granite countertop and double sinks. She saw the tub and separate oversize shower. "This is crazy. Five people can fit in that shower."

"There's more," Arykah said.

Lance and Arykah showed Gladys the other two bedrooms and bathrooms before returning to the living-and-dining-room combination.

"Well?" Lance said to Gladys. "What do you think?"

She looked all around the living and dining rooms. "I'm speechless."

"It comes furnished," Arykah said. "And there's a rooftop deck with a swimming pool. All you gotta do is move in."

Lance removed the keys from his front pants pocket and held them out for Gladys to take. "Welcome home," he said.

Gladys didn't take the keys. She glared at him and Arykah. "You know I can take care of myself, Miranda, *and* my grandson just fine. I really don't appreciate the two of you getting in my business."

Lance and Arykah looked at each other.

"But I'm so glad y'all did," Gladys said smiling. She accepted the keys from Lance and hugged him tight. "I'm so grateful for this, Bishop." She looked at Arykah. "And you, I don't know what to say about you, Lady Arykah. You've been so good to me and Miranda."

"Well, you and Miranda have been good to me as well. What goes around comes around."

"I thank both of you so much. I know Miranda will love this place. Whoever thought that I'd be living on Lake Shore Drive?"

"Jennifer Hudson and Oprah own condos within walking distance from here," Arykah informed her.

Gladys was floored. Her mouth dropped open. *"You mean I'm amongst the elite?"*

Lance and Arykah laughed out loud.

Gladys's cellular telephone rang. She looked at the caller ID and frowned. "This is Miranda's last day before summer break. Why would the school be calling?"

Seconds after Gladys answered the call Arykah and Lance saw the color drain from her face.

Gladys, Arykah, and Lance rushed to the maternity ward at Northwestern Memorial Hospital. They could hear Miranda screaming for her mother as soon as they exited the elevator. Gladys followed Miranda's screams. When they entered her room, they saw Miranda lying in a bed with an IV in her arm. A nurse stood next to Miranda monitoring the baby's heartbeat.

Arykah and Lance stood at the foot of Miranda's bed.

"Hey, Baby," Gladys said to Miranda.

Miranda was sweating profusely. "It hurt so bad, Momma. It hurt so bad."

"She'll be given an epidural shortly," the nurse informed Gladys.

"Has she dilated?" Arykah asked.

The nurse nodded. "Her doctor just examined her. "She's already eight centimeters."

"Already?" Lance shrieked.

The nurse laughed at the fear on his face. "Yes. Apparently she'd been in labor for the past two days."

"Two days ?" Gladys and Arykah shouted out.

Lance looked at the nurse. "How could she have been in labor for forty-eight hours and not know?"

"She ignored the slight stomach pains," the nurse answered.

"I thought I had to poop," Miranda said wincing at the pain in her lower abdomen. A sharp pain pierced her back. She screamed out. "Oh, it hurts. It hurts."

Arykah went and stood on the opposite side of the bed and held Miranda's hand in her own. "It won't be long now." She wiped the sweat from Miranda's forehead.

Lance came and stood next to Arykah. He looked at Miranda. "Let's pray."

"Bishop," Miranda started. She was panting and incoherent. "I ain't got time for that right now. You gon' have to get me some pain medication." Miranda looked at her pastor. "Please, Bishop. Get me something now. Cocaine, crack, anything, Bishop. I promise I won't tell nobody."

Gladys gasped. *"Girl, what?"*

Lance chuckled. "I won't be able to do that, Daughter."

The nurse laughed at Miranda. Every day she witnessed women lose their cool and say wild things while in labor. That was the first time she'd heard someone beg for cocaine or crack, though. "The anesthesiologist is on his way."

Miranda screamed again.

The anesthesiologist rushed into the room and tended to Miranda. Lance and Arykah stood out of the way and watched Gladys try to comfort her daughter while a needle was stuck in her back.

"The pain should cease," the anesthesiologist said to Miranda as he inserted the epidural in her spine. "And your legs will go numb in a few seconds."

Moments later Miranda calmed down and lay back on the bed.

"How are you feelin' now, Baby?" Gladys asked her.

"Okay," she answered.

Her doctor came in to examine Miranda again. Lance and Arykah stepped out into the hallway and waited.

Suddenly Gladys opened the door to Miranda's room and rushed out to them. "She's ready to deliver! Miranda's gonna start pushing now." She looked at Arykah. "She wants you in there."

"Me?" Arykah asked excitedly.

"Yes," Gladys said. She grabbed Arykah's hand and pulled her. "Come on."

Arykah shoved her purse against Lance's chest and ran after Gladys. Lance went toward the waiting room.

Gladys and Arykah quickly dressed in hospital garb, then stood on opposite sides of Miranda's bed. They each held up her legs and forced them into her chest.

"Come on, Baby," Gladys encouraged. "Push, push."

Miranda inhaled and pushed with all of her might. She lay back on the pillow exhausted. "I can't no more," she cried. "I can't do it."

Her doctor looked up at Miranda. "Come on. Give me another big push. You're almost there. Come on."

"You can do it, Miranda," Arykah encouraged.

"No," Miranda cried. "Please, I can't."

"You can't stop now," the doctor said. "The baby is coming. Give me a big push right now."

Miranda inhaled and pushed. *"Arrrrrrrrrgh."*

"The baby is crowning," the doctor announced.

Arykah couldn't resist. She left Miranda's side and looked for herself. *"Oh my God,"* she cried out. "I can see the top of his head, Miranda."

"One last push," the doctor said. "Come on, Miranda, let's have a baby."

With every fiber of her being Miranda inhaled and pushed her son out of her womb.

"It's a boy," the doctor announced.

Miranda heard her son cry and started to cry herself.

"You did it," Gladys said with tears in her eyes. She kissed Miranda's wet forehead. "My baby has a baby."

"Congratulations, Grandma," Arykah said to Gladys.

The doctor put the screaming boy on Miranda's stomach. "Who's gonna cut the umbilical cord?"

"I think the godmother should do it," Gladys said to Arykah.

"I think so too," Miranda confirmed.

Arykah shook her head from side to side. "Uh-uh. It's too messy."

The nurse put a pair of small shears in Arykah's hand. "This is nothing compared to the soiled diapers you'll have to change. Cut directly beneath the clamp," she instructed.

Arykah cut the cord and frowned. "Oh, Jesus. Oh, Jesus. Oh my God."

"Perfect," the nurse said when Arykah had completed her task. She picked up the baby and brought him to Miranda's face. "You have a beautiful son. We're gonna weigh him, get him cleaned up, make a print of his feet, tag your name on his plastic ankle bracelet, and bring him right back to you."

Everything was done in Miranda's room, then her son was placed in her arms. Miranda looked down at his face. His eyes were open. "You tried to kill me, didn't you?"

Arykah and Gladys chuckled.

"What's his name?" the nurse asked Miranda.

"Maximillian Aristotle Blackmon."

"What?" Gladys and Arykah shrieked at the same time.

Even the nurse was shocked. "Where did you get a name like that?"

"From a soap opera."

"Maximillian Aristotle," Gladys repeated. She couldn't process it.

"A big name for such a little guy," Arykah said.

"Yeah, but he'll grow into it." Miranda added.

"Are you sure?" Gladys asked her. "That boy has to go through life with that name. Why not choose something simple like 'James' or 'Richard' or 'William'?"

Miranda looked at the nurse. "My son's name is Maximillian Aristotle Blackmon."

"His last name should be Williams," Gladys told Miranda.

Miranda shook her head from side to side. "I don't want Max to have Titus's last name, and I don't want Titus on his birth certificate either."

"Miranda," Arykah started, "Titus is Max's father, and he should be held responsible for him as well as you. You're gonna need support from Titus."

Maximillian would be entitled to support from Titus no matter what his last name was, but Arykah felt that it would help the legal process if Miranda gave the baby Titus's last name.

"But his parents doesn't want him anywhere near his son."

"So what?" Gladys asked her. "Eventually, Titus will have to face the fact that he fathered this baby. Give Max his last name."

Miranda exhaled and looked at the nurse. "Maximillian Aristotle Williams."

"You'll be glad you did that, Miranda," Arykah said to her.

"Okay," the nurse said. "Williams it is. Will he be circumcised?"

Miranda frowned. "What's that?"

"Yes," Gladys answered the nurse. "Definitely."

The nurse nodded and exited the room just as Lance was entering. "I heard Freedom Temple's newest member has arrived."

Miranda was happy to see her pastor. "Come on in, Bishop."

Lance entered and gave Arykah her purse. He then went to see the baby boy in Miranda's arms. "Wow, what a handsome li'l dude."

"Miranda, tell your pastor what your son's name is."

She looked at her mother. "I'm not ashamed."

"Clearly," Gladys said. "Tell him."

Miranda looked at Lance and said, "Maximillian Aristotle Williams."

With her camera phone Arykah took a picture of Lance's mouth that hung open.

He chuckled. "Maximillian Aristotle?"

Miranda nodded. "We'll call him 'Max.'"

"Whatcha think of that, Bishop?" Arykah asked Lance.

He shrugged his shoulders. "I kinda like it."

Gladys's eyes grew wide. *"You do?"*

"Yeah," Lance said. "It's a cool name. He may not get any chicks with it, but it's a cool name," he chuckled.

"Bishop, are you angry with me for getting pregnant?"

Gladys and Arykah looked at each other.

Lance sat on Miranda's bed. "No, I'm not angry."

"Were you disappointed when you found out?"

He looked at her. "I won't lie and say that I wasn't a little bit upset. You are a straight-A student, Miranda, and you had your whole life ahead of you. A baby will only slow you down."

Miranda looked at her son and kissed his forehead. "Max may slow me down, but he won't stop me from graduating high school next year. I'm going to keep my grades up, Bishop. I promise."

Lance couldn't ask for any more than that from her. "And I'm gonna hold you to that promise."

The nurse came back into the room. "It's breast-feeding time, Miranda."

"Well, I guess that's my cue to leave," Lance said as he stood from the bed.

"Bishop, before you go, can I ask you a question?"

"Sure," he said to Miranda.

She had been holding back a question that she wanted to ask Lance for quite some time but would have been devastated if he turned her down. Miranda knew her pastor was disappointed when he learned of her pregnancy. When the news broke and the gossip started to spread, Miranda distanced herself from Lance. She had stopped visiting him in his office after morning worship service. She avoided him in the sanctuary. But at her baby shower, Lance gave Miranda his personal number and made her promise to call him if she or her baby needed anything. That gesture reminded her that Lance was still her pastor; a man who cared for and saw after his flock. She swallowed, then asked, "Would you like to be Max's godfather?"

Tears filled the eyes of Gladys and Arykah.

Miranda had just melted his heart. Lance smiled and said, "I thought you'd never ask."

***

The following Friday evening Arykah and Monique were shopping in the baby section at Target.

"I'm looking for a small bassinette for Max," Arykah informed Monique.

"For Max? He already has one, doesn't he?"

"Yes, but I need one for *my* house. Gladys and Miranda are moving into their condo tomorrow. Lance and I offered to babysit Max all day and overnight so they can do what they have to do and get some rest."

Monique nodded. "I know that's right. Moving is no joke. They're gonna need a good night's rest after all of the unpacking and organizing they'll have to do."

"True," Arykah agreed. "The last thing Miranda needs to deal with is a fussy, hungry baby while she's getting his bedroom set up."

Monique saw blue Superman onesies and couldn't resist removing one from the rack. "Now isn't this the cutest little thing?" She held it up for Arykah to see.

Arykah cooed. "That is adorable. Max would look so cute in that."

"I gotta get this." Monique placed it in the buggy she was pushing.

"He is so spoiled already," Arykah said.

"I know," Monique chuckled. "I can't walk by anything and not get it for him."

"I'm the same way," Arykah laughed. "And Gladys appreciates it." She pointed to the bassinettes on a shelf. "There they are, Monique."

Monique pushed the buggy in the direction Arykah was walking. "Adonis and I stopped by the hospital to see Max on Tuesday just before he and Miranda were released. I have to say that he is the most handsome baby boy I've ever seen."

"I know, right? I just can't stop kissing those fat cheeks." Arykah saw a bassinette almost identical to the one she purchased from Babies 'R' Us. "Girl, look at the price on this thing. I paid three hundred twenty dollars for one just like this, and Target has it for only one eighty." She shook her head from side to side. "A doggone shame."

"Miranda should've registered here in the first place. Target got it going on."

Arykah put the bassinette in the basket. "Now I need newborn diapers, formula, and bottles."

"Why formula?" Monique asked. "Isn't Miranda breast-feeding?"

"Uh-uh. Not anymore. Max stopped suckling her boobs when they got home from the hospital. Gladys has him on Enfamil with iron."

"I'm sure Miranda is glad about that. When Adonis and I were at the hospital, she complained about the pain."

Arykah laughed. "I guess it would hurt if someone was pullin' on your nip all the time."

"Humph," Monique commented. "Depends on who you ask and who's doing the pullin'."

Arykah looked at Monique shamefully. "You is nasty."

Monique shrugged her shoulders. "I'm just saying."

When Arykah had piled the buggy with plenty of diapers, baby powder, formula, and more baby clothes for Maximillian, she and Monique proceeded to the checkout counter.

"Arykah?"

They were standing in line when Arykah turned to look at Monique.

"You wanna do it?" Monique asked.

It took a moment for her to realize what Monique was talking about. She shook her head from side to side. "No."

"Come on, Arykah," Monique said. "You know you want to."

Arykah shook her head no again. "We're too old for that now."

"What?" Monique shrieked. "We just did it six months ago."

"Well, now we're wives, and I'm somebody's first lady. I can't be acting a fool with you."

Monique saw a woman coming their way. "Here she comes. Pleeeeease, Arykah," she begged. "This will be the last time, I promise."

Arykah saw the woman getting closer to them. When the woman stopped to glance at something Arykah looked at Monique. She couldn't resist. "Okay, go ahead. Hurry up before she sees you."

Monique left the line and went to stand a few feet away. She and Arykah were excited when they saw the woman push her buggy to the line and stand behind Arykah. Monique grabbed a small bag of chips from a rack she stood next to. She went and cut in line right in front of Arykah.

Arykah looked at Monique as though she was crazy. "Excuse me. Don't you see me standing here? You can't jump in front of me."

Monique looked at the contents in Arykah's buggy. "Your buggy is full. I only have a bag of chips. You can wait."

By now, the two of them had the woman's full attention.

"I don't care what you have," Arykah fussed. "You gotta wait in line like everyone else."

"That's right," the lady behind Arykah said to Monique. "Where is your respect?"

Arykah turned around, frowned at the woman, and yelled, "Who are you talkin' to? Do I look like I need your help?"

The woman was taken aback. She didn't know what to say. "I . . . I . . . was . . ."

"You . . . you . . . was . . . *what?*" Monique asked the woman mimicking her. "Does she look like she needs your help?" She glared at her.

"You need to mind your business," Arykah said to the woman.

"Yeah," Monique agreed. "This is between us. It ain't got nothing to do with you."

The woman quickly pulled her buggy back and went to another line.

Arykah and Monique laughed until their bellies ached.

"We are two whole fools," Monique said.

"I hope you got that out of your system, Monique, 'cause I ain't doing it again."

Early Saturday morning, Arykah and Lance drove up to Gladys's house at the same time the movers arrived in a forty-foot truck. Arykah and Lance exited their car. Lance went toward the movers that he hired, and Arykah went to ring Gladys's doorbell.

"It's moving day," Arykah sang when Miranda opened the door.

Miranda held Maximillian in her arms. "Good morning, Lady Arykah."

Arykah stepped inside. "Give me my godson."

Miranda did as she was told. "He's been up since four this morning. Momma said newborns sleep a lot. Well, this one doesn't."

Arykah chuckled. "You are experiencing the new adventures of motherhood." She placed Maximillian on her right shoulder, then looked around the cluttered living room. "Where's your mom?"

Miranda looked outside and saw Lance speaking with the movers. "She's in the kitchen packing up the dishes."

"I'm gonna say 'hi' and 'bye' to her, then we'll be out of your way." Arykah went toward the kitchen. "Hey, Gladys," she greeted when she saw Gladys rolling glasses in sheets of newspaper.

Gladys looked exhausted. "Girl, I'm glad you're here. That boy ain't been to sleep since he left the hospital," she complained.

"That was five days ago," Arykah said.

Gladys's eyes rose. *"That's what I know,"* she shrieked. "That Enfamil must have steroids in it. Thangs have changed. When Miranda was an infant, all she did was eat, poop, and sleep." Gladys looked at her grandson snuggled comfortably on Arykah's shoulder. "I don't know where that boy came from."

"Well, you and Miranda can get plenty of rest tonight. Lance is outside speaking with the movers right now."

"They're here already?" Gladys asked. She picked up the pace of wrapping the glasses in newspaper. "I am so far behind."

"Why are you doing that anyway? The movers are being paid to pack everything."

Gladys exhaled. "Why didn't you tell me? Girl, I'm runnin' around here like a maniac trying to cram things into boxes."

"I'm sorry. I thought I told you when we hired the movers. They have boxes too."

Just then Lance entered the kitchen. "Mornin'," he greeted Gladys. "You ready to make the transition?"

"Yep. More than I was five minutes ago. I just learned that the movers will take care of everything."

"That's right," Lance confirmed. "The movers know what to do. They know where they're going, and you don't have to give them a dime. Arykah and I have taken care of everything."

"I can at least tip them, Bishop. There's a lot of stuff to pack and move."

Arykah shook her head no. "They're only packing up your dishes, clothes, toiletries, and personal stuff. You're leaving all of the furniture behind, right?"

Gladys nodded. "Yes. All of the furniture is staying."

"The movers have already been tipped handsomely," Lance added.

"Well," Gladys said, "you two have thought of everything."

"Yep," Lance agreed. "The only thing you and Miranda will have to do is unpack when you get to the condo."

The three of them heard commotion in the living room and left the kitchen.

"Okay, well, the bishop, Max, and I will get out of y'alls way," Arykah stated when she saw Miranda directing three movers on what to do. "Where are Max's things?"

"There it is, Lady Arykah," Miranda said pointing to a light blue duffel bag on the sofa. "I packed extra diapers."

"I bought diapers, a bassinette, and a car seat yesterday," Arykah stated. It was wise for Arykah to have purchased the bassinette and car seat. Since she and Lance were Maximillian's godparents, he'd be spending a lot of time with them. Switching his car seat and bassinette from Miranda's possession to theirs would be time-consuming. "You can take the extra diapers out of his bag and keep them."

Lance removed all of the diapers from the diaper bag and gave them to Miranda. He then placed the strap of the bag on his shoulder. He looked at Gladys. "Call us when everything gets settled at the condo."

Gladys hugged her pastor. "Bishop, we are truly grateful for you and Lady Arykah. We appreciate everything."

"Everything," Miranda emphasized. "I can't wait to see the condo. Momma says it's to die for."

"And there's a swimming pool on the roof deck," Arykah said to Miranda.

Miranda's eyes lit up. "Wow. Really?"

"It really is something else," Gladys said to her.

Arykah wrapped Maximillian in a receiving blanket. "Miranda, how often does he take a bottle?"

"Every three hours or so. I prepared and packed ten bottles in his bag but they gotta be refrigerated when you get home."

"His li'l weewee is still irritated from the circumcision," Gladys said to Arykah. "And his umbilical cord hasn't completely fallen off."

"Poor dude," Lance sympathized.

"We'll take good care of him," Arykah said. She looked at Gladys. "Will you be at church tomorrow?"

Gladys shrugged her shoulders. "I ain't making any promises. We'll see how my arthritis responds to this move, unpacking, and situating."

"I understand," Arykah chuckled. "Call me in the morning. If you and Miranda wanna sleep in, Lance and I will bring Max to the condo afterward."

Lance and Arykah left Miranda and her mother alone. They were overly excited to spend the entire day and night with their godson.

Gladys and Miranda stood at the bay window watching Lance settle Maximillian in his car seat. Gladys chuckled at the thought of black bags that'll be under Lance and Arykah's eyes the next morning. Neither of them will get an ounce of sleep that night.

Thirteen

It wasn't until five forty-five Saturday evening when Gladys had called the Howell home to say that she and Miranda had finally unpacked everything, decorated Maximillian's nursery, and settled in.

"The condo is stunning, Lady A," Gladys said. "We love the furniture, the hardwood floors, and the spacious closets that Miranda and I needed so badly. I can't wait for everyone to see the nursery. Everything came together perfectly. And what newborn has a walk-in closet?" Gladys chuckled. "Max is already so blessed."

"I'm excited to see the nursery," Arykah stated.

"How is Max doing?"

"He's napping. He had a bottle about thirty minutes ago. He is a happy baby."

"Yeah, he is."

"Where's Miranda?"

"Girl, I give you one guess where she is."

Arykah laughed out loud. "Already?"

"A tornado couldn't have kept that girl and Natasha from the pool."

"Oh, Natasha's there too?"

"Uh-huh. She came to help Miranda unpack and set up Max's nursery. I promised them that once they were done they could visit the pool."

"Miranda's not swimming, is she?"

Arykah couldn't see Gladys shaking her head no. "She had better not be. I told Miranda that she could only put

her feet in the pool. Her vajayjay is still fresh and suscep-
tible to all types of bacteria. She needs to be resting, but
what am I gonna do? By the way," Gladys said changing
the subject, "I've already been down to the lobby and got
myself a cup of mojo from Starbucks. I am going to love it
here. Our doorman, Stewart, is so nice and helpful."

You get what you pay for, Arykah thought. "That's
great, Gladys. It's good that you, Miranda, and the
baby are someplace where you're comfortable and not
cramped."

Gladys sat in the living room on the dark brown leather
sectional as she talked to Arykah. She looked out over
Lake Michigan. "I can't get over this view. I mean, the
water doesn't end."

"Are you happy and content?" Arykah asked her.
She really hoped that Gladys was comfortable with the
condominium. She and Lance had chosen that very one
with care.

"Are you kidding me? Of course, I'm happy. I'm elated,
to be honest. But I'm worried about what folks will think
about me residing here."

"What do you mean?"

"Come on now, Lady A. Everyone knows that I can't
afford to live like this. Folks are gonna be talkin'."

"First of all, it ain't nobody's business where you live
or how much anything costs. No one balances your
checkbook but you. Girl, look, don't get me started, okay?
You need to be like me, Gladys. You gotta carry yourself
in a way that folks would already know not to get in your
business."

"I hear you. But how do I explain how I got here?"

"You ain't gotta 'splain nothing to nobody. You're
blessed and highly favored. That's all folks need to know,
and you wouldn't even be lying. See, you're trying to get
my blood pressure up talkin' about stupid folks, but I

ain't gonna let you. My godson will be up in another hour and I'm looking forward to loving on him."

Gladys chuckled. "Well, I'm getting ready to draw me a bath in my brand-new Jacuzzi tub and relax. Hey, did Miranda even call you to check on her baby?"

"No, but it's okay."

"That's not okay, Lady A. I told that girl to make sure she called you before she and Natasha went to that pool. I can already see that the pool is gonna get Miranda into trouble."

"Gladys, take your bath and leave that girl alone. She is a teenager, and she knows she has a great support team behind her." Arykah decided to change the subject. "Hey, listen, keep Stephanie Nichols in your prayers. She called us to say that her mother has taken a turn for the worse."

"Oh no," Gladys responded. "She's battling ovarian cancer, right?"

"Yes. The bishop went to the hospital to be with the family. The doctor told Stephanie her mother may not make it through the night."

"Oh my God. Poor Stephanie," Gladys said. "And Stacy too. I know they're devastated."

Arykah thought back to when Stephanie confided in her that she had caught Stacy in bed with her husband, Kenneth. "Yeah, Stacy too," Arykah said.

"The way my body is feeling, Lady A, I can already tell you that Miranda and I will not make it to church in the morning."

"Okay, that's fine. The bishop and I won't mind bringing Max home after church."

Lance entered the master suite at 2:34 a.m. Sunday morning. He was so exhausted that the only thing he could do was strip from his clothes and crawl into bed and snuggle up next to Arykah.

"What happened?" Arykah asked him.

Lance exhaled. "She passed about an hour ago. She went peacefully."

"My goodness," Arykah sighed. "So we plan another funeral at Freedom Temple."

"No. Stephanie and Stacy's mom wasn't a member of Freedom Temple."

"Oh, I didn't know that."

"I supported Stephanie and Stacy because they're *my* members. Their mother was of the Apostolic faith. I'm not sure what church she belonged to. I did hear Stephanie telling her cousins that her mother wanted to be cremated. There may or may not even be a funeral service for her."

As the first lady of Freedom Temple, Arykah felt that something should be done to support Stephanie and Stacy. She could only imagine how they must be grieving for their mother. Arykah sighed again. "How are Stephanie and Stacy doing?"

"Stephanie took it very hard. But Stacy and Kenneth didn't arrive at the hospital until after their mother was pronounced dead."

"What?" Arykah asked loudly. She sat up on the bed and clapped her hands. The bedroom lit up, and she glanced at Maximillian sleeping in his bassinette next to the bed hoping that her shriek hadn't awakened him. Diva Chanel lay on the floor next to him. She glared at Lance. "Stephanie called us at three this afternoon. Are you telling me that she sat at her dying mother's side—alone—all this time?"

"Well, I was there, and Stephanie's cousins were there as well."

"But not Stacy or Kenneth?"

"No."

"And Stacy arrived at the hospital *with* Kenneth *after* her mother was pronounced dead?"

"Yeah, what are you getting at?"

Arykah shook her head in disgust. "Wow," was all she said.

"What's wrong, Cheeks?"

Arykah knew she had to keep her promise to Stephanie to not tell Lance about Stacy and Kenneth or the divorce. "I'm gonna have Stephanie talk to you."

Arykah lay down and clapped her hands together. As soon as their bedroom went dark, Maximillian woke up crying.

Lance put his pillow over his head. "Oh my God."

Arykah chuckled. "It's your turn. I've already been up with him twice."

"Arykah, I'm exhausted," he mumbled.

"So am I."

"I gotta preach in eight hours."

Maximillian's cry got louder. "Do you want this one or the next one?" Arykah asked Lance. "He will be up again at four."

Lance threw the covers from his body, walked around the bed, and picked the baby up from the bassinette. He turned to leave the master suite.

"Make sure to powder his bottom when you change him, and the milk in his bottle has to be lukewarm, not too hot. Test it on your wrist first."

"Oh sure," Lance said. "Never mind the fact that I just got home from a hospital and I gotta preach in the morning. I don't need your help. I got this."

"Go on and get it then," Arykah said. She lay down and closed her eyes. She didn't care that Lance had to preach in a few hours. He was the one who suggested that Maximillian stay the day and night with them while Gladys and Miranda moved and unpacked. As the godfather,

Arykah was going to make sure that Lance shared in the overnight sleep interruptions. If Lance thought that he was going to be bright eyed and bushy tailed on Sunday morning while Arykah sat on the front pew with bags beneath her eyes from lack of sleep, he had another thing coming.

The alarm clock on Lance's nightstand buzzed at seven o'clock. He stirred, then reached over and pressed the SILENCE button. Lance turned to his side and saw Arykah sitting in a chair across the bedroom. She was feeding Maximillian a bottle of milk. Though she was fifteen feet away from him he saw the dark circles beneath her eyes.

"Good morning," he said to her.

She tried to smile. "Mornin', Bishop."

Watching Arykah cradle the baby in the crease of her arm warmed Lance's heart. He regretted that he and Arykah didn't get the chance to be parents. Just looking at her love and care for Miranda's son told Lance that whenever he and Arykah conceived a child again, she'd make the perfect mother.

"How long have you been up?" he asked her.

Arykah shrugged her shoulders. "I don't know. Awhile." She looked down at the precious face in her arm. "He's so fussy."

"You look tired."

She nodded her head. "I am." She removed the empty bottle from Maximillian's mouth, then placed him on her shoulder. Arykah patted his back until he belched.

Lance chuckled when he heard the noise come from the baby's throat. "That boy sure eats a lot."

"That's what growing boys do." Arykah stood and brought Maximillian to his bassinette. She lay him down and covered him with a blanket. Then Arykah got in bed and snuggled up to Lance. "I'm exhausted, Bishop."

Lance pulled Arykah in his arms and kissed her forehead. "We both are. Max must've gotten up seven times throughout the night."

Lance and Arykah had taken turns changing Maximillian's diapers and entertaining him until he took his next catnap. Neither of them had slept for more than an hour at a time.

"I'm not going to church," Arykah confessed.

Lance laughed out loud. "I knew that was coming."

"I think Miranda should be the one to debut her baby on his first Sunday at Freedom Temple. It wouldn't seem right for me to carry him in the sanctuary like he's *my* son."

"I can understand that," Lance said.

"And besides," Arykah started, "Max is barely a week old. A portion of his umbilical cord is still attached to his navel. It's too soon for various folks to be handling him and kissing on his face. You know what I mean?"

"Yeah. I agree. We don't wanna expose him to germs."

"Well, I can take Max home this morning. I know the team is meeting at Gladys's condo after church. Why don't you come by?"

"I can do that, but I need you to get some sleep 'cause you and I got a date tonight."

Arykah smiled. "Really? Tell me what you got planned."

"I can't. It's a surprise."

"Give me a hint."

Lance thought for a moment. "Our backyard."

Arykah frowned. "Backyard?"

"Yep," Lance said. "And that's all you're getting from me."

Arykah looked at Lance seductively and kissed his lips. "You don't wanna give me anything else?"

Lance knew by the sultry look in her eyes that she was flirting with him. He looked at her. "You ain't too tired?"

"Never."

Lance pulled her closer and kissed her passionately. As soon as he removed Arykah's nightgown from her shoulder Maximillian cried out. Lance lay on his back and looked up at the ceiling. "Oh my God."

Arykah laughed, then tended to the baby. "You better get used to it, Bishop," she said as she cradled Maximillian in her arms. "Eventually, this will be us on a daily basis."

Lance exhaled. "Oh my God," he said again.

After feasting on Gladys's mustard and turnips greens, fried chicken, homemade macaroni and cheese, and potato salad with Team Arykah and Deacon Marshall, Lance and Arykah arrived home late Sunday evening.

"I'm beat, Bishop," Arykah said when they entered the kitchen from the garage. "It's been a long day. I'm going to bed."

"What about our date?"

Arykah yawned. "Can I take a rain check? I'm exhausted."

"No rain checks, Cheeks. This is the perfect night for our date and the special surprise that I have for you."

"In the backyard?"

Lance smiled. "Yep." He needed time to set everything up. "Go and change into something more comfortable and join me and Diva Chanel out back."

Arykah looked at Lance suspiciously, then went toward the master suite.

"Come on, Diva," Lance said to her. He opened the kitchen patio doors and Diva Chanel ran outside. He followed and closed the patio doors behind him.

Ten minutes later when Arykah stepped onto the patio, she saw Lance and Diva Chanel lying on one of two hammocks. "What in the world?"

Diva Chanel left Lance and ran to Arykah.

"*Surprise!*" Lance yelled out. "Remember a couple weeks back when we were out here getting drunk?"

She chuckled. "Yeah. Are we getting drunk tonight?" Arykah was hopeful.

"No. Do you recall what you said about how perfect the weather was that night?"

Arykah looked at the hammock and put two and two together.

"*It is nights like this one that I wish we had a hammock out here. It would be so nice and romantic to lie in your arms and watch the stars.*"

Arykah smiled. "I love it when you listen, Bishop."

Lance reached behind his back and pulled out a scroll. He extended it to Arykah. "A gift for you."

"What's this?" she smiled.

Next to his leg on the hammock Lance had a small flashlight. He gave it to Arykah. "This should help."

Arykah untied the red satin ribbon and unrolled the paper. Lance stood from the hammock and took the flashlight from Arykah. He flashed it on the paper so she could read the words.

"It's a star certificate," she said.

"Read it out loud."

"*This star with the coordinates RA: 15h17m31.2s JUN: 31 degrees 17m31.6s was successfully entered into the star-naming registry on June eighth, twenty thirteen. The star has been named Lady Arykah. Registry number five zero two eight seven zero zero zero nine four three eight.*" Arykah looked up at Lance. "Aw, Babe, this is so nice." She kissed his lips.

"Read the rest," he instructed.

Tears were filling Arykah's eyes, and the words on the paper became blurry. "*This star will always shine for you and show you the way to my heart. I will love you forever, Lance.*"

Lance grabbed Arykah's hands and led her farther out in the backyard where she saw another hammock next to a telescope.

"Oh my God ," she shrieked. "You didn't."

"I did," Lance said. "Look through the lens."

Arykah knelt down and looked for her star. *"I can see it, Lance,"* she yelled out. She laughed. "I can see my star. It's so bright and big. I can really see it."

"It's a binary star, Cheeks, and it's made up of two stars orbiting around each other."

Arykah stood upright and looked at her husband. "Like you and me."

"You said you wanted to lie in my arms and watch the stars. Well, let's do it."

Arykah watched Lance retrieve the hammock from the patio and drag it to where she stood. He lay down on one hammock and Arykah lay on the other.

"I can't believe it," Arykah said. "My husband bought me a star."

"If I could afford it, Cheeks, I'd buy you the moon too."

Diva Chanel jumped onto Arykah's lap and settled down. Lance and Arykah held hands and watched the stars all night long.

Fourteen

On the second Sunday in July, after morning worship, Lance dedicated four babies before he called Miranda, Maximillian, Gladys, and Arykah, all dressed in white, to the front of the church. Lance left the pulpit and joined them next to the altar.

Minister Weeks, dressed in a white robe decorated with metallic gold braided trimming around his wrists and collar, stepped from the pulpit and took Maximillian from Miranda's arms. He held Maximillian and sprinkled holy water on his forehead. Maximillian squirmed in his white satin bonnet and white satin jacket and shorts. Arykah designed his lace tailored-made socks and satin booties as well.

"Father, we surrender little Max to You," Minister Weeks started. "We ask that You guide him, teach him, and lead him." He gave the baby back to Miranda and looked at her and Gladys. "God has blessed you both with a miracle. Do you promise to protect Maximillian and train him in the way that he should go so when he is grown, he will not depart from it?"

"Yes," they responded.

Minister Weeks looked at Lance and Arykah. "As godparents, do you accept the responsibility to see after Maximillian, to make sure he is safe and cared for? Do you promise to step in and become parents if Miranda can no longer be there for him?"

"We do," they stated.

Minister Weeks smiled and looked at all of them. "Today, we dedicate Maximillian Aristotle Williams to the holy Trinity. May he forever be blessed. Amen."

"Amen," everyone responded.

After Maximillian's christening, Lance and Arykah treated the team, Adonis, Miranda, Natasha, and Deacon Marshall to Italian food at Leona's Restaurant on West Ninety-fifth Street in Chicago Ridge. They were seated around a large round table in the center of the restaurant.

Arykah looked across the table and noticed that Deacon Marshall and Myrtle were chatting and smiling in each other's faces. They had been spending a lot of time together. They rode to church together in the limousine that Lance hired for Myrtle's use and whenever the team got together, Deacon Marshall was always in tow now. Monique had informed Arykah that she had called Myrtle's house late one evening and Deacon Marshall answered.

"For real?" Arykah asked Monique. "He's answering her phone? You think they're shacking up?"

"I can't say for sure. I asked her why Deacon Marshall was there so late and she told me to stay out of grown folks' business."

"What going on over there?" Arykah asked Myrtle.

Everyone at the table heard Arykah and followed her eyes.

"What y'all over there hee heeing and haw hawing about?"

Both Myrtle and Deacon Marshall looked like deer caught in headlights.

"Yeah," Monique added. "That's what I wanna know."

Everyone seated at the table waited to see what would happen next.

"Why are you two always in my business?" Myrtle asked Arykah and Monique.

"Because you're always in our business," Monique answered.

"You both have wonderful husbands. Now it's time for me to have one."

The entire table yelled out. *"What?"*

Diners nearby heard the members of Freedom Temple and turned to look their way.

"For real?" Chelsea asked Myrtle.

"Let's show 'em," Deacon Marshall said to Myrtle. He and Myrtle held up their left hands and revealed matching gold wedding bands.

Deacon Marshall smiled. "We gat mard at the coathas las tooday."

The table shrieked again. *"What?"* Deacon Marshall's Southern accent was strong, but every word he spoke had been understood.

"And you said nothin', Deac?" Lance asked him.

He looked at Lance, then he nodded his head in Myrtle's direction. "She say it wadden y'alls bitness."

"You robbed us the chance to throw you a bridal shower," Darlita said to Myrtle.

Gladys nodded her head in agreement with Darlita. "Mmm-hmm."

Myrtle just shook her head. "That's for you young folks. When you get to be my age, you're just thankful for the husband."

"Were you *ever* going to tell us?" Adonis asked the newlyweds.

"Probably not," Myrtle answered.

Arykah didn't understand why Myrtle was so secretive. "Why?"

Myrtle looked at her. "'Cause you too damn nosy and bossy and opinionated and controlling. We wouldn't have a moment's peace."

Arykah's eyebrows shot up in the air. Everyone at the table looked at her.

Miraculously, the waitress appeared at the table.

"We ain't ready to order yet," Arykah told her while glaring across the table into Myrtle's eyes.

The waitress sensed hostility in Arykah and walked away.

Arykah was huffing and puffing.

"Calm down, Cheeks," Lance said.

Arykah's inhaling and exhaling didn't move Myrtle at all. "You ain't gotta tell her to calm down," she said to Lance. Myrtle looked at Arykah. "What you gonna do, Cletus? Come on over here, but you're gonna limp back."

The table yelled out laughing at Myrtle's imitation from a scene in the movie, *The Nutty Professor*.

Arykah was offended by Myrtle's words. "I don't think anything is funny."

"All I'm saying," Myrtle started, "is that you would have wanted to throw us a big, lavish, over-the-top, blinged-out wedding. You wouldn't have taken no for an answer. The deacon and I did thangs the way we wanted. Yes, you are the first lady of Freedom Temple, Sugarplum, and everybody knows that you're rich and love to spend money, but you can't be in control of everybody's everything all the time.

"When folks come and confide their problems in you, that don't mean you gotta find resolutions to them all. Some people just wanna get stuff off their chests and know that you ain't gonna take their secret nowhere else. Learn to sit down and let folks fend for themselves and do what they wanna do, even if it ain't big like you would do it."

Arykah heard everything Myrtle had just said, but she didn't care. "But you ain't even give me a chance to buy you a cake."

Myrtle waved her hand at Arykah. "Girl, go on somewhere. All you think about is cake. If somebody die, you wanna have a cake. If somebody gets married, you wanna have a cake. I'll tell you what to do. If you want cake so bad, get that waitress that you so rudely dismissed to bring you a slice."

Lance clapped his hands together one time and looked around the table. "Okay, anybody else wanna share some shocking news?"

"I'm pregnant."

Everyone gasped and looked at the person who just blurted the words out. The table shrieked again. *"What?"*

There was another baby coming and that meant a baby shower would have to be thrown and Arykah would get to have her cake.

Book Club
Discussion Questions

1. Why was Arykah so reluctant to see a therapist? Was it wrong for Lance and everyone else to force her to go?
2. Why was it so difficult for Arykah to stop cursing? Do you think she really wanted to?
3. Arykah and Monique were as close as sisters. Was it wrong for Monique to jump Angela Moore?
4. Do you agree with Monique that it was necessary for Lance to tell Arykah about Angela Moore?
5. Did Lance do the right thing when he blackmailed Angela to drop all charges against Arykah and Monique? Even though Lance and Angela are no longer a couple, should he continue to pay for her brother's medical bills and therapy?
6. Was Arykah out of order when she spoke to Lance about traditions in the church? Do you agree with the changes that Lance had made?
7. Lance fired Sharonda as the church secretary. Do you agree with his decision? Was it wrong for Lance to ban Angela from Freedom Temple?
8. Did Lance and Arykah overstep their bounds when they took it upon themselves and leased an expensive condominium for Gladys, Miranda, and baby Max?
9. How do you feel about Arykah bringing her dog, Diva Chanel, into the sanctuary?

10. Lance and Arykah drank Bacardi rum together. Was that appropriate?

11. Why didn't Arykah want to reveal how large her bedroom closet was?

12. As the first lady of a church, should Arykah have accepted the role as godmother to Maximillian? Was it wrong of her to want to throw Miranda a baby shower at the church?

13. Arykah kept Stephanie's secret when she learned of her husband and sister's indiscretion. Should Arykah have told Lance?

14. Do you think Arykah is the perfect wife for Lance? Is she the perfect first lady for Freedom Temple?

15. In the last chapter, someone revealed that she was pregnant. Who do you think it was?

UC HIS GLORY BOOK CLUB!

www.uchisglorybookclub.net

UC His Glory Book Club is the spirit-inspired brain-child of Joylynn Ross, Author and Acquisitions Editor of Urban Christian, and Kendra Norman-Bellamy, Author for Urban Christian. This is an online book club that hosts authors of Urban Christian. We welcome as members all men and women who have a passion for reading Christian-based fiction.

UC His Glory Book Club pledges our commitment to provide support, positive feedback, encouragement, and a forum whereby members can openly discuss and review the literary works of Urban Christian authors.

There is no membership fee associated with UC His Glory Book Club; however, we do ask that you support the authors through purchasing, encouraging, providing book reviews, and of course, your prayers. We also ask that you respect our beliefs and follow the guidelines of the book club. We hope to receive your valuable input, opinions, and reviews that build up, rather than tear down our authors.

What We Believe:

—We believe that Jesus is the Christ, Son of the Living God.

—We believe the Bible is the true, living Word of God.

—We believe all Urban Christian authors should use their God-given writing abilities to honor God and share the message of the written word God has given to each of them uniquely.

—We believe in supporting Urban Christian authors in their literary endeavors by reading, purchasing and sharing their titles with our online community.

—We believe that in everything we do in our literary arena should be done in a manner that will lead to God being glorified and honored.

We look forward to the online fellowship with you. Please visit us often at *www.uchisglorybookclub.net*.

Many Blessing to You!

Shelia E. Lipsey,
President, UC His Glory Book Club